THE MASTER LIGHTNING BOLT

SEA OF INK PRESS

WAR ON THE GODS

3

THE MASTER LIGHTNING BOLT

A. P. MOBLEY

SEA OF INK PRESS

For my beloved readers.

Thank you for sticking with me this long,
and for waiting so patiently for this book.

I hope you love it as much as I do.

CHAPTER ONE
HOME

March 2nd, 2000

Calliope dashed through what seemed to be the twisting, turning passages of a pitch-dark cave, her only light source the candle she'd fished out from her robes and lit with her flint and stone. The Goddess of Eloquence clasped the taper with one hand, and with the other she held up her skirts, trying not to topple over because of them again.

The scrapes on her knees still stung from when she'd tripped over the billowing silks mere minutes ago.

Her breaths came in shallow gasps, and feverish sweat seeped from her pores. Despite the heat, the golden ichor that flowed through her veins—the same fluid that coursed through all Greek immortals' veins—ran cold. "H-hello?" she called, panting. "Can—anyone—hear me?" No one replied, her voice echoing back several times before fading away completely. *Where in all the universe am I?* she thought, her heart hammering against her rib cage.

Wherever she was, it was certainly no place for gods. She had already attempted to transport herself back to Mount Olympus twice. She'd even tried to contact her lover, Anteros, but to no avail. And it wasn't just because she'd been weakened from centuries upon centuries of dwindling worship—no, she couldn't tap into her power at all. It was as if the magic lacing her cells had been neutralized, rendering every enchantment she concocted futile in this black maze.

Finally, she paused. Perhaps it was better to stop and regroup, to figure out *how* she'd gotten here, rather than continue sprinting through winding passageways in a panic. She dropped her skirts and wiped the perspiration from her brow, racking her memory as she attempted to recall the details from before she'd arrived. It was strange that she couldn't in the first place—the gods didn't usually experience amnesia. Surely, if she could just remember what had transpired, she could piece together the situation and get home. "What happened?" she asked herself between breaths, pressing her cheek against the damp stone wall beside her. "Think. Think. *Think.*"

My vellum, she suddenly recalled, and shoved her free hand into her robes, searching for the document. Something told her it held the answers she needed.

After what felt like whole minutes, Calliope's fingers brushed the parchment, and she pulled it out and unrolled it. The words written upon it with crisp black ink were in her handwriting.

My fellow immortals, after all we have discussed today, do you still believe the Olympians should dismantle the modern world?

Should they not preserve the natural progression of the universe?

Should they not maintain humanity's choice and free will?

*What if they, even with all their power,
have no right to sway this fate?*

*What if choosing violence leads
everyone down an even greater
path of destruction?*

*I propose that the Olympians and
their loyal followers be*

The message cut off, left unfinished, but Calliope didn't need to read any more to know what she'd been about to add. *I propose that the Olympians and their loyal followers be stopped,* she thought, her memory of the message flooding back like water gushing through a ruptured dam, *before they disrupt the balance of the universe, sending all of us spiraling into chaos.*

For I may not be King of the Gods, nor can I see visions of the future—but I am positive that if we take this road, we will find only hardship at the end.

"That was the conclusion of the speech I was going to give to . . . to . . ." The events leading up to this moment rushed back to her, and finally she remembered how she'd arrived in this place. She inhaled sharply, dropping her vellum. Zeus, King of the Gods—*her father*—had sent her here.

She recalled Zeus bursting into her bedchamber on Olympus. She'd been preparing for her speech. Somehow, he'd discovered what she planned to do.

"You dare act with such insolence? You dare speak out against my will?" he'd said. She'd shoved the vellum into her robes, but before she'd been able to do anything else, he'd clamped meaty fingers over her throat and snapped her neck. Once she had regenerated, she woke to find herself surrounded by the greenery of the Garden of Olympus. Zeus had bound her with some of his lightning-rope.

The King of the Gods had dragged Calliope through the garden, all the way to the edge of Mount Olympus itself, where one could see the galaxy in which mortals who had once worshipped the gods lived—or, at least, the galaxy in which their planet was located. Even in Calliope's groggy state, she'd found the view to be breathtaking. Stars twinkled against light-years of black, and vibrant planets orbited a blazing sun.

"How do you plan to punish me for my 'insolence,' Father?" she'd asked Zeus with a chuckle. Her voice had been barely more than a whisper, her throat raw. *"Kill me? I'll only regenerate again and again. Throw me into Tartarus? You cannot do so without the vote of the other Olympians—and Hades's and Poseidon's help."* Her

last comment made Zeus's scowl deepen. *Yes, Father*, she'd thought, *I know of your secrets.* "Surely, *the other gods will not agree to such a cruel penalty,*" she'd continued, "*considering the insignificance of my crime. I didn't want to overthrow you, after all. I only wanted to stop what you plan to do to humanity.*"

Zeus had laughed, dangling her over Olympus's edge. As he'd spoken his next words, Calliope had finally felt a twinge of fear. "*Witless daughter, I do not need anyone's permission to rid myself of you.*"

"*How will you do it, then?*"

"*I always believed the only way a god could die and stay dead was if no one believed in him and he, over time, faded into nothingness,*" Zeus replied. "*However, I now know that is not true. Goodbye, Calliope.*"

Then he'd pitched her into space. She'd soared toward Earth, electrifying pain arcing through her body until it had grown too much to bear. She'd fallen unconscious, and when she'd opened her eyes next, she'd found herself lying in a dark, muggy passageway.

How had Zeus discovered her intention to convince the minor gods to stop the Olympians and their allies? To prevent them from dismantling the modern world humanity had created, from forcing people to worship the gods again?

Had someone exposed her schemes? A smaller deity hoping to win Zeus's favor? The other Muses? Anteros? *No, it wasn't Anteros. He would never do such a thing to me. But the others . . .*

Calliope shook her head, picking up the vellum and tucking it back into her robes. It didn't matter who had revealed her plans to Zeus; all that mattered now was figuring out where she was so she could escape and get her power back, then transport herself to Olympus. Something about this place—other than the fact that it rendered her magicless—made her uneasy.

The only place that can steal away godly abilities is the deepest pit of Tartarus, she thought. *That's why it makes for such an excellent prison. But Zeus couldn't have transported me there, and he said that wasn't what he planned to do with me. Also, this place doesn't look how Tartarus is described. So where am I?*

There was only one way to find out. Calliope raised her candle once again and started down another cavern.

HOME

Now . . .

Summer, Year 500 AS

Peridot-green lightning flashed across the night sky. Rain poured from the inky clouds and pelted Karter in the face, thunder rumbling as he trekked through the forest toward New Mount Olympus with heavy legs. For the last week he'd led his party to their destination, hardly eating or sleeping the whole way for fear of his attention being focused somewhere other than on the prisoners. He couldn't lose them. At least, he couldn't lose one of them—Diana, the Daughter of Apollo.

More green lightning blasted across the sky, and thunder roared, cold water dripping down the crevices of his body. *I'm almost there*, he thought. *It's nearly time to fulfill my destiny.*

Zeus had appeared to Karter several times over the past few days. He'd explained that once the party arrived on Olympus, the twin grandchildren-of-Hephaestus would be killed. Then everyone else would gather for Diana's execution, and later on, Zeus would act out Apollo's punishment, which he had recently revealed was casting the traitorous god into Tartarus.

Zeus had also asserted Karter must kill Diana by conjuring a green lightning bolt and shooting her with it. The lightning would end her life instantly, as all green bolts made by Zeus and children-of-Zeus were fatal, and afterward Karter would be made an immortal god for his heroic efforts against the Dreaded Prophecy.

Easy enough, if I were able to create and control green lightning, he thought, running a trembling hand through his shaggy black hair. His father had assured him he'd be able to make it despite the fact he'd never done so before, but he wasn't sure how. *I suppose I'll simply have to trust Zeus's judgment.*

He glanced back and peered through the pines to check that no one had fallen behind. The four Cyclopes, three of whom had been blinded in battle by their adversaries several days ago, still carried the cage that held the captives, the ground tremoring as they marched on. The demigods Layla and Xander, a lone centaur *astynomia*, and the only Cyclops who hadn't been blinded guided those who couldn't see, shoving vegetation out of the way as they traveled.

Violet, Daughter of Aphrodite, walked next to Karter. Her hips swayed with every step, and she twirled a few strands of her soaked blonde waves in her fingers, offering him a dazzling smile. Even drenched and illuminated only by the bolts above, she was a vision of beauty. "We're nearly there, love. Are you ready to finally be home?"

Karter sighed. It seemed like forever since he'd been on Olympus. The last time he had, Spencer and Syrena had still been alive. "Home. Right. Yes, I suppose I am."

She leaned over and kissed him, and he didn't object, pressing his lips against hers. Despite how sour she tasted, this was . . . nice. He wasn't sure if she was interested in him because he was to be made an immortal god or if she'd actually missed him while they'd been broken up, but how much did that matter? She'd been helping him keep his mind off things.

Violet pulled away, and Karter gazed down at her, at the pleasing lines of her face, into her shining opalescent irises. Did she believe he was in love with her because of this? Because he'd given up and looked into them? Maybe that had happened all those years ago, had been why, at one time, he'd believed he was in love with her. But no, not any longer. For a reason he had not yet come to understand, she couldn't cast her spell on him any longer.

His stomach twisted, and he glanced back at the rest of the party, his stare locking on Xander. The Son of Hermes glared at Karter so intensely he thought perhaps the demigod was planning to strangle him.

"What's Xander's problem?" Karter asked.

"He's been acting like this the entire trip."

Violet took Karter's hand as they continued walking. "Oh, he's just jealous I'm giving you so much attention. You know how my teammates get around me—or at least how Xander gets around me. I'm pretty sure Layla's never been in love, and I'm not sure she ever could be, considering she's about as affectionate as the statues in Zeus's palace. Anyway, don't mind Xander. He can't help himself."

"Wait, did you force him to fall in love with you?" Karter asked, tensing.

"Of course not," Violet answered, squeezing Karter's hand in reassurance. "You have nothing to worry about, love. I don't use that trick on anyone but my enemies." She batted her eyelashes and flipped her hair half-dramatically, half-flirtatiously. "But do you really think most demigods spending day in and day out by my side would be able to resist falling for me?"

Karter chuckled, rolling his eyes. As far as appearances went, no, he imagined it would be difficult for anyone to *not* find themselves attracted to Violet at one point or another. "I don't think they could resist you," he said, and that must have been what she wanted to hear, because she giggled in reply.

Still, despite the levity of their exchange, he

couldn't help but remember how badly she'd broken his heart all those years ago. How, after he'd gained the lightning scar on the right side of his face, she'd told him she didn't care to surround herself with ugly, unlovable things like scars. Could anything she'd said to him these past few days be trusted? Considering how angry Xander was about them spending time together, could Karter really believe her when she said she didn't use her love-trick on anyone but her enemies?

Another half hour passed before the trees began to grow sparse. New Mount Olympus emerged in the distance, Zeus's pearlescent palace standing high atop the giant mass of floating rock it had been located upon for centuries. Stormy clouds hovered around the palace, its tall columns glistening beneath the flashes of lightning and sheets of rain.

Karter halted and swung around to face the party. Violet did the same. "Xander," Karter called to the Son of Hermes, "it's time to contact Zeus. Ask him if he'll send down pegasi so we can transport our prisoners the rest of the way."

Xander barked orders at the Cyclopes. They nodded, and with the guidance of Layla and the centaur *astynomia*, they lumbered toward Karter and Violet and dropped the enclosure holding the hostages onto the grass. The ground grumbled at the force.

The three prisoners—Diana, Troy, and Marina—knelt near the front of the cage, hands clenched around its bars. Diana glowered at Karter, her expression full of fire even after defeat. At her stare, sharp pain seared in his chest, stealing the air from his lungs. Suddenly the faces of his two dead best friends, the faces of Spencer and Syrena, appeared in his mind. He clamped his eyes shut, trying to get Spencer and Syrena out of his head. *Don't focus on them*, he thought, but he couldn't escape the memories as they came tumbling back to him.

First, he saw Syrena on the night of her execution. Her expression as Karter held Spencer back from helping her. How she put her face in her hands and wept before Zeus shot her with a green lightning bolt, rendering her chest a crater of ash. Her deep-olive skin growing pale. The few last tears trickling down her cheeks.

Then Spencer as the boy struggled to stay alive in Hades after Persephone stabbed him. How he held out his golden apple to Karter, blood dribbling from his lips. *"Take it,"* he said.

"I refuse," Karter replied. *"I won't let you die because of me. Syrena already did."*

"I'm not afraid of death anymore," Spencer said. His eyes glazed over, and Karter lost both of his best

friends forever.

Karter bit his lip so hard he drew blood. Hadn't Syrena and Spencer uttered the same thing in their last moments? *Not afraid of death anymore . . . How could either of them say such a thing when they knew they'd be punished in the afterlife?*

He shivered. *It doesn't matter. I have to stop thinking about the past and about death.*

It's time to let go of all fragile mortal emotions. Let go and forget.

Karter opened his eyes and straightened himself, buried his memories as best he could, and returned his attention to the party before him.

Xander waved a hand. "Zeus, I ask to speak with you." At once all sound dissipated, the area suddenly drowned with silence, and Xander began to glow with purple light. The space around him rippled as though it were a lake with rocks skipping over it, and a familiar figure materialized before him: Karter's father. White silk robes were draped over Zeus's bulging muscles, his silver hair and beard careening about as if he were standing within violent gusts.

Xander bowed. "Thank you for accepting our call, my king. We're just outside of New Mount Olympus, and we request pegasi so we can finish transporting the hostages."

"Good work, warriors," Zeus boomed.

Instinctively, Karter shrank back at his father's voice. It sounded like cracks of thunder. "I grant your request."

As quickly as Zeus appeared, he disintegrated, and shortly afterward, three winged horses soared from the palace toward the party. Within a matter of minutes, the creatures landed. "We'll have to ensure the prisoners can't escape on our way up," Layla said. The Daughter of Ares brushed back her wet burgundy coils as she sauntered toward the prisoners' cage door. "Maybe Violet should knock them out?"

"My pleasure," Violet said, and before Karter could blink, the Daughter of Aphrodite had pulled three darts from her robes and thrust them at the hostages. The weapons pierced them in their necks. They swayed for a few moments, then toppled to the enclosure's floor. Xander unlocked the cage, and then he, Violet, and Layla gathered Troy and Marina and hoisted the grandchildren-of-Hephaestus onto the backs of two pegasi.

The Cyclops who hadn't been blinded stumbled forward, hands clasped. "Good demigods, before you go, please tell us if we have earned our freedom. If we may roam the forest now."

Violet snapped her fingers at the creature. "You'll have to wait for Zeus's orders regarding that. He might still need your assistance before you go free. As for the *astynomia*"—she pointed at the centaur—"it's time for you to go back to Hephaestus City. If there are any supporters of the Daughter of Apollo and the Chosen Two of the Prophecy, the gods will need you to help calm things down once word of the execution spreads." The *astynomia* nodded, and he turned around and clopped into the trees without a word.

The demigod trio began mounting the pegasi, and Violet gave Karter a sly smile. "What are you waiting for, love? Grab the Daughter of Apollo and let's go."

Karter braced himself and faced Diana. Although tiny, she had never been fragile. But now, as she lay in this cage, her freckled skin a sickly shade of gray, her blonde waves plastered to her scalp, she looked more delicate than ever before . . .

All at once the memories came rushing back.

"Bastard!" Diana screamed at Karter after his betrayal in Hephaestus City. *"We tried to rescue you from them, and this is how you repay us?"*

Karter picked up Diana and hoisted her over his shoulder. *Yes*, he thought. *This is how I repay you.* But before he could leap into the night, before he could fly toward the palace, a final memory plagued him, the face of a pretty girl materializing in his mind. She was a few years younger than him, with tan skin and long, curly brown hair. Her eyes shone a brilliant blue, like a clear midday sky.

"Why are you doing this?" Zoey asked Karter as they fought in the forest outside Hephaestus City, after he'd decided to help Violet, Layla, and Xander instead of her, even after she'd risked life and limb to save him. *"You could have helped us."*

"I'll do as my father commands me," Karter replied. *"What destiny has planned for me."*

"Why would you help a person who murdered millions of innocent people for power? Who killed one of your best friends right in front of you? Who mutilated your face?"

At the memory of Zoey, at the memory of his time spent with her in the Hephaestus City jail cell, Karter's chest ached. He clenched his jaw, snarling and balling his free fist at his side. After everything she'd done for him, he hadn't wanted to hurt her, but he had no choice. *Let go and forget*, he thought, over and over. *Let go and forget.*

And so he did just that, flying toward New Mount Olympus with Diana in custody. He suppressed the memories, suppressed the emotions.

After all, why would he allow such mortal frailty to control him, when he'd always been fated to become so much more?

Two days had passed since the Not-So-Pocket-Sized Submarine Troy and Marina gave the group had broken down. For an entire day after they'd stolen Poseidon's Trident and escaped the sea god and the Trojan Cetus, the vehicle had worked fine. Great, even. Andy and the rest of his friends had been traveling west across the Atlantic Ocean, hadn't encountered a single sea monster, and seemed to have been on time in reaching Olympus before Diana's execution.

Despite all this, it took only one morning for everything to go to shit. Andy had pressed down on the gas pedal, and for some reason the submarine wouldn't budge. *"Troy and Marina told us it was highly experimental,"* Zoey had said, the color draining from her face. *"I'm not sure what we're going to do now, though."*

However, Andy had soon discovered a way to keep them moving west. He kept the sub at the ocean's surface, the top door propped open, and stood on the vehicle's back seat so that his head, shoulders, and arms were outside. Then he used Poseidon's Trident to steer. All he had to do was wave the Trident in circular motions and concentrate on the direction he wanted the waves to take them. He'd taught Zoey, Darko, and Kali how to do it, and they'd taken turns steering for the next few days.

This at least pushed the submarine onward, but constantly keeping their thoughts on the right direction and gesturing with the Trident had proven to be a difficult feat for long periods of time. All four of them had accidentally veered off course at least once, and that was even when their thoughts didn't meander.

Basically, losing track of where they were going was super easy. Especially at a time like this, with the sky nearly black from a storm.

Lightning streaked across the clouds. Rain teemed, the endless ocean surrounding them churning. Frigid saltwater sprayed Andy's face, his white feathered wings already sopping and weighing down his back. The submarine tipped side to side, and he had to focus even more than normal so they wouldn't capsize, nausea bubbling in his gut. He guessed if there were anything in it, he would have thrown up by now, but they hadn't eaten since their food supply ran out yesterday. At least they still had a little bit of drinking water left.

Down below, Darko heaved. "Do you see any land yet?" he asked, and thunder roared in the distance.

"No, not yet," Andy replied. "I'll let you guys know when I do."

"I feel like we should have gotten to shore by now," Kali said. "Diana's running out of time."

"And Troy and Marina," Zoey added. "If they're still alive."

At the mention of Diana and the twin grandchildren-of-Hephaestus, Andy felt as though his heart were splitting in two. Land was nowhere in sight, and once they reached shore it would take even more time to arrive at New Mount Olympus.

He estimated around five to six days had passed since he'd awoken from that weird dream with Asteria and discovered he had wings. That same evening the group had headed toward the Labyrinth leading to Poseidon's palace. If Andy guessed right, Karter and the demigod trio were on schedule to have already made it to Olympus.

What if Troy and Marina were long gone, Diana already executed? What if it was too late to save any of them? *You can't let your mind go there*, he thought. *There's still a chance. As long as there's a chance, you have to do your best. You have to try.*

Andy pressed on, twirling the Trident and focusing on moving the sub forward without tipping it over. However, more and more dread filled him every second land remained out of sight.

What seemed like hours passed before finally the storm ceased and the waves calmed. The sky cleared to reveal the moon and stars as they gleamed down, the ocean twinkling as though it hadn't pitched a monstrous fit earlier.

Zoey climbed up from below and rested her hand on the roof of the sub, right next to Andy, and smiled at him. "*So* freaking glad that's over."

He gulped. The last time he'd talked to Zoey alone, he'd told her he was in love with her, and rather than clarifying how she felt toward him, she'd told him the truth about her past, and he hadn't reacted appropriately. Honestly, he'd pretty much screwed everything up. He'd been waiting for the best moment to apologize since.

Bringing it up when Darko and Kali can hear what we're talking about would be awkward, though, he thought. *And I have to focus. Plus, we smell like fish. Right now is a no-go for sure.*

"Uh—yeah, definitely," he said. "Me, too."

"Sometimes it feels like the storms will never end."

"Agreed. It majorly sucks."

She glanced out at the shimmering sea. "I

figured I'd watch for land with you. I really hope—I mean, I'm not sure we're gonna make it before the execution, you know? I'm worried."

Her voice cracked as she spoke, and Andy wished he could hug her. He wished he could carry on a real conversation with her, as well, but he had to concentrate. "I get it."

"Sorry," she said quickly. "I know you need to focus. I just . . . wanna talk to you."

"It's okay. I wanna talk to you, too." For a long while they didn't speak, simply standing next to each other in the serene quiet, a soft breeze blowing past them.

Out of nowhere, Zoey jumped and gasped. "What's wrong?" Andy cried. He wasn't sure he had the strength to fight a god or some crazy sea monster right now, but he'd do whatever he needed to to protect his friends.

Zoey pointed to the left, bouncing in place. "Look, there's the coastline! We did it! We're here!"

Andy glanced that way and blinked in disbelief. Zoey was right. Even in the night a solid landscape was visible in the distance—hills and trees and jagged cliffs barely illuminated by the moonlight.

"Darko, Kali!" Zoey shouted. "Get up here! We're nearly to shore!"

The satyr and the future chief of Deltama

Village clambered up to poke their heads out, grinning ear to ear. Darko whistled, and Kali pumped a fist. "Yes!" she cheered.

Andy twirled the Trident and focused on pushing them faster toward the coastline, and soon they'd nearly made it. The dark outline of a cliff hung overhead. *This is it*, he thought, relief and elation flooding his senses. *We finally made it to land. Now it's time to save Diana and the twins.*

The group's enthusiasm didn't last long, though. The waves began pushing the sub backward despite Andy's best efforts.

"What's happening?" Zoey asked. "Andy, don't lose your focus. Land is *that* way."

Andy frowned. "I know. I don't understand . . ." He swung around, gaze on the ocean, and soon discovered what was pulling them back. At the sight of the creature, his breath caught in his throat.

The monster floated only a couple hundred feet away and was unlike anything he'd seen before— mostly because the only parts of the creature he *could* see were long writhing tentacles and a gaping mouth the size of his old high school gym. Rows upon rows of crooked, sharklike teeth jutted out from the mouth, and water from every direction swirled into it like one giant whirlpool.

Andy's pulse raced. "Crap. Crap, crap, crap!"

"What the hell is that thing?" Zoey yelped.

"I think it's Charybdis!" Darko cried. "She's a sea monster who swallows a bunch of water three times a day, then spits it back up later. She—she sank *a lot* of ships in the old days."

Kali pounded a fist against the submarine. "Well, we better get to land, and fast, or we're next!"

Andy waved Poseidon's Trident faster and faster. He was trying to stop the submarine from being pulled any closer to Charybdis, but his efforts seemed to be of no use.

Panic gripped his senses as waves carried them toward the creature's cavernous jaws.

CHAPTER TWO
SHORE

Moments after Karter and the pegasi holding Violet, Layla, Xander, and the twins landed at the front of the palace, past the glistening steps that led toward the building's doors, the creatures flew in the direction of the stables, and nine demigod warriors burst from the palace's entryway. Some of them held iron chains for the prisoners, while others had large bundles of blankets in hand.

The demigods swarmed Karter, his remaining party, and the unconscious captives. A few of the warriors, the ones holding manacles, seized the grandchildren-of-Hephaestus and shackled their wrists and ankles, while the others undid their bundles and draped Violet, Layla, and Xander with blankets.

One of them approached Karter, and he quickly recognized Iro, a daughter of his godly half-brother Heracles. Iro was three years younger than Karter and stood nearly as tall, the bones beneath her taut olive skin structured like a series of sturdy columns and sharp blades. Her chestnut hair fell in waves over broad, armored shoulders, two pairs of iron chains hanging from her belt. She peered cautiously at Karter, her brown eyes—the same shade Karter's used to be before his father struck him in the face with a golden lightning bolt—nearly black in the night.

Karter and Iro had been closer when they were small children, but at the beginning of their training to become Warriors of the Gods they'd grown apart, as they were required to prioritize their teammates above everyone else. Karter had been grouped with Spencer and Syrena, while Iro had been joined with Corinna, Daughter of Demeter, and Liam, Son of Dionysus.

"Welcome home, Son of Zeus," Iro said. She gestured at Diana, who lay unconscious on Karter's shoulder. "Why don't I take the Daughter of Apollo so you can rest before her execution?"

Karter nodded and handed Diana over to Iro, his body numb with cold. From behind, another demigod placed a blanket over his shoulders.

Iro locked Diana into her manacles. "Warriors," Iro shouted, Diana in her arms as she started for the palace's entryway, "to the king!"

The other demigods repeated Iro's words and followed her lead, and Karter plodded after them, his sandaled feet sopping wet. *This is it*, he thought. *I'm really here. I'm really about to do this.*

The Warriors of the Gods made their way through the doors and into one of the palace's front halls, thunder roaring from outside. Marble statues of deities stood along the walls, their lifeless eyes glaring down at all who passed. The sky outside was visible through the hall's arched windows, and peridot-colored bolts blasted again and again, casting zigzags of bright light across the golden tiled floor.

After passing many chambers and trudging through several more halls, the demigods reached the throne room. Marble pillars with swirls winding all the way up and twelve sleek thrones lined the curved white walls. However, only ten of the Olympians were seated in their respective chairs—Zeus, Hera, Demeter, Hestia, Poseidon, Hephaestus, Ares, Hermes, Athena, and Aphrodite. Apollo was missing, as he would be put in Tartarus soon, and Artemis was hunting Zoey and Andy, the Chosen Two of the Dreaded Prophecy, alongside her loyal Huntresses. Images of shooting stars and constellations gleamed across the black ceiling, while beyond the room's dome-shaped windows, the storm raged on.

The warriors carrying Troy and Marina stepped forward and flung the grandchildren-of-Hephaestus onto the floor, the prisoners' chains clanking, then stepped back. In the dim light of the throne room, Karter recognized them as Ebony, Daughter of Nyx, the Goddess of Night; Justine, Daughter of Nemesis, the Goddess of Retribution; Luca, Son of Hemera, the Goddess of Day; and Griffin, Son of Kratos, the God of Violent Strength and Power.

Zeus climbed down from his throne, the muscles of his arms twitching as if he were preparing to choke someone, and Karter shivered.

The King of the Gods conjured two green bolts in his giant hands, sparks of electricity dancing around the lightning. "Welcome home, my son," he said, looking to Karter. "The execution of the Daughter of Apollo will commence shortly, but first I wish to take care of something."

Karter's father stepped toward Troy and Marina. Troy stirred as if he was about to wake up, but Marina was still out cold.

Zeus held his green bolts high. Karter's stomach plummeted to his feet. Despite his efforts to suppress it, the memory of Syrena's execution appeared in his mind.

He wanted to clamp his eyes shut. He wanted to turn around, to never witness someone die the way she had again. But he knew he had to watch if he was going to execute Diana this way, if he was going to become an immortal god among the rest.

And so he did.

Zeus prepared to strike. However, before he could, one of the Olympians on the left side of the throne room yelled, "Zeus—Father—stop! Please, do not go through with this. Not yet." Despite the god's pleading words, his deep voice was as fiery as boiling lava simmering across a bed of rocks.

Zeus paused to peer at the Olympian who'd spoken out, as did everyone else, and when Karter realized who it was, their identity didn't surprise him. It was Hephaestus, the Blacksmith of the Gods and the God of Fire and Metalworking. Troy and Marina's grandfather.

Compared to the rest of the perfect, glowing Olympians, Hephaestus was quite unattractive, his eyes bulging in his head like a deformed hound's, the rest of his features entirely asymmetrical. Soot covered his brown hair, face, and hands. As he hobbled toward Zeus he leaned on a thick metal cane, one of the legs beneath his tunic shriveled and misshapen. Karter recalled from history lessons that this was a permanent injury obtained from the day Hera gave birth to him. The Queen of the Gods thought he was an ugly baby and cast him off Olympus.

"Hephaestus, what is the meaning of this?" Zeus asked.

The Blacksmith of the Gods opened his mouth to reply, but Hera sprang from her throne and rushed in front of him, her long hair and flowing dress swelling out behind her, her nostrils flaring. "Hephaestus, you are a wretched excuse for a son," she began, the words like venom spewing from her lips. "Sit down and keep quiet. You must respect Zeus's ruling. Above all else, he is your king."

The sight of the Queen of the Gods and the sound of her voice made Karter sick. He closed his eyes, but still, his mother's face flashed before them. Usually, he could remain neutral with Hera, but Asteria had given him a vision a few days ago—a vision of the night his mother had been killed.

"Hera has sent Ladon," his mother had said, moments before the monster slashed her throat. He'd barely escaped the same fate. *"This is the work of Hera!"*

Karter clenched his fists at his sides and focused

on shoving the thoughts from his mind. *Let go and forget*, he thought. *That's only a ghost of your past. A ghost that will fade with time, just like Spencer and Syrena. Just like Diana.*

Even Zoey's kindness toward you will fade, too.

Focus on your destiny, the one written by the Fates long ago. Let go and forget.

Hephaestus pushed past Hera. "I will say my piece, 'Mother.'" But before the god could speak again, Troy groaned and opened his eyes. He glanced around, his jaw dropping as he digested the scene before him, and then he began to shake Marina. Once she awoke and took in her surroundings, her gaze locked on her grandfather. Troy glared at the god as well.

Marina snarled, orange flames flickering in her bound hands. "You ratted out our father, you bastard!"

Troy struggled against his chains. "How could you do that to us? He was all we had!"

Thunder *craaack*ed, and Zeus stomped his foot. "*Silence!*" Everyone quieted, turning to him. He allowed his green bolts to disintegrate and crossed his arms. "Hephaestus, why must you always insist on speaking out against me when it comes to these insufferable descendants of yours? First when Helen gave birth to them and now. You are a valued Olympian, and since Apollo betrayed us, you've become even more important, but these two have broken the law. They have conspired against us, lied to us, just as their mother did. Helen was a traitor, and it is time her legacy ends."

Hephaestus licked his lips. "You misunderstand, Father. I . . . agree with you, in that they have committed heinous crimes against the gods, and that they must be punished accordingly. However, they are the Master Blacksmiths of the forges in my *polis*. They run everything there. I need them spared, if only for a few more days, so that they can wrap things up, so to speak. Appoint others to take the mantle. If I am to be . . . well, absent, on my mission for you, and they are killed now, without any chance to settle their final affairs, the forges—my *polis*—will descend into madness."

Karter raised a brow. What was Hephaestus talking about? What mission was he going on for Zeus? Also, wasn't there some kind of chain of command in the forges of Hephaestus City? Did the god actually believe what he was saying, or was he trying to stall for Troy and Marina?

"Very well then, Hephaestus," Zeus said, stroking his beard. "For the six days you are absent, I will allow your descendants to sort out what they must in their forges. But, once the six days are up, once you have returned, and despite whether they've finished wrapping up business or not—

they will be killed."

Hephaestus bowed to Zeus and thanked him, but Marina only glared at the gods, and Troy spit at their feet. "You might as well just kill us now," he said.

"That's right," Marina added. "Execution is a welcome consequence for our rebellion."

Zeus sneered. "Imbeciles. Even after death, your punishment won't end. A swift message to Nyx and Thanatos as they look after the Underworld in Hades's absence will ensure you'll be sent straight to Tartarus, where you will remain for all eternity. That is, if you refuse to do as you are told."

The twins shared a knowing look. They nodded and reached for one another, their chains clanking. They clasped hands, and, together, they inhaled deeply and looked up at Zeus.

"We won't help with the forges," Marina said. "We won't help you."

Troy shook his head. "We don't serve tyrants any longer, no matter what we're threatened with."

The King of the Gods chuckled, and the lightning scar on the right side of Karter's face throbbed with the memory of old pain. Despite what the grandchildren-of-Hephaestus said, Karter was sure Zeus would get what he wanted from them, one way or another.

The god conjured two golden bolts and raised them above his head. "Your bravery is commendable. However, it will be in vain. You insects will do as I instruct you to until you take your dying breaths."

Zeus brought the bolts down onto the grandchildren-of-Hephaestus—onto their backs, their spines—and they screamed.

Zoey's heart hammered against her rib cage as the group approached the mouth of Charybdis. In no time at all, they would be swallowed whole.

Beside Zoey, Andy slapped the Trident against the water, probably to try another method of escape, but to no avail. Meanwhile, Kali launched one of their daggers at the monster, and Darko shot an arrow. That didn't help, either. The weapons only slid down Charybdis's gullet without so much as a cough or splutter. "Nothing's working!" Darko cried. "What do we do?"

My voice-powers, Zoey thought. She took a deep breath and focused on what she could say to get this creature to let them go, her throat tingling. "Mighty Charybdis, monster of the sea," she began. Her body thrummed with the power of a goddess, with the power of Calliope, Goddess of Eloquence. "Allow us safe passage to shore, and you will be rewarded greatly. Do not sink us, and in return, we will give you anything your heart desires!" Moments passed, and nothing changed. Either the creature couldn't hear Zoey, or she was immune to Zoey's abilities.

Zoey cursed through gritted teeth and glanced around for another idea, spotting the cliff that had just been overhead. The rocks were farther away now, but if the group could reach them . . .

She grabbed Andy's arm and gestured at the precipice with her handless wrist. "Andy, fly us to that cliff!"

"What about the sub?"

"We've reached the coastline. We don't need it anymore—just let this thing have it." She looked over to see they were less than fifty feet away from the creature's toothy maw. "Andy, you gotta fly us outta here! Now!"

Resolve came over his expression, and he shoved the Trident into Zoey's hand. He seized the sack holding the Helm of Darkness and slung it over his shoulder like a backpack, then grabbed Zoey under the armpits and jerked her into the sky.

Andy darted toward the precipice with Zoey in his arms. Just as they neared its edge, he pitched her toward it. She tumbled onto the rocks. Aches spasmed in her shoulder, but she kept her hand clasped tight around the Trident's handle.

Moments passed before Darko toppled next to Zoey. He groaned in pain. Her head spun, but she forced herself to sit up and look at him. He clutched his wrist, the joint twisted at an odd angle.

Zoey gasped. "Oh my God! Darko, are you okay?"

Before he could reply, the scream of a young woman pierced the air behind them, and Zoey and Darko locked eyes. "Kali," Darko said. Zoey swung around, her stomach clenching.

Sure enough, the cry belonged to Kali. Andy held the tall, dark-haired girl by the wrists, his white feathered wings flapping frantically, but Charybdis had reached up with one of her tentacles and wrapped the appendage around Kali's ankle. Below, the monster's massive mouth sucked in ocean like a high-speed vortex. The Pocket-Sized Submarine crashed into a few of her teeth before disappearing into her esophagus.

Zoey scrambled to her feet, Trident in hand. Days ago, she'd discovered she was a goddess incarnate, and in this moment, she held one of the most powerful objects in existence. Yet as she watched the scene before her unfold, she felt completely helpless. *Please*, she thought. *I'm begging whatever god might be listening, please let Andy and Kali be okay.*

Charybdis tugged on Kali with her tentacle, pulling the girl down, and she slipped from Andy's grasp. She screamed. With one hand Andy grabbed her before she could fall. With the other, he reached for the sword at his belt.

The appendage yanked again. Kali kicked it with her free leg. At the same time, Andy unsheathed his sword. He reared his weapon back, then sliced the blade clean through the tentacle.

A hiss like a waterfall sounded from Charybdis's throat. She closed her mouth, rows of teeth disappearing, and slipped beneath the surface.

Andy and Kali soared toward the cliff. Once they landed safely, Zoey dropped the Trident and hurried to them. She threw her arms around Andy's and Kali's necks, and they hugged her back. "I thought you guys were goners," she said.

Kali chuckled and gave her a little squeeze. "Would I seem less impressive if I told you I thought so, too?"

Andy laughed. "Man, c'mon, you guys. Have a little faith in me, will ya?"

Darko groaned behind them, and Zoey broke away from their embrace and turned to the satyr. In all the commotion she'd forgotten he'd been injured.

"It hurts," Darko said as he sat holding his wrist.

Andy rushed to Darko's side. Zoey and Kali followed his lead. "What happened?" Andy cried.

"When you threw me onto the cliff, I think I landed wrong."

Andy cursed under his breath. "I'm so sorry, Darko. I can't believe I—"

"It's okay," Darko interrupted. "Don't be sorry. You were just trying to get everyone to safety."

Zoey eyed the satyr's injury. It was already swollen and bruised. She grimaced, the fleshy stump where her right hand had once been aching. The excruciating pain she'd felt when it had been cut off seemed to have lasted forever, even though Diana had healed her once they escaped from Hades. But the group no longer had the luxury of Diana fixing their every ailment, which meant Darko would suffer much longer than she had, even if the injury wasn't as severe.

Kali squatted and rested a hand on Darko's shoulder. "Do you think it's broken?"

He nodded. "Yeah. Kind of looks like the time my—my brother broke his arm during training. It really, really hurts."

"We're gonna have to figure out how to set it," Zoey said.

"How do we do that?" Andy asked. "I don't

even know where to begin. I wish Diana was here."

Darko grunted. "I might have an idea of what we can do. At least until—until we rescue Diana. Then she can heal it the rest of the way. When Phoenix broke his arm—well, I didn't want to leave him by himself at the healing shrine. So I—I stayed in and watched what they did to him. I just have to try and remember how . . ."

Before the satyr could finish his sentence, deep rumbles sounded from within the earth beneath them, and the ground trembled. Zoey's pulse quickened. What god or monster was after them this time?

"What now?" Andy said with a sigh. He grabbed Poseidon's Trident and climbed to his feet. All the while, Zoey knelt next to Darko and Kali, ready to defend them.

Darko's eyes went wide. "Uh-oh. 'To be between Scylla and Charybdis . . .'"

"What are you talking about?" Kali asked.

"We avoided Charybdis." As Darko spoke, the words came out at a rapid pace. "But opposite of Charybdis is Scylla. In the old days, the hero Odysseus had to choose whether to sail closer to Charybdis or Scylla, since they weren't avoidable for where he needed to go. If he chose Charybdis, she'd sink his whole ship, and if he chose Scylla, she'd eat some of his men. Odysseus chose to sail closer to Scylla, since it was better to sacrifice a few men rather than the whole ship. I—I don't think he even tried to fight Scylla." Panic rose in his voice. "Actually, if I remember right, Scylla can't be defeated at all. Maybe she could be with the Helm of Darkness and Poseidon's Trident, but—we need to run!"

Zoey and Kali shot to their feet and helped Darko stand. Andy was already ushering them closer to the mainland. "Let's go, let's go, let's go!" he yelled.

Growls and barks like those of a pack of vicious hounds echoed from somewhere inside the earth beneath their feet. From the right, something jolted out of the darkness and shot in front of them. They stopped dead. Even in the night Zoey could see it was a moss-colored eel—that is, if eels had heads as large as motorcycles, complete with glowing amber eyes and the jaws of a wolf.

Andy leapt into the air and brandished the Trident at the creature. "Don't get any closer unless you wanna be skewered." The monster let out a deep, rumbling growl, shaking the ground. "Go back to wherever you came from!"

As if in reply to Andy's words, more eels slithered into view until six of the slimy serpents hovered before them. The creatures snaked all around them, surrounding them on every side.

Then the eels emitted a series of odd barking noises, baring their sharp, canine-like teeth.

"Yeah, that's definitely Scylla," Darko squeaked.

Zoey couldn't waste another moment. She was supposed to be a *goddess*, and just a few days ago, she'd taken down Poseidon by manipulating the Trojan Cetus with her voice-powers. Charybdis might not have been able to hear her, but surely Scylla could. It was time to end this. "Stop!" she shouted at Scylla, her throat tingling as she focused on her voice-powers. "In the name of the gods, I command you to *stop!*" To her surprise, Scylla quieted and paused, puzzled expressions on her several heads.

"Good work," Andy said, Poseidon's Trident still in hand.

"Thank you for your cooperation, Scylla, great monster of the, er, cliff," Zoey went on. "I'm sure you recognize that"—she gestured at the Trident, but kept her gaze locked on the monster—"as it is one of the most powerful objects in existence. Whoever wields it controls the oceans and the seas, and I believe that might include you, since you're by the sea. Therefore, it is in your best interest to not engage violently with us. Simply leave us alone and allow us safe passage onto the mainland. In return, you will be rewarded greatly. We can do that because we are gods, and we promise to . . . to grant you whatever you desire."

Scylla blinked a few times, her heads sharing confused looks. She glanced back and forth between Zoey and Andy. *Please work, please work*, Zoey thought, balling her hand at her side. *If what Darko says is true, and she can't be defeated in battle, we're toast.*

After what felt like an eternity, the group received an answer to their request, but it didn't come from Scylla, and it certainly wasn't the reply anyone expected.

From somewhere ahead of them, somewhere farther onto the mainland, the soft and unfamiliar voice of a young woman echoed. "I suppose I can tell Scylla to let you go, so long as I receive something in return. However, you stand on no mainland. In fact, you are not even close to any mainland.

"My name is Circe, and you should know that you stand on an island. *My* island."

CHAPTER THREE
ISLAND

Karter grimaced, his scar still throbbing as he watched Troy and Marina wail on the floor, Zeus's bolts disintegrating. The twins' earsplitting shrieks bounced off the walls, and Karter's body racked with shudders, the scent of scorched flesh assaulting his nostrils.

Troy and Marina writhed their heads and arms in pain, and Karter suspected they would have twisted their legs as well if they could. However, it seemed they could no longer move those limbs. Hot tears welled in Karter's eyes. He blinked hard to hold them back, his heart pounding. *This is only a fragile human emotion*, he told himself. *Let go of it. In time it will pass altogether.*

Hephaestus rushed toward his grandchildren, his deformed face contorted with what looked like worry. "Father, what have you done to them?"

"If my punishment went as planned," Zeus began, "and my punishments generally do, Troy and Marina will be paralyzed from the waist down for the remainder of their miserable lives. That's what they get for disobeying me."

Only a few of the gods and demigods present appeared genuinely concerned for Troy and Marina—Hephaestus and Hestia, then Luca and Corinna. Karter thought he himself probably seemed worried for them as well, but he was doing his best to make himself as emotionless as possible. Several others looked downright pleased with the outcome, though—among them were Ares, Hera, Poseidon, Xander, Violet, and Griffin. However, a majority only sighed and shook their heads.

"Take them away," Zeus ordered. Iro, Corinna, and Liam stepped forward to do as he demanded, their expressions fearful. "Lock them in the dungeons. I'll come for them tomorrow so they can begin setting the forges straight."

As the trio of warriors dragged a sobbing Troy and Marina out of the throne room, the rest of the gods and demigods broke out into gossipy whispers, and Karter had to take deep breaths to calm his racing heart. He glanced around the room, scanning other people in an attempt to forget his own panic for a moment. And, as he focused on everyone else's faces, he quickly found there was one person whose reaction he couldn't read. One person whose face remained an impassive mask—not a trace of delight or sorrow in her eyes.

It was Violet and Xander's "friend"—the girl who had once been Diana and Pearl's close companion, before Pearl's untimely death and Diana's consequent betrayal.

It was Layla.

Karter watched Layla curiously for a few moments as the gods and demigods continued whispering, forgetting about himself for a time and wondering why her expression was so blank as she observed Troy and Marina be carted off.

A second later Layla glanced his way, and, surprisingly, he thought he spotted a hint of emotion in her eyes, her brow furrowing. Was that guilt? Anguish? Something else?

Before Karter could decipher what he saw on Layla's face, she turned away from him, and a giant hand clamped down on his shoulder. He flinched and turned to find his father standing over him. "Now we must prepare for the execution," Zeus said.

Karter's tongue suddenly felt heavy in his mouth, and he found he couldn't form a coherent response. Would he be able to create and control green lightning? Would he be able to do this? He managed to nod in reply, his only choice to try and trust his father.

Zeus nodded back. "It is almost time," he announced, never taking his gaze off Karter. "Time for all to watch the Daughter of Apollo die. To watch the end of the Dreaded Prophecy."

Everyone in the throne room went quiet. Zeus guided Karter into the halls of the palace, the rest of the gods and demigods following close behind.

Andy craned his head, trying to spot Circe, but he couldn't see anything past Scylla's snarling eel-dog-monster heads that surrounded him and his friends. "What do you mean, we're on your island?" he yelled. "This can't be happening. You're insane!"

"Shhh, Andy," Darko hissed from behind the boy, his voice still strained with pain. "I've heard about Circe, back in my history lessons and trainings. She's an enchantress, and whenever people have made her mad, she turns them into animals. You *do not* want to offend her, so calm down."

But Andy couldn't do that, panic brewing in his chest. If what Circe said was true, if they weren't near a mainland, if they weren't near Olympus or any of the twelve cities, then what in the world were they supposed to do? How would they reach Diana and the twins in time, if ever?

Zoey rested her hand on his shoulder, probably to ease his senses before he did something rash. However, it had the opposite effect on him. His heart pounded even harder than before. "I think what my godly companion here is trying to express," she began, "is that surely this coastline couldn't be an island. We've been traveling toward the mainland—toward Olympus, more specifically—for days now, and that's where we need to go so we can complete our mission."

"Hmm, most curious," Circe replied. "You say you are gods, and I am inclined to believe you, considering you have somehow obtained Poseidon's Trident, and considering the divine essences I sense you possess. Yet you do not know your way to Olympus? Most curious, indeed."

Andy opened his mouth to reply, but Zoey beat him to it, laughing nervously. "Yeah, well, you know how it is. I'm sure you've run into your fair share of minor gods and goddesses." It seemed her voice-powers had worn off, or she'd lost concentration. She didn't sound as regal as she had a few moments ago. "Anyway, since you say we're on an island, and since our mission is pretty time sensitive, it's probably best we head out and find a way to reach Olympus."

"Ah ah ah, not so fast," Circe replied. "You will not go anywhere until I receive my payment. Not unless you care to be eaten by Scylla."

"You forget," Zoey started in a singsong way, sounding a bit more self-assured now, "that we are gods, and with a snap of our fingers we could end your very existence. So let us go without a fight, and we will repay you when it suits us." At this the woman laughed, but it couldn't be in jest. There was something sinister to it. Andy shivered.

"You have no power over my existence," Circe said with another cackle. "You should know that. How can you be a goddess yet have no idea who I am? Curious, curious, curious."

Who the hell does she think she is? Andy wondered. *And why isn't she afraid of us? We've got gods living inside of our bodies. Or, I guess, we're gods reincarnated? Plus, we have the Helm of Darkness and Poseidon's Trident.*

Zoey took a step in the direction of Circe's voice, and Kali grabbed her hand. "Wait. Remember what Darko said? Maybe we shouldn't—"

"I can handle this," Zoey interjected. She gave Kali's hand a squeeze, as if to reassure the other girl, and pulled away. "I don't think you quite understand who you're up against, Miss Circe. We most certainly have power over your existence, regardless of whoever you *think* you are. After all, we are gods, and we possess not only Poseidon's Trident, but also the Helm of Darkness. With these items, we rule over the Underworld and the seas. You have to do what we say. What *I* say." Andy had to admit, Zoey sounded pretty convincing. Those voice-powers of hers sure were getting strong again. He almost had to force himself to stay standing instead of bowing at her feet and asking her what her first order of business was.

Circe chuckled again. "The items you speak of are useless unless the wielders know how to properly utilize their powers. I suspect you fools have not yet unlocked their secrets, considering you're still attempting to persuade me rather than using them to make your escape." Andy blinked in surprise. Zoey's abilities really weren't working on Circe. Not only that, but she made some seriously good points.

"Maybe we should just do what she asks," Darko whispered. "Before anyone else gets hurt?"

Andy took a few deep breaths, his head finally

clearing, his heart and stomach calming. The last thing he wanted to do was comply with this Circe person, but it didn't seem they had any other choice. He looked to Zoey. "We're cornered, exhausted, and starving," he said. "Darko can't fight with a busted wrist, and the rest of us are so weak there's no way we can take on this 'Scylla' thing without getting seriously hurt—or an 'enchantress' who turns people into animals when she's mad, for that matter. We don't exactly have the upper hand here."

"But we have Poseidon's Trident and the Helm of Darkness, not to mention my voice-powers," Zoey replied, turning to him. "If we can't even fight some woman and her pet monster with them, how are we ever supposed to use them to steal the Master Lightning Bolt and take down an entire pantheon of gods?"

Andy shared looks with Darko and Kali and mulled over Zoey's words. The Helm of Darkness and Poseidon's Trident were supposed to grant them incredible powers that helped them rule over parts of the world, but Circe was right: the objects were useless in many ways unless Andy and Zoey could wield them properly and use them to their full capacity. The two of them didn't know how to do that yet; otherwise, they would have already done it and escaped.

In fact, it seemed as if the pair had only touched the tip of the iceberg when it came to unlocking the objects' secrets. After all, the only reason they'd defeated Poseidon was because Zoey manipulated the Trojan Cetus with her voice-powers. If they hadn't had an advantage like that, they would have been totally screwed. Not to mention the fact that they didn't have anyone to teach them or anyone who knew much about the objects ever since Diana had been captured. Until they could save her, or until they could do some research of their own and get serious amounts of training under their belts, they were pretty much stuck in this stagnant state of knowledge regarding the gods' toys.

We might be legitimately hopeless, Andy thought. *Which is kinda funny, considering how far we've gotten . . . somehow making it out of the Underworld and Poseidon's palace alive. What if this is where it all comes to a halt, and we let down the world because we were too stupid to think about learning more regarding how to use the gods' objects of power ahead of time?*

He finally whispered to Zoey, "Think about what Circe said—the items are pretty much useless if we don't know how to properly utilize their powers. I think there's some truth to that. If there weren't, we wouldn't be arguing with her right now. Or am I missing something?"

Zoey knit her brow, pushing a few loose curls behind her ears. "You're not wrong. I just . . . I'm worried about what's going to happen when we finally face off with the gods. Like, if we can't do *this* the way we're supposed to, how will we ever do *that?* I thought by this point, we'd be pretty much invincible. But we're not, are we?"

"You might be to some," Darko said. "But you'll still have to deal with every situation we come across a little differently. Maybe this is one of those times?"

Kali shrugged and jutted a thumb in Darko's direction. "I mean, I see where you're coming from, Zoey, but Darko's not wrong."

Zoey sighed and smiled a little, Andy's stomach flip-flopping. How could a person go through hell and back multiple times—in a literal postapocalyptic world, no less—and still look so beautiful? "Thanks for talking me down, guys," she started. "I keep thinking this is going to get easier, but it isn't. The odds are still against us, it seems."

"But at least we're doing it together, right?" Andy asked.

"Right," Zoey replied. She offered everyone a nod, then faced the direction of Circe's voice once more. "All right, Miss Circe. What would you like from us as payment? We'll give you whatever you want, within reason. For instance, you can't have the magical objects in our possession—we're, um, we're delivering them. To Zeus, I mean. Once we give you what you want, though, we'd like directions to Olympus, and advice on how we can get a new method of transportation, if it's not too much of a hassle."

"You're a goddess who gets down to business, I see," Circe replied with a chuckle. "You'd fulfill any request I have and then be on your way without even knowing who I am? Who I really am?"

"Who are you, then, exactly?" Andy piped up, squaring his shoulders and tightening his grip on the Trident as he stepped forward.

"You're an enchantress, right?" Darko asked.

"Yes, that's true," Circe replied, and the dog-eel-monsters, or Scylla or whatever, parted to reveal her.

When Andy laid eyes on Circe, he had to focus on keeping his jaw from dropping. Not because she was unbelievably gorgeous or anything like that. She was pretty, yeah, and she looked as if she could be around his age even though he knew she wasn't. But what immediately stood out to him was that she couldn't just be an enchantress—she also had to be a goddess.

She was fairly short, maybe an inch or so taller than Diana, unlike many of the other gods and goddesses they'd met before. However, her presence remained commanding all the same. Inexplicable energy rolled off her deep-olive skin in droves. Silky knee-length robes draped over her slim figure, bracelets and necklaces dotted with precious gems snaking around her limbs and throat. She held a large pointed branch like a wand, which had wires and raw crystals wrapped all around it. What startled Andy the most, however, were her eyes and hair. Her pupil-less orbs glowed like molten gold, and her long red locks flowed all around her head like the flames of a bonfire.

Circe must have been amused by the way Andy was staring at her. She gave him a little wave, her lips curling up in a flirtatious smile. Immediately he tore his gaze away.

"You're also a goddess," Zoey said matter-of-factly.

"Mm-hmm," Circe replied. "A daughter of Helios and Perse—so a minor deity, just like you. Although I still thought you'd look much more impressive than you do. Your companion, on the other hand . . ." She gestured at Andy with her stick or wand or whatever it was and winked. "Very handsome. I *love* the wings." Andy's cheeks went hot. He glanced at Zoey. She only rolled her eyes at the goddess.

Kali must have sensed Zoey's annoyance and

Andy's embarrassment because she trudged ahead of them. "Okay, so you're a goddess who dabbles in witchcraft," she said. "That's real impressive, and I mean it. Now please, name your price for our safe passage out of here. We're—we're trying to rescue someone, and she's running out of time." Kali's voice cracked as she uttered those last few words, and Andy recalled the moments before they'd all been separated from Diana.

Kali had begged Diana not to leave the group to battle Karter and the rest of the asshole demigods, but Diana had insisted she needed to so everyone else could escape. Then Kali had kissed Diana, right on the lips, and Diana had kissed her back. It had been a cute moment between them, and Andy would probably remember it a lot more fondly if his wings hadn't been breaking through the skin of his back to grow in the same moment. The pain had been so intense he'd passed out. *At least those two finally acknowledged they like each other*, he thought. *Maybe the next time we're all together, they won't bicker anymore, unless that's just the way they'll always flirt.*

If they can *always flirt. If we reach Diana before the execution . . .*

Circe tapped her chin. "Hmm. You know, I'm not sure what I want from you yet. Follow me home and let's chat while I think about it. Once we arrive, I can use some natural remedies to heal his bones"—she pointed at Darko—"and provide the four of you with food and drink." She snapped her fingers, and Scylla slithered back beneath the cliff without hissing or barking or anything else. Circe twirled around and started heading farther down the cliff.

At the mention of food and drink, Andy's stomach growled, but he still shared looks of bewilderment with Zoey, Darko, and Kali. What was Circe's deal? First she threatened them with being eaten by her pet dog-eel-monster if they didn't somehow pay her, and now she was offering to fix up Darko and feed everyone. Was this some kind of trap? Did she know Andy and Zoey were the Chosen Two of the Prophecy and were planning on saving humanity from the tyranny of the gods? Was she planning on turning them in to Zeus?

At any rate, what other choice did they have, other than to follow her?

"I guess let's go?" Zoey said. The rest of them agreed, and with that, they trekked after the goddess.

They reached the bottom of a hill that sloped upward toward the cliff. Down here, a forest of cypress trees beckoned them into total darkness. "Uh, how're we supposed to see in there?" Andy asked Circe as they approached the woods. "It looks pitch black.”

“Not to worry,” Circe replied, and slapped the tip of her crystal-wrapped wand against her palm. In an instant, a sphere of yellow illumination glinted into existence on the branch’s end like a flashlight. “I know most others cannot see in the dark.”

Andy scratched the back of his head. “You can see in the dark?”

“Why, yes,” she said, and giggled girlishly. Andy gulped. He wasn’t sure how he felt about the tone in her voice when she talked to him. “I’m surprised you didn’t pick up on that when you saw my glowing golden eyes, you striking creature.” Andy blanched and paused for a second. *Uh, gross*, he thought. *She’s, what, thousands of years old? Even if she only looks a little bit older than me?*

Someone pinched Andy’s arm, and he turned to see Kali. “Hey,” she whispered. “Remember what Darko said? Don’t offend her.”

“Yeah,” he whispered back, although the fact that she turned people who’d upset her into animals couldn’t change how weird he thought her flirting with him was.

As they walked into the trees, following Circe so they didn’t trip or get lost in the darkness, the goddess started to ask them questions. “So, what are your names? Other than your detour on my island, how is your mission for Zeus going? And what does the mission consist of, exactly?"

"I'm . . . I'm Zoey," Zoey began, and Andy wondered, due to her pause, whether she'd considered saying Calliope instead. "And our satyr friend here is named Darko. Then there's Kali and, um, Andy." She gestured at them as she said their names. "As for our mission for Zeus, well . . . he doesn't exactly want us telling too many other gods about it, if you know what I mean. He was pretty clear about that when he sent us away."

Circe snorted. "I know exactly what you mean. Zeus has always been an idiot. Why make you keep your mission a secret, when those around you could help if they only knew what you are meant to do? It's always a game of loyalty with him. If you ask me, there's no one less worthy of being King of the Gods. But what can any of us do about it, right? We still have to follow his every last order."

Andy blinked hard. *What the hell?* he thought. *If she buys the story about us being gods and on a mission for Zeus, why is she trash-talking him right now? What if we were super-loyalists to him? Shouldn't she be worried about us tattling on her or something?*

Also, was she suggesting that if she knew what our mission was, she'd help us? What about the fact that we're on her *island, and we have to repay her for safe passage out of here, or else she'll sic Scylla on us?* His friends seemed equally taken aback by Circe's contradicting words and actions. They raised their brows and shared looks with him.

Finally, Zoey let out a nervous laugh. "So, I take it you don't like our king?"

"Not particularly," Circe replied. "I cannot say I care for any of the Olympians, really. I suppose you can see, then, why I'm asking you for something in return before letting you go so you can finish your little excursion for them."

"I suppose I can," Zoey replied.

A few minutes of awkward silence passed before there was a rustling in the woods to their left. Everyone but Circe halted in their tracks. "What was that?" Darko whispered.

Gray fur that must have belonged to an animal flashed between the trees up ahead—there and gone in an instant. A howl sounded in the air, echoing across the sky, and goose bumps prickled on Andy's skin, the hair on the back of his neck standing straight. "Circe, are you sure it's safe out here?" he asked. "For our mortal friends, I mean."

The goddess giggled again, and Andy shivered. "Of course, handsome winged beast," she said. "That was just one of my pets you heard." He gulped. *One of her pets?* It was probably better to keep his mouth shut from here on out. He didn't want to be turned into a pet, and he didn't want to be turned into pet-kibble, either.

When it began to feel as though they'd been walking through the black forest for ages, they reached a massive clearing at the bottom of another hill. A trio of long, vertically stacked stone staircases led to the top of the mound, marvelous gazebos and fountains spouting shimmering water lining the three flights of steps. And, at the top of the stairs—at the top of the hill—one of the most magnificent structures Andy had ever laid his eyes on beckoned them.

The building was a round ivory palace supported by tall columns, the marble it had been fashioned from glistening beneath the dim light of the moon and stars. Even at the bottom of the hill, Andy could make out the designs carved and painted into the palace's exterior; they reminded him of pictures he'd seen in his high-school art classes that featured ancient Greek pottery.

Circe paused and spun around. "Gorgeous, isn't it?"

Darko released a low whistle, and Kali said, "Sure is."

Circe sighed contentedly, and her gleeful gaze wandered over all of them before fixing itself on Andy. She flashed him a dazzling smile, seizing his free hand with hers. "Come, come. Welcome to my home!"

Her palm was warm, feverishly so, and Andy had the very strong urge to yank away from her grip. However, remembering what Darko had said about how she punished those who offended her, he did no such thing. Instead, he let her entwine her fingers with his, allowed her to begin dragging him up the stairs leading to her palace.

For a brief moment, he glanced over his shoulder to shoot his friends a helpless look as they followed behind him and the sorceress. Darko offered him a pained shrug, while Kali gave him an awkward smile. It was as if they were saying, *"Sorry, there's nothing we can do. You're on your own."* The only expression he couldn't read was Zoey's. She pressed her lips into a thin line. Was it just him, or did she almost seem *annoyed* with Circe? With him?

Circe tugged hard on his arm, pulling him up onto the second flight of steps, and he turned away from his friends, an uncomfortable feeling settling in his stomach.

Soon they reached the top of the stairs. Circe led them past tall columns and the front doors, then into the entryway, still clutching Andy's hand. As they walked, the sorceress twirled her wand. Flames burst to life atop sconces attached to the walls, one by one as the group passed, casting flickering shadows along the gem-encrusted tiles making up the floor.

It was because of the dancing fires that Andy could finally see the interior of the palace. He drank it all in with wide eyes. The high, arched ceilings. The colorful paintings embellishing the white walls. The lavish, gold-trimmed furniture. The lions and wolves that were lounging on said lavish, gold-trimmed furniture . . .

Wait, he thought, *what the hell? Am I seeing things?* He stopped in his tracks to further inspect the palace's insides, blinking hard, but no, he wasn't imagining it. Twelve wild animals—seven sleek gray wolves and five fluffy yellow lions, to be exact—were sitting on Circe's plush rugs and cushions and chairs and couches as if they owned the place.

In fact, it seemed as if the animals *did* own the place, and Andy suddenly felt as though he'd intruded on a sacred space. When the animals spotted him and his friends, they went rigid where they sat. Low growls escaped a few of the wolves' throats, the fur on their backs standing straight, lips pulled back to reveal gleaming fangs. All the while, the lions flicked their tails back and forth, glaring at Andy and his friends with soulless black pits for eyes.

Worst of all, though, was the stench. When it finally hit Andy's nostrils, he wrestled with the urge to plug his nose. It smelled like a barnyard in here.

Darko and Kali yelped from behind Andy and Circe as the wolves' growls grew louder, and Zoey stepped up next to Andy. She side-eyed his hand intertwined with Circe's. "I'm guessing these are more of your pets?" she asked.

"Now you're catching on, Goddess of Eloquence," Circe replied.

Zoey's eyes narrowed. Her hand lingered over the bag holding the Helm of Darkness. The bag was draped over her shoulder, and it dangled at her waist. "How did you—"

It was then that the wolf closest to them—it had been sprawled out on a royal-blue rug with intricate, sewn-in designs—released a series of barks and snarls and pounced for Zoey.

At this point, Andy didn't care about pissing off Circe. He yanked his hand from hers, brandished Poseidon's Trident, and jumped in front of Zoey.

However, before he ever needed to use the Trident, Circe snapped her fingers. "Back, Agamemnon!" she ordered. Her voice echoed through the chamber, through the whole palace, it seemed. "Back!" The wolf—Agamemnon— heeded Circe's command. It backed away, shrinking in on itself, whining all the while.

Circe wagged a finger at the rest of the wild animals around them. "My pets, these are our . . . our friends. Our *guests*. And you will respect them as you respect me and my nymphs." She twirled around to face Andy; he still stood protectively in front of Zoey, and he didn't plan on leaving her side again. "That is," Circe continued with a wink, "unless I say otherwise."

Andy gulped. There was something in the tone of her voice that made him nervous. *But what else can we do, other than give her what she asks for and go? We're in no shape to fight, and Zoey's voice-powers didn't work on her.*

They strolled through more chambers in the palace, each larger and more magnificent than the last. As they walked, they passed what must have been dozens more lions and wolves. They even passed some young girls who looked like forest and sea nymphs; the girls stayed quiet and kept their heads down as the group went by, focusing on their chores.

All the while, Andy wondered where the lions and wolves came from. Had they once been people? People who'd angered Circe and been turned into "pets"? Or had they been born as animals and simply flocked to the goddess? Seriously, though, where had they come from? How big was this island, exactly? It couldn't be all that large. And wasn't there some kind of prey-to-predator ratio? Was that a thing? If so, where were all the animals the lions and wolves ate?

Finally, they reached a chamber that looked like a kitchen—that is, if one managed to fuse a kitchen with a witch's potion room. Regular kitchen utensils, ovens and stoves, and pantries stuffed with food inhabited the room. So did a number of animal and human skulls and bones, along with several wooden racks filled to the brim with bottles of colorful glowing goo. *Potions?* Andy wondered. The thorned vines of plants unlike any he'd seen grew over everything, and the scents of fresh bread and juicy produce mingled with the smells of aromatic herbs and smoky concoctions. Hot air blasted Andy in the face as he entered, sweat forming on his brow.

Circe sauntered over to a rack of what Andy thought could be potions and grabbed a bottle shining a tranquil shade of green. "Come here, satyr," she said. "Let me treat your injury."

Darko looked at Andy, Zoey, and Kali as if asking for reassurance. They all nodded at him. "We're right behind you," Andy said, and Darko headed tentatively over to Circe, the rest of them following close behind.

When Darko made it to Circe's side, she seized his injured arm and began work on it. He yelped in pain, his wrist *crack*ing. "Don't hurt him more!" Andy cried, lunging forward. Someone grabbed Andy's hands from behind to stop him from getting any closer. He swung around, saw it was Zoey and Kali.

"She's not hurting me," Darko assured Andy, though he was breathing heavily, his voice laced with pain. "She set the bone."

"Quite right," Circe said. "Though your compassion for this creature is quite attractive, Anteros, try not to worry. He'll be just fine."

Andy stepped back, blinking hard. Had he heard her right? Had she really just called him Anteros? "What the hell?" he shouted.

"I knew it." Zoey released Andy and stomped past him toward Circe and Darko as Circe continued her work on Darko. "I knew you'd figured out who we were when you called me the Goddess of Eloquence."

Circe uncorked the bottle of mint-green goo she'd grabbed from her rack and handed it to Darko. "Drink this fast," she ordered. "It will accelerate the healing process. In fact, once you finish it, you should be completely healed within a few minutes." Darko did as Circe said, guzzling down the brew with a few quick gulps, and Circe turned to Zoey. "Of course I know who you are," she went on. "I knew it from the moment I saw you—both of you." She faced Andy, and suddenly her expression was pleading as she gazed at him. "After everything we've been through, do you really think I wouldn't recognize you, God of Requited Love?" Andy took a few more steps back, his stomach turning. He wasn't sure why, but Circe was really, *really* freaking him out right now.

Zoey's hand hovered above the bag slung over her shoulder. "What do you mean, after everything you've been through? What are you talking about?"

"You really don't remember?" Circe asked Andy, her shoulders slumping, her expression crestfallen. "The time we spent together?" Darko's jaw dropped, his eyes going wide as he watched them, and Andy figured Kali probably had a similar expression on her face.

Andy shook his head. "Lady, I don't have a freaking clue what you're talking about. I don't know whether Anteros—whether I—knew you before . . . well, before I was in this body. But I'm . . . I'm Andy now, okay?" He glanced over at Zoey, who offered him a quizzical expression. "Yeah, I'm Andy. Andy Regan." He turned back to Circe. Standing straighter and with more confidence now, he felt surer of himself. "And I might be Anteros reincarnated—really, I have no idea how all this works. I just found out I have his wings and stuff a few days ago. But what I do know is I grew up like any other regular kid, with my own family and friends and no memories of Anteros's life. So . . . yeah. I don't know you, okay?"

Circe turned away. Andy wasn't sure whether he'd seen it right, but he thought she'd been . . . smiling? Slightly? "Of course you don't," she said. "How foolish of me. You are, after all, not just Anteros, God of Requited Love. You are also one of the Chosen Two from the Before Time, brought back to life five hundred years after your deaths in the Storm to avenge humanity by leading a war on the gods. That is why you possess the Helm of Darkness and Poseidon's Trident. You stole them to battle the gods. You weren't tasked with returning them to our half-wit king on some ridiculous quest. Correct?"

Andy felt as though someone had socked him in the gut. *She knows we're leading a war on the gods? Why'd she pretend not to know who we are when we first met her?*

"Shall I begin preparing dinner for everyone, then?" Circe asked, and she started toward the other side of the "kitchen."

Zoey threw her hand into the air. "Hold on a sec! You don't just know we're Calliope and Anteros—you also know we're the Chosen Two of the Prophecy. Then why . . . why are you helping us? Why haven't you turned us in to Zeus?"

Circe looked over her shoulder, narrowed her fiery eyes straight at Zoey. "As I've already told you, I'm not particularly fond of the King of the

Gods, and I'm not helping you out of the goodness of my heart, anyway, considering you'll be giving me something I want in return." She proceeded toward the nearest stove and stirred whatever was brewing in the steaming pot on it. "Besides, it's not as though Zeus has allowed me to erect a city in my name, as he has many of the other gods. It's not as if I have worshippers offering me sacrifices and spreading word of my great deeds, as many of the other gods do. One of the only reasons I haven't faded away from lack of worship—as we all thought Anteros and Calliope had—is my association with Odysseus in the old days. Because I turned his men into pigs and eventually became his lover, my name was known by many in the Before Time. And now, because the gods have taken back humanity and spread their stories far and wide, including their involvements with Odysseus's quest, I am still often spoken of to this day. Other than that, my own methods of survival seem to work just fine."

"Why didn't you just tell us all this in the first place?" Zoey pressed. "Why the smoke and mirrors? Why pretend you had no idea who we are and go along with our story?"

Circe snorted. "I could ask the same of you. You're the one who tried to trick me from the very beginning, after all. So, what is it I should call the two of you? Your human names? Your divine names? Or something else entirely?"

"We use their human names, and they respond just fine, if that's any help," Kali chimed in with a shrug. "Need some help with the food? I've been told I'm a great cook, and the herbs and spices you've got have been calling my name ever since I stepped foot in here."

"Go right ahead," Circe replied, making room for Kali at her side. Kali headed that way, grabbing a few things from one of Circe's pantries before reaching the goddess's side, and Andy gave the future chief of Deltama Village an incredulous look.

Kali merely shrugged at him and started helping Circe. "What? I'm starving."

Had dehydration and hunger finally gotten to Andy? Was he hallucinating all of this? How had their interactions with this immortal sorceress led to something as whacky as helping her prepare dinner?

Before he could form his next sentence, Darko clopped to his side. The satyr's wrist looked good as new, and he seemed to be feeling much better. The color had returned to his face, and he was moving his previously injured arm as though it had never been broken. "It worked," he said to Andy and Zoey, grinning ear to ear. "Circe healed me as easily as Diana would have!"

Zoey raised a brow at Darko as if still skeptical of Circe and her intentions, and Andy couldn't help but feel the same. Something told him Circe couldn't be trusted. *We need to find out more about her.* "So," he started, "why hasn't Zeus let you have a city of your own? And worshippers, too? I thought the more minor gods and goddesses had cities and worshippers across the world. Wasn't that the whole point of the gods sending the Storm anyway? To take back humanity's worship? Why's he excluding you?"

Circe sneered as she worked alongside Kali. "Only the gods and goddesses who blindly agreed to Zeus's plans of world domination were given such special treatment. The rest of us—the ones who were less enthusiastic about his idea—were left to fade and die with time."

"That's pretty messed up," Zoey remarked. "It makes sense that you don't care about whether we lead a war on the gods, then." She shared a knowing glance with Andy. He guessed they were on the same page regarding their curiosity about Circe. Zoey seemed to be prying.

"I care little about politics," Circe replied. "I keep to myself, look out for myself. And Zeus's efforts to destroy me have not yet worked, have they? I'm still here, after all." She clapped her hands, opened the cupboard above the stove she was at, and pulled out four clay cups with symbols and people and pigs painted on them. Then she lifted her and Kali's pot and filled the cups with some kind of stew, the sweet and savory aromas of the gravy dancing in the air, teasing Andy's nose.

His mouth watered, his stomach growling. *That smells so good*, he thought. *When was the last time we ate?* The effects of hunger finally overtook him, and he swayed to the side, feeling as if he might pass out.

Circe handed each of them a cup. Andy's hands shook as he held his container, trembled so much his stew sloshed from side to side. "Please eat, my guests," Circe said. "You are famished. After your hunger has been satiated, we will proceed with our bargaining." Andy looked around at his friends. They were suddenly shaking from hunger as well.

"We need our strength," Kali said, and before anyone could argue with her and point out that it might be laced with poison, she brought the cup to her mouth. Her dinner went down in just a few big gulps, and once she finished, she licked her lips and grinned at Circe. "Delicious. Thanks."

Circe winked at her. "Don't thank me. *You* helped with the finishing touches."

Apparently, Kali's act of bravery gave Darko the courage to trust Circe's intentions, because he slurped down his meal next. "Darko!" Zoey scolded.

"What?" the satyr asked once he finished. "Kali's right. We need our strength so we can save Diana, Marina, and Troy." Andy shared another knowing look with Zoey. Even though Darko and Kali trusted Circe just fine, something felt off. Still, Darko made a good point: they needed their strength to save Diana and the twins. How would they ever rescue their comrades if they were starving to death? How would they ever even get off this island if they were starving to death? Worse than that, if he refused this meal, would it offend Circe? Would she turn him into one of her pets if he didn't eat?

With dozens of worst-case scenarios running through his head, Andy gave in. He lifted the cup to his lips and sucked down the stew. It tasted just as delicious as it smelled. A delectable fusion of meats and vegetables and spices—this was the best food he'd had since the party at Deltama Village before he and his friends had traveled into the Underworld. Even before he was done, a blissfully warm sensation started to spread from his stomach into the rest of his body. *I already feel so much better*, he thought, and he really did. For the first time in God knew how long, he felt almost . . . euphoric. His head and limbs suddenly didn't feel so heavy, all the pressure and stress dissipating from his tired muscles. *Is there more of this stuff?*

"Now, then," Circe began, "would any of you like seconds, or shall we proceed with the bargaining?"

"Seconds, please," Darko and Kali said almost in unison, and Andy held out his cup for more as well. Zoey stared at Circe, her lip curled with distrust. What was her deal? Sure, at first this had seemed too good to be true. But Circe had healed Darko, had allowed Kali to help prepare the meal—and the stew felt *incredible* going down, made Andy so warm and light and comfortable. Everything was fine; Circe was trustworthy. Couldn't Zoey see that?

Andy elbowed Zoey in the side. "Go on, eat. It's okay."

"Their speech is slurred," Zoey said to Circe. "Did you drug this?"

"I use red wine in all my cooking," Circe replied to her, waving a hand dismissively. "Under the right conditions there's enough to intoxicate. But go on, Goddess of Eloquence—er, Goddess of Eloquence *incarnate*, I suppose. As your companions said, you'll need your strength for what comes next."

Despite her shaking hand, Zoey set her cup aside. "I'll wait and eat something else later.

Thanks, though." Andy opened his mouth to argue, to tell Zoey she should eat now, but she shot him a glare that told him he should keep his mouth shut.

Circe offered Zoey a smile sweet as candy and took the cup back. "Suit yourself, dear." She got Andy, Darko, and Kali their seconds, and soon they'd slurped those down, too. Circe asked them if they wanted thirds, but by that point they were too stuffed, and they declined. If Andy hadn't been so full, he would have had more, though. He felt better than ever, as if he'd been pampered at the world's greatest spa all day rather than steering a broken-down submarine with a magical pitchfork across the Atlantic.

"So, have you determined what you want from us yet, Circe?" Zoey asked.

"I think I might have," Circe replied as she began to clean up the mess from dinner.

Zoey raised a brow. "What is it, then?"

For a while Circe didn't say anything. Finally, however, she turned toward the group. "My guests, I have made my decision. Once you have promised to fulfill my wish, I will not only grant you safe passage from my island, but I will also lend you a boat to reach the mainland, and I will give you directions to New Mount Olympus."

Andy grinned, sharing grateful looks with

Darko and Kali. However, when he looked at Zoey, she had a skeptical expression on her face, her arms crossed. He frowned. Did Zoey still think Circe was too good to be true? Did she believe the enchantress would betray them? That she wouldn't hold up her end of the bargain?

"Stop dragging this out," Zoey snapped. "Tell us what you want."

Circe gave them a childlike smile, and she nodded at Andy. "What I want is for the God of Requited Love incarnate—for Andy, or as I knew him, *Anteros*—to stay with me on my island. Forever."

Suddenly all the good feelings in Andy's body fled. His stomach clenched, his muscles tightening once again, and before he could stop himself, he blurted out, "Wait, what? Why—why the hell do you think I'd ever stay on this island with you?" He cringed as the words came out. His speech really was slurred, as Zoey had pointed out.

Circe's golden eyes flashed. "What did you say? That you won't oblige?" She took a few steps toward him. "No, that can't be correct. After all, I have shown you such hospitality. Perhaps I misheard you?"

"Oh, you heard me right," Andy said, hiccupping. "Maybe you should get your ears cleaned if you're having trouble, though."

Apparently, that hadn't been the right thing to say, because Circe's fiery hair crackled, burning higher, higher, higher, and suddenly she was raising her crystal-wrapped wand and—

"Our greatest and most sincere apologies," Zoey exclaimed, running in front of Andy. She stood straight, her shoulders back. She was using her Calliope voice again, and she sounded every bit like a fierce goddess. "You *have* shown us great hospitality, Circe. You've given us food, healed our friend, and spared us from Scylla. But your request . . . it simply cannot be done. We cannot let you have Andy. Or Anteros, as you knew him."

Circe's hair snapped and popped, not calming in the slightest. "Oh, and why is that? Initially, you asserted the only request you could not grant was giving me the Helm of Darkness and Poseidon's Trident. You said nothing regarding handing over someone belonging to your party."

"You know why," Zoey said, her voice growing higher pitched and panicky. "He and I—we have to lead a war on the gods. Please, ask for something else."

Circe circled the group, tapping her wand against her palm. "I don't want anything else."

There was a long pause—whole minutes where everyone was quiet. Finally, hooves clacked against the tiled floor as Darko stepped forward. "I'll stay with you on your island forever, Circe." Though the satyr's speech was slurred, he sounded sure of himself. "I'll be your payment so Andy and Zoey can leave."

Andy grabbed Darko by the shoulder. "Are you crazy?" he cried. "You can't stay here. We need you." He shot Zoey a hopeless look, but she only stared back at him with wide eyes, her mouth opening and closing in shock.

Circe tapped her chin with her wand. "Hmm. No. I don't want you, satyr."

Darko hung his head. Andy breathed out a sigh of relief, but the solace didn't last long. Kali stepped forward next. "I'll stay. Take me, Circe." She turned back to look at the rest of the group, her expression full of sorrow. As she spoke her next words, Andy's eyes welled with tears. "Just . . . if I do this, promise me that when you save Diana, you'll tell her that . . . tell her that, more than anything in the world, I wanted to see her again."

Andy extended his hand. "Kali—"

Kali yanked out of his reach. "This is what must be done. Eventually, word will spread to my village, and in time they'll understand." She winked at them, and Andy knew exactly what she was trying to tell them. Because Kali was the future chief of Deltama Village, this decision would leave her people without a leader. They'd have to appoint someone else, and until they found that someone, there would be chaos among her people. But it would mean Andy and Zoey could go on to save the world, which would ultimately improve the lives of her people, which was why she'd come with them in the first place. It would give her village a better chance at a free and prosperous future.

"Presumptuous, aren't we?" Circe said with a giggle. "I respect your bravery, mortal, but I don't want you, either. You will not make a suitable lover. However, Anteros will. I want Anteros."

Andy balled his fists at his sides. He'd had enough of this. "First of all, I'm not Anteros anymore. I'm Andy. Second, you can't just ask people to be your obedient little dogs. We're human beings." He cast Darko a quick shrug. "Uh, most of us are. Some of us are satyr beings, I guess. Anyway, the point is, I'm a person. You can't just ask me to be your love-prisoner on this stupid island. It's weird. You're gonna have to ask us for something else. You can't have the Helm of Darkness, Poseidon's Trident, or any of us, though."

Circe raised her wand. It glowed with golden light, sparks hissing and popping around it. "Even in this weak, mortal form, you still refuse to submit to me, Anteros?" She narrowed her eyes at Zoey.

"And for that unremarkable whore, no less."

Zoey flinched, and Andy clenched his jaw. "Don't call her that!" he shouted.

"After all our years of involvement," Circe went on. "After all the times you'd sneak into the palace while my husband was out—"

"You have a husband?" Andy interrupted. "And you want me, a sixteen-year-old kid, to stay with you and be your lover? What the heck is wrong with you, lady?"

"You didn't seem to have a problem with it while you were still immortal," Circe retorted. "Not until *she* came along, at least." The goddess jerked her head at Zoey as she uttered that last sentence, and Andy swallowed hard. When he'd been a god, had he been a player? It sounded so unlike him now that it was hard to believe, but the pieces were starting to come together. From what he'd gathered here, he'd broken Circe's heart.

"Look, I don't remember any of what happened between you and Anter—uh, you and me," Andy said. "I'm really sorry if . . . if I hurt your feelings. But you need to understand, I'm not Anteros anymore. I'm Andy. And I'm not going to stay here with you. I couldn't even if I wanted to. I'm too important to our mission."

"In that case, I'll do what I should have long ago," Circe said, pointing her wand at Andy. "I'll punish you and your whore for everything you've done to me." Andy raised the Trident, but he was too slow, his reflexes dulled from Circe's stew. The golden light emanating from Circe's wand shot straight for him.

As the light rammed into Andy, his friends screamed his name, and strange, sharp pains overcame his body. His gut bubbled with nausea, and his skin felt as though it was pulling itself tighter and tighter around his insides, as if it was shrinking. His bones *crack*ed and *creak*ed, and he cried out and collapsed, his limbs involuntarily jerking at inhuman angles. The Trident fell from his hands, clattered to the floor.

Circe stood above him. She suddenly seemed much taller than before. "You should have done as I asked, my pet," she said with a cackle.

Andy's pain began to subside, but still he couldn't climb to his feet. He groaned. Clawed at the tiles beneath him. Extended a hand for the Trident. Found he couldn't reach the object of power, couldn't even grip the floor properly. What had Circe done to him? What was she going to do to his companions?

What felt like whole minutes passed, the shouts of Andy's friends ringing in his ears, before the strangely familiar voice of a man sounded in his mind. *"Do not worry, child. I have been waiting for an opportunity like this since you were born, and finally my time has come."*

Who are you? Andy thought at the voice. *What are you talking about?*

"In time, you'll come to understand that we are the same being. For now, allow me to take control of our body."

It was then that a buzzing feeling—the same buzzing feeling Andy had experienced when he'd been drawn to the statue of Anteros in Aphrodite City—hummed in his chest, and a flash of silver light blinded him.

CHAPTER FOUR
SKY

The amphitheater Syrena had been killed in looked just as Karter remembered it.

It was massive, half the size of a city, with plates of inclining gray rock bent into a crescent shape. It provided hundreds of rows which were now filling with gods, demigods, nobles, and aristocrats. Everyone was gathering to watch the execution tonight. The execution of a traitor, which Karter himself was supposed to act out.

And that traitor, of course, was Diana, Daughter of Apollo.

Karter couldn't see Diana—she hadn't been

brought out yet. Even still, as he stood at the edge of the columned temple in front of the amphitheater, as he watched the people filing in and listened to their incomprehensible murmuring, he felt light-headed, his heart racing, his breaths coming in shallow gasps. Though the storms had not ceased, he had dried off in the palace. But now sweat dripped down his forehead, down the back of his neck. It formed in every little crevice on his body and made him smell sour.

Could he create a green lightning bolt, let alone control it? And even if he could, could he bring himself to kill Diana?

Memories of Spencer's and Syrena's smiling faces plagued him. Where were their souls located in Hades? Had any form of mercy been extended to them?

He usually pushed thoughts like these away the moment they cropped up, considering the punishments his friends probably had to face because of their choices. However, Zoey and Andy certainly caused quite the commotion in the Underworld by stealing the Helm of Darkness, not to mention Hades and Persephone were now trapped in Tartarus, so perhaps Spencer and Syrena had managed to slip past a harsh judgment and were spending their days together.

No, the logical side of his mind argued. *Even with*

Hades and Persephone in Tartarus, Zeus mentioned that Nyx and Thanatos are watching the Underworld for now, so it's not as if Spencer's and Syrena's souls could have escaped.

What does it matter, anyway? Nothing can be done to change it. Even if something could, I am destined to become a god. And gods do not concern themselves with trite thoughts such as the ones I'm entertaining.

Someone smacked him hard on the back, and he turned to find his father towering over him. Zeus smiled, but it wasn't jovial. His eyes glinted wickedly as he extended an arm toward Karter. "Take my hand. You are about to make your grand entrance."

Karter gulped and placed a palm in Zeus's. In an instant they dissolved like clouds in a scorched atmosphere, and suddenly they were hovering hundreds of feet above the amphitheater. Karter yelped in surprise, focusing on his power of flight. He caught himself midair before he could plummet toward the ground. Within seconds the rain had soaked him again.

"Once all of this is over," Zeus began, "I will transform you into an immortal so that you may spend eternity with the rest of us on Olympus. Think of that, and do not be afraid. Allow that reasoning to wash your terror away."

Karter shot his father a fearful glance. To the

bystanders below, Zeus must have looked like a glimmering star among the rest in the sky. "Why would I . . . be afraid?" Karter asked. "This is . . . this is a joyous occasion. Is it not?"

"Of course it is. However, I . . ." Zeus hesitated as if searching for the right words. "I know I've been hard on you in years past, my son. Especially regarding your usefulness. Or, more specifically, your ability to create and control green lightning. I know you fear whether you will be strong enough to do so, despite that I have seen into the future myself, have seen that you will do it easily. I'm sorry for that."

Karter blinked in surprise. His father rarely apologized for anything, much less for pushing anyone to be a better Warrior of the Gods. To be more useful. More powerful. "There is, um, no need to apologize, Father. You . . . were only doing what was necessary to make me the demigod I am today. You must have known from the beginning that I was meant to fulfill a spectacular destiny. You only wanted me to realize it rather than squander it, I'm sure. You are a great and fair king."

"Yes, all of that is true," Zeus replied. "But your confidence in your abilities has suffered because of me. There were other ways I could have made you strong."

"Such as?"

Zeus stroked his beard for a moment before taking Karter's hands in his. However, he didn't do so briskly or harshly—his touch was gentle. Suddenly the King of the Gods' expression seemed almost affectionate, and Karter wondered if his father had ever treated him so tenderly. A part of him was comforted by this, but another part of him questioned whether the exchange was genuine. Was Zeus acting this way because he cared about Karter, or because of what Karter could do for him? "Such as simply giving you a taste of my own power," he answered. "So that you may understand what green lightning feels like. Then, hopefully, you'll be able to make it yourself."

Peridot electricity sparked around Zeus's wrists, just inches from Karter's skin, and Karter's jaw dropped as realization set in. His pulse quickened. He tried to jerk back, even implemented his divine gift of strength to get away, but Zeus kept a firm hold on him. "No, no! It will kill me, it will—"

"It will not kill you," Zeus interrupted, squeezing Karter's hands in reassurance. His tone was surprisingly calm considering what he was about to do. "Close your eyes and listen to me."

"Please, Father—"

"*Do as I say.*" There was the Zeus Karter was used to. The one who barked orders. The one who struck fear into people's hearts. The one who scarred his own son's face to prove a point.

Karter didn't argue further. Instead, he closed his eyes and trusted in his father's judgment. Perhaps if he lived through this and succeeded in becoming an immortal, he would one day understand the reasoning behind his father's decision.

"Green lightning is the most powerful thing a child-of-Zeus can wield," Zeus started. "It is more beneficial in battle than its red and gold counterparts, and it is even better to have than strength and flight. When a child-of-Zeus becomes capable of making it, of holding it, they are an unstoppable force to all except the gods."

"Yes, I know," Karter replied, trying to keep his voice from shaking.

"Because green lightning is formed from such raw energy," Zeus went on, "a child-of-Zeus can more easily conjure it when they are near what gives them strength—the sky. You must stay close to the clouds and focus, my son. Think of the sky, of the storm. Allow their energies into your body. Allow them to invigorate you. Only then will you live when the green bolts touch you."

As if on cue, thunder rumbled, and Karter flinched. The last thing he wanted to do right now was hover hundreds of feet in the air alongside the clouds, rain pelting him in the face and chilling him to the bone, bolts flashing all around him, thunder roaring in his ears. *But there must be some truth to what Zeus says*, he thought. *After all, it's true that demigods are strongest when they are close to what gives them power.*

I am a son of Zeus. A descendant of the sky. And that is what gives me power. If I'm truly meant to do this for the first time, it only makes sense that high in the air is where it will happen.

"Prepare yourself, my son," Zeus boomed, and every muscle in Karter's body tensed. "Focus on the forces giving you energy. Draw strength out of the atmosphere and into your body so I do not stop your heart. And remember, you can do this. You are ready. I know you are."

Karter clenched his jaw, trusting in his father's words and doing as he was told. He thought of the storm clouds hovering above him, the black sky all around him, the lightning bolts flashing overhead. He imagined the magic and mystery and raw power they possessed, concentrated on making himself a conduit for it all. A familiar energy lurched in the center of his chest, spread through his abdomen, his limbs.

Hisssss, hissssss, hissssss. Suddenly his hands were burning white-hot, as if they'd been lit on fire. He cried out in pain, his eyes shooting open, and spotted little peridot-green bolts crackling and arcing around his and Zeus's fingers. They curled up his arms, as did the blazing sensations on his skin. Heart racing, he tried to pull away. *I'm going to die*, he thought. *This is it.* But his father wouldn't let him go. "Focus!" Zeus bellowed. "Focus or you'll lose control, and this *will* end your life!"

Karter threw his head back, his breaths replaced with shallow gasps, and gazed up at the clouds. They were moving, stirring and shifting and spinning before his eyes, bright electricity whizzing out from them. All the while, the heated sensations from the green lightning spread toward his chest, toward his heart. He should have been panicking—after all, he was surely about to meet his death—but instead, as he stared up at the atmosphere, a feeling of calm enveloped his senses. *I am a son of Zeus*, he thought. *The sky gives me strength. Gives me power.*

Invigorates me.

The familiar pulsing energy spreading through his body—the power he was used to, the kind he'd possessed most of his life—burst. At first all Karter knew was he hurt, bad. It was as though all the pieces inside him were rupturing, as though all the cells of his body were exploding. Then they swirled beneath his skin and through his veins in a stinging, prickling chaos. He screamed until his throat ripped raw.

What could be happening to him? Was he

dying? Would he find himself in the Underworld shortly? *I must have made a mistake*, he thought. *I must have lost focus.*

After what felt like forever, the agony dissipated. It was then that he knew he wasn't going to lose his life, then that he knew his fractured cells were coming back together and rebuilding themselves into something new. He could feel them as they piled on top of one another, stitching and mending themselves back together. Soon his discomforts ceased, aside from his sore throat and racing heart.

Zeus released Karter. "Congratulations, my son. You've done it. You're holding it. Look."

Sure enough, when Karter glanced down, he had the bolt in his hands. It seethed with peridot light, sparking and hissing and flickering, except when the green electricity grazed his skin, nothing happened to him. He didn't die, didn't even burn.

He released a long breath and laughed in disbelief. He'd done it. He'd actually, really done it. Granted, he hadn't created the lightning, but the fact that he was controlling it was a miracle in and of itself. Now that he'd held it, experienced it, surely he'd have no problem recreating it and following through with the execution.

As the bolt fizzled out, Karter realized the horror and suffering he'd endured throughout his life was about to end. Every gut-wrenching memory—the heartbreaks, the punishments, the deaths—they would, with time, become distant memories. He could finally relinquish the torturous recollections of Spencer's and Syrena's and his mother's deaths, finally abandon his grief and worry and culpability regarding them. He'd never have to relive the way Diana had yelled at him when he'd betrayed her and her friends, never have to reconceive the look in Zoey's blue eyes when she'd discovered the same.

Eternal youth coupled with incomprehensible strength and power were about to be his. The world was about to be his.

And all he had to do was end Diana's life.

"It appears most of the seats have been filled now," Zeus said. The King of the Gods snapped his fingers, and the rain around them slowed to a drizzle. "I think that was a warm enough welcome for everyone, don't you?"

Karter smiled. He didn't remember the last time he'd felt this good. "Yes, Father. I do."

"Are you ready to kill the Daughter of Apollo, then?"

Of course he was ready. And even if he wasn't, he didn't have a choice. This was his destiny. But now, with his father's encouragement, he knew he'd be able to create and control a green lightning bolt. All the uncertainty he'd experienced earlier was gone.

"I'm ready," Karter answered.

Zeus guided him toward the center of the dirt floor of the amphitheater, where he would finally meet his spectacular fate.

Zoey wasn't sure what had just happened, and quite frankly, she couldn't believe her eyes.

With a wave of her wand, Circe had transformed Andy into a pig. A *literal swine*—fat and pink, with hooves and a curly tail. He lay on his side, his legs flailing as though he was trying to regain his footing.

"No!" Darko cried from behind Zoey. Her nostrils flared, her muscles going taut. Suddenly her hunger had dissolved, her hand no longer shaking. Swiftly, she retrieved the Helm of Darkness from her bag and pulled it over her head, chills charging through her body as the object turned her invisible. Then she dove toward Poseidon's Trident and clasped the handle tight, the weapon disappearing in her grip.

Kali stomped toward Circe, her fists raised.

"Turn him back, you evil witch!" Her words slurred together. "Turn him back *right now*. Make him as he was before, or I'll—"

"Or you'll what?" Circe replied, a nefarious grin on her lips. "Considering you're about to share the same fate, I imagine you won't be able to do anything, mortal girl." Kali's expression morphed from angry to confused. "Were you really moronic enough to trust that I wouldn't lace your food with my potions?"

"Kali, Darko, get out of here!" Zoey screamed, sprinting toward Circe, ready to impale the sorceress with the Trident. Perhaps she could "kill" Circe, find a way to hold her hostage, and, when she eventually regenerated, force her to turn Andy human again. But before Zoey could reach the sorceress, Circe waved her wand, and Darko and Kali began transforming just as Andy had. Zoey stopped dead, gasping as she watched them squirm and shrink and squeal, and then they too were turned into pigs.

Circe tapped her wand against her palm. "Oh, Calliope," she said in a singsong voice, glancing around the chamber. "Where did you run off to, dear? I'm sorry I couldn't turn you into swine as well. You were clever enough to avoid taking my potion. Even still, I think it's better this way. After all, I need someone to sacrifice these disgusting creatures in my name. That's how I keep from fading away, you see. Now come out of hiding and hand over those precious objects of power, before I call on my pets and have them track you down with their noses."

Zoey gripped the Trident tight; she had no other choice. She had to kill Circe, trap the goddess, and find a way to—

The shrill scream of Andy, Darko, or Kali—Zoey wasn't sure which one—pierced the air. Blinding silver light flashed in her peripheral, and she covered her eyes.

Once the light faded, she glanced over. And, to her surprise, she found Andy standing before them. He looked completely normal—at least, as normal as one can look when they have giant feathered butterfly-shaped wings spread out wide from their back. Also, there was a strange luminosity to his skin, making him appear as though he were glowing from the inside out.

What the hell just happened? Zoey thought, gazing at Andy in wide-eyed shock. *How did he turn himself back?*

Am I seeing things? Is this another one of Circe's tricks?

Andy flapped his wings and leapt into the air. He soared straight for Circe, whose lips were spread in a leering grin as he approached her. "Anteros," she said, drawing out each syllable in a way that made Zoey's skin crawl. "I see you—the *real* you—decided to make an appearance. Have you finally come to your senses? Have you finally decided to stay here with me?"

He stopped flying, hovering above Circe. "Calliope, come here," he ordered, keeping his eyes trained on the sorceress. "Hand over the Helm and Trident." Except he didn't sound like himself, not really. For one, he'd never called her Calliope—he'd only ever called her Zoey—and he'd never asked her to "hand over" anything. For two, his voice was far deeper than usual, and it reverberated across the room, sounding less like a teenage boy's and more like a grown man's. No, even more than a grown man's, it sounded like . . .

A god's, Zoey realized. *It sounds like a god's voice.*

"Andy?" Zoey called. Was this a new Anteros power, or had something else happened to him?

He held out a hand in her direction. "Now, Calliope! Hand over the Helm and Trident! I've taken control so I can perform the Descent Spell. Don't you remember it, how it works? It's the only way to defeat this witch and escape the island!"

"Oh, it seems you haven't come to your senses," Circe said, grimacing. She raised her wand once again. "I suppose I'll have to follow through with your punishment, then. Whether you've made an appearance or not, Anteros, you're still trapped in that weak, mortal body. You're no match for me."

Zoey didn't have any more time to waste. She couldn't let Circe hurt Andy, but she couldn't "hand over" the objects of power to Andy, either, because it was clear he wasn't himself right now.

So she did the only thing she could think of. She charged for Circe, brandishing Poseidon's Trident, and stabbed the sorceress through the chest with its prongs.

Zoey wrenched the still-invisible Trident through Circe, then pulled it back to her side. Circe's fiery eyes went wide with surprise. Coughing sounds escaped her throat, golden liquid spewing from her lips. The same color of fluid leaked from her wound, and she looked up at Andy, who still hovered above her. "I loved you, you know," she choked out, and collapsed face-first onto the tiled floor.

"Good work," Andy said, drifting down onto the tiles. Thankfully, his voice had started to go back to normal. *Maybe it was just his Anteros power coming out*, she thought. "Now, please," he continued, "hand over the Helm so I can perform the Descent Spell, unless you'd like to take over and do it yourself." He winked. "Or I suppose we could always perform it together."

Something twitched at the back of Zoey's mind when he said "perform the Descent Spell," as if it was something she'd known about years ago but had since forgotten the details of. However, she could hardly focus because of the look on his face when he addressed her—flirtatious and confident. Granted, he couldn't see her because she was still wearing the Helm, but she knew the look was for her. After all, he'd just confessed his crush on her a few days ago. *Then again*, she thought, *something could still be going on with him. He's never called me Calliope before, and his voice has never sounded so strange, either. Did he receive more visions of Anteros and Calliope when Circe turned him into a pig? Like how he saw those visions when he touched the statue of Anteros in Aphrodite City?*

Is he mixing up memories of the past with what's happening right now?

At any rate, her heart skipped with anxiety as she looked at Andy. The last time he'd behaved so flirtatiously toward her—well, it had been when they'd danced together at the party in Deltama Village. Though she was pretty sure she didn't like it, then or now. In fact, the most she could remember of their dance was how Spencer had cut in so he could show her how her father died, and then how Karter had ruined the beautiful moment of clarity by showing up and kidnapping her.

Spencer, she thought, half tempted to whisper his name just so she could hear it, the memory of his death still agonizingly fresh in her mind. *And Karter.* She could hardly process the fact that the Son of Zeus had betrayed her in Hephaestus City after she'd risked everything to save him, and especially after they'd found common ground while trapped together in a Hephaestus City jail cell. *The next time I see that asshole . . .*

"Calliope?" Andy called out. "Are you still there? Is something wrong? We must make haste. We need to perform the Descent, return our companions to their previous state, and escape this island."

Zoey groaned in frustration. *Something* is *wrong with him, then.* She set the Trident down and pulled the Helm off her head, shooting Andy a glare. "What's going on with you? Why are you talking so formally? And why do you keep calling me—" However, she didn't finish scolding him. When she reappeared and he spotted her, his eyes went so wide it frightened her, his head jerking to the side. "Andy?" she said, reaching out for him.

But Andy didn't respond. Instead, his head kept twitching, and it seemed as though he wasn't in control of the movements, either. His gray irises flashed a brilliant shade of silver, and then the silver melted into his pupils and the whites of his eyes like luminous molten metal.

"Andy!" Zoey cried, louder this time, and raced

to his side. She took one of his hands in hers, squeezed it hard. She needed to ground him, to bring him back from whatever was taking him away.

Several seconds passed before the glow in Andy's eyes dissipated and his head stopped jerking around. He glanced at Zoey, his lips parted slightly. He looked as if he'd just woken up from a long nap.

Zoey gave his hand another squeeze for good measure. "Are you okay? What just happened?" But instead of answering her questions, Andy did something she never expected.

He yanked his hand from hers, grabbed her face, and kissed her on the lips.

Karter watched as Violet, Layla, and Xander dragged Diana by the chains on her wrists across the muddied floor of the amphitheater.

Zeus stood beside Karter and had been talking for the past few minutes, rattling off a series of sentences meant to prepare the audience for Diana's death. Karter was sure it had something to do with her crimes, how the gods were going to eliminate a threat to their peaceful reign by having her killed, but he couldn't be sure. It was difficult to pay attention to speeches when his ears were ringing incessantly, when his adrenaline was running rampant.

I held green lightning, he thought. *I really did it, and I'm still here.* Never in his life had he thought he'd achieve such a feat.

The audience clapped and cheered, their collective roar snapping Karter back to reality. ". . . and now, she will pay for her transgressions," Zeus said, finishing his sentence as they went quiet again. He rested a hand on Karter's shoulder and nodded, and Karter's palms grew slippery with sweat. He still had to manage creating green lightning by himself—just holding it wouldn't do. Not only that, but even though he'd killed whenever the gods had ordered him to, he'd never been ordered to execute a fellow demigod.

He focused on the space ahead, catching sight of Diana.

She was soaked from head to toe, her blonde hair plastered against her scalp, her freckled skin the palest he'd ever seen it. She held her head high *that's how Syrena looked* though, as if she had no fear *when she said she wasn't afraid of death anymore* walking toward the demigod meant to take her life. Instead, she only *right before Spencer tried to save her* glared at

Karter, her bright-green eyes *then I lost both of them forever* boring into him, making his stomach *and now I'm executing their friend* twist and turn.

All at once, the confidence he'd mustered slipped away.

"Furthermore," Zeus boomed at the audience, "she will pay for these misdeeds at the hand of my son. I received visions of his destiny, and he is meant to end this war on the gods. He is meant to restore balance and peace. He is meant to become an immortal among the rest."

More cheering and clapping. *I have to get ahold of myself,* Karter thought, turning away from Diana. *Let go and forget.*

"It's a shame your mortal life had to end this way," Zeus said, and Karter snapped his attention back to the Daughter of Apollo. "Any last words?"

Diana was only feet away from Karter now, her fierce stare trained on him. Wasn't she scared at all? "No," she said, then spat at their feet. "Not one." As she spoke, her voice didn't waver, her defiant tone solid as stone.

Zeus faced Karter, a grin on his lips. "Then by all means, let's not waste any more time. Go ahead, my son. Annihilate this traitor." Karter nodded and raised his arms above his head. He was almost there—he just had to work through the last of his emotions and get this over with. *Let go and forget.*

He kept his arms raised, closing his eyes and recalling what his father had said about the sky being his source of power. He concentrated on its energy, allowed it—no, invited it—to flow through him, invigorate him. In an instant, hot power pulsed in his chest, spread through his limbs. He focused on centralizing that power into a green lightning bolt.

Suddenly it felt as if thousands of needles were pricking his skin, and the crowd went wild. Karter opened his eyes. Peridot electricity hummed in his palms.

In his peripheral he spotted Zeus cheering. "Marvelous job!" His voice echoed across the amphitheater. "Spectacular! You've done it! Karter, *you've done it*!"

A shiver of glee snaked down Karter's spine. Who would have thought that in just one night, he'd learn to create and control green lightning? Who would have thought his father would be so proud? Who would have thought his father would forget about keeping up appearances with the rest of the gods, demigods, and aristocrats, and cheer him on with reckless abandon?

Who would have thought that after everything he'd been through, he could still feel this magnificent?

"Now, Karter!" Zeus shouted. "Kill the

Daughter of Apollo *now!*"

Diana, Karter thought. *That's right.* He held tight to the bolt and faced Diana, preparing to pitch it at her. However, once he laid eyes on her again, he stopped dead.

It wasn't that she appeared any different. She was still chained up, and her hair was still flat against her scalp, and she was still drenched and white in the face. She still held her head high, held her shoulders back. Proud until the very end, just like Spencer and Syrena. But somehow, despite how invincible Karter had felt moments ago—how *glorious*—when he looked at Diana, *really* looked at her, it was as if he were seeing . . .

Someone seized Karter's free hand and jerked him to the side. The crowd gasped, and Karter glanced over to see it was Zeus.

The King of the Gods squeezed Karter's wrist so hard the demigod thought his bones might break. Zeus pulled Karter close, his skin wrinkling as his expression morphed into one of fury. "What were you waiting for?" he whispered. "You allowed the lightning to fizzle out!"

Karter stared at his father in shock for a few moments before looking down at his hand. He had, in fact, lost the peridot bolt, his palm bare. "I . . . I don't know what happened," he finally said. "I had it, and then—" He stopped, wincing when Zeus reared back an arm as though to smack him. The crowd broke into fits of gossipy whispers, and Karter braced for his father's colossal hand to collide with him and send him sprawling to the ground.

What felt like whole minutes passed, and when the hit never came, when the crowd's murmurs dwindled, Karter chanced a glimpse up at his father.

Zeus had lowered his hand. His angry expression had waned, replaced with something that looked almost kind, almost tender. However, Karter couldn't be sure if that's what it really was, as vexation seemed to twitch at the corners of his father's face. "Apologies," the King of the Gods said, although it wasn't clear whether the sentiment was for Karter's benefit or the crowd's. Still, Zeus released Karter and continued, "I only wish for this war to end. It is of the utmost importance that *you* finish off the Daughter of Apollo, my son. In my visions, when she died by *your hand* specifically, the war on the gods ended quickly and easily, while in other scenarios, the outcome was not clear. Now, please, try again."

Stomach churning, Karter nodded, his shoulders slumped as he drew further into himself. He glanced at the crowd. They'd gone deathly quiet, watching him with bated breath.

He tore his gaze from them and faced Diana, taking her in. She no longer looked brave and proud, as she had before. But somehow she didn't seem frightened, either. No, another expression had made its way onto her face. She watched Karter with something that looked like pity, and that made him feel even smaller and more insignificant than before.

"Go ahead," Zeus boomed, interrupting Karter's thoughts. "You are ready, my son. You are capable of this. You are strong enough. I know it." His father sounded sincere for the most part, but still, he wasn't sure if this was a genuine exchange.

It doesn't matter, he thought. *It's time to show him I'm capable, whether he believes it or not. It's time to show him I'm strong enough.*

It's time to realize my destiny.

Once again, Karter raised his arms and closed his eyes, concentrating on the energy of the sky. He invited it to flow through him and invigorate him. A searing force throbbed in his chest and darted through his limbs. He focused that power, centralizing it into a green lightning bolt. He waited for the prickling sensation. Soon he felt it dance across his skin. He looked to Diana, preparing to launch the killing blow.

Diana's gaze *don't do this don't kill her* bore into him, *Spencer, no* and then all *please Zeus I beg you I love her I want nothing more than to be with her for all time* he could see *she has committed unforgivable crimes against the gods the punishment is death* was Spencer *restrain him my son* and Syrena *stop it's no use.* And then . . . and then . . .

Nothing.

Karter looked down at his hands. Sure enough, there was no electricity crackling in his palms.

He tried to summon a peridot bolt again.

And again.

And again.

But no matter how many times he tried, it was no use. He couldn't manage the feat a second time—at least not right now, and whether he could do this right now determined whether he'd become an immortal god.

I knew it, he thought. *I knew I wouldn't be able to do it.* And truly, he had. Ever since Spencer's and Syrena's deaths, he'd lost all hope, and he'd realized what he truly was: a murderer, a monster. His mother was dead because of him, and so were his best friends in the whole world.

Not only that, but he'd betrayed the gods to try and save Spencer in some desperate attempt to keep his last companion alive, and, at the same time, to somehow make it up to Syrena for what he'd let happen to her. How could the gods forgive him for such a transgression? Especially considering he hadn't even succeeded at it? Sure, his father had seen into the future, had seen that Karter would become something incredible. But obviously fate could be wrong sometimes. Tonight was proof of that.

Fate be damned, anyway, because as far as Karter was concerned, he wasn't worthy of greatness. He couldn't make himself worthy of the pantheon, couldn't make himself worthy of Spencer or Syrena or his mother, couldn't make himself worthy of anyone else, either.

He fell to his knees and hung his head, allowing the tears to flow freely, not caring about keeping up with appearances or impressing his peers or anyone else. He was ready to accept whatever punishment awaited him now. He'd been torn between duty to his gods and loyalty to his friends for too long. It seemed he could never give all of himself to one or the other, no matter how hard he tried, and it had made him tired. So, so tired.

At one time, he'd told Asteria that it might have been better if he'd never been born. Now, he just wanted to die.

Someone rested a gentle hand on Karter's shoulder, and he jerked his head up. To his surprise, it was his father. Even more startling than that, not a trace of rage showed on the King of the Gods' face. "I have placed too great a weight on your shoulders after your long and perilous journey," he said. "I apologize and ask you not to worry. We'll reschedule this execution for another night, after you have had enough time to rest."

CHAPTER FIVE
KISS

Borderline-painful electricity crackled on Zoey's lips as Andy kissed her. It whizzed through her limbs, along every inch of her body. He lowered one of his hands from her face to rest it at the small of her back, lifted the other to stroke her long brown curls.

A part of her wanted to pull away, to end this kiss right here and now. However, as the electricity continued arcing through her, something in the back of her mind twitched again. Suddenly Andy kissing her didn't seem like such a foreign concept, and she found herself kissing him back.

She closed her eyes. Dropped the Helm and leaned into him. Buried her fingers in his hair.

No, stop, she thought. But Zoey found she couldn't stop, found she'd been starved for oxygen and Andy's lips on hers was the only way to satiate her aching lungs.

Yet still, she knew deep down this was wrong. This wasn't her. She'd never acknowledged it— truly acknowledged it—maybe because she feared hurting Andy. But the fact was, she didn't reciprocate his feelings for her. There was nothing wrong with him—he was adorable and funny and sweet and brave—but he didn't make her heart skip. Didn't make her shiver at a single touch. Didn't make her light as air.

Jet, her ex-boyfriend from the Before Time, had done all those things. At least before he'd shattered her heart and she'd broken up with him. Then there'd been Spencer . . .

Well, she had certainly felt *something* that resembled romance for Spencer, but she'd also felt connected to him in ways she'd never felt connected to Andy. Sure, Andy had become one of her best friends and she loved him dearly, but he didn't make her feel as though she could speak about the darkest parts of herself without receiving backlash or judgment. He didn't help her piece together the scattered bits of her past, didn't help her heal the broken parts of herself. *But even if Spencer were still alive*, she thought, *he'd still be in love with Syrena.*

My feelings for him never really mattered. They never could have amounted to anything.

A long while passed before Zoey finally managed to break whatever trance she was in that made her kiss Andy back so passionately. Or, maybe, what made her kiss him back at all.

She yanked her lips from his and shoved him away. All the electricity in her body dissipated instantly. "What's gotten into you?" she cried. "You don't get to—you don't get to just kiss me without . . . without . . ." She almost said *without me wanting you to* or *without asking me first* but found she couldn't form the words, her tongue heavy in her mouth.

Andy stared at her, blinking in confusion. His irises flickered between normal gray and blazing silver like lightbulbs going in and out until he clenched his jaw, looked away, and put his face in his hands. "No," he whispered, his voice hoarse. "No, no, no! This is *my* body. Give it back!"

When Andy said *this is my body* and *give it back*, the gears began turning in Zoey's head. She'd known something strange was going on with him—for instance, how had he counteracted

Circe's pig-potion? Why had his voice sounded so different earlier, and why had he called Zoey Calliope? What about the weird glow-y thing going on with his eyes? Most of all, he was such a shy person; it had taken a lot for him to confess he had a crush on Zoey. Where had the confidence to outright grab her and make out with her come from?

He's not in control of his own actions, Zoey realized, watching him as he wrestled with himself, his arms clawing at his own chest, stomach, and legs. She wasn't sure why this was happening to him, or to what extent he'd lost control, but it was the only explanation. Something must be possessing him, though she couldn't recall any possession tales from the Greek mythos. Then again, she hadn't been well-versed in it in the first place. Had Circe's magic caused this, perhaps? Was there an anecdote somewhere in this room?

"You know you enjoyed it." The oddly familiar voice of a woman rang through her mind, and she winced. Where had *that* come from? *"You know you loved the feel of his lips against yours,"* the woman continued. *"Loved how he grabbed at your waist and played with your hair and—"*

"Stop!" Zoey shouted, clamping her eyes shut and rubbing her temples. "Be quiet! None of that's true!"

The squeals of swine sounded to her left. Zoey looked over to see Darko and Kali wriggling on the ground, trying to gain footing, and her cheeks went hot. Had they seen her and Andy kissing? If so, when she and Andy turned them back to normal, would they remember it?

"I have been silent for eighteen years, little girl," the woman went on. *"Trapped in the labyrinth of your mind and unable to speak. Placed in this prison by my own father, no less. I will not be quiet. I will say my piece."*

"Then at least tell me who you are," Zoey snapped back, shooting Andy a quick glance. He still seemed to be wrestling with whatever was possessing him. "While you're at it, tell me what's going on with him, since you think you know so much about us."

"I do not think I know so much about you two. I know more about you than you know about yourself, for I am you. And he—well, he is our lover, Anteros. Banished into that puny mortal body—by Zeus, I am sure—because I imagine he tried to save us. That is something he would do. Though, I suppose you already know that of his character, do you not?"

Zoey's throat grew drier than ever, her head spinning, and suddenly she felt as though the ground were tilting beneath her feet. "You're Calliope? You're the Goddess of Eloquence? And you're trapped in the—in the labyrinth of my mind? But I thought—I thought *I* was Calliope. Well, Calliope reincarnated, at least. But then how do I have powers and that divine essence everyone keeps talking about? None of this makes sense."

"Of course none of it makes sense. It is more complex than what you just described. We are a goddess, yes, though frail and mortal now. We have powers and a divine essence, yes, though they are weakened because of the body we inhabit."

"What do you mean, 'we'? 'We' seem pretty separate right about now, wouldn't you say?"

"I would not. We share all, little girl. My powers are your powers. My divine essence is your divine essence. Though I am trapped in the labyrinth of your mind, it is also my mind.

"And that is how I know you are in love with Anteros—Andy, as you call him—because I am, too."

Zoey shook her head, trying to keep her balance. This was too much to take in. Greek gods bringing on the apocalypse and destroying everything she knew? Easy to accept once Spencer showed her the visions to prove it. Being transported five hundred years into the future to fulfill a prophecy because she was one of two "chosen ones" selected for the task? A bit more difficult to wrap her head around, but she'd wanted to escape her old life, so it had been an opportunity to do something great, to make something of herself. Being a goddess incarnate, which explained *why* she was one of two "chosen ones" meant to fulfill said prophecy? Yeah, that detail was even crazier than everything else, but it explained her voice-powers and the divine essence Prometheus, Amphitrite, Poseidon, and even Circe said she had.

But a goddess living inside of her, and somehow she and said goddess were one and the same? They both had powers, both had divine essences, both seemed to have minds of their own, yet at the same time they shared all those things? A line of logic needed to be drawn somewhere, and Zoey decided this was it. "No," she said. "Sorry, but no. You must be lying. Everything you just said—it's too outlandish."

"Outlandish, yes. Yet somewhere deep down, you know it to be true."

Andy's voice tore Zoey from her "conversation" with Calliope. "Oh my God, Zoey—I'm so freaking sorry. I—I didn't mean to—to kiss you. That was so messed up. I . . . I . . ." She looked up at him. He hesitantly stepped toward her, his expression as apologetic as his words. "Wait," he went on, glancing around, "where're Darko and Kali?"

"Circe turned them into pigs," Zoey replied. "That's what she did to you, too, but somehow you turned back."

He stood closer to Zoey now, looking more confused than ever, and for some reason he seemed . . . taller? Was it possible to go through a growth spurt in just a few hours? She could have sworn he'd been around her height earlier today. But now he stood several inches taller than she did.

She gulped. This had to be because of Anteros. What was the God of Requited Love *doing* to him?

"Forcing him to realize his true potential," Calliope answered, unsolicited. *"That is what Anteros is doing to your precious Andy. However, despite your limited human perception, they are one and the same."*

"Shut up!" Zoey yelled at Calliope.

Andy flinched as if those words had been meant for him, hurt flashing in his eyes. "Uh. Um. I—I'm sorry." He backed away. "I get why you wouldn't wanna talk to me right now. You probably don't wanna see me, either. I'll try to explain later, once I figure it out for myself. Just, uh—"

"No, not you, Andy," Zoey interjected, throwing up her hand.

Andy glanced at Darko and Kali awkwardly, both of them still squealing on the floor. "Oh, yeah, okay," he started. "To be fair, though, I don't think they can understand y—"

"No, I wasn't speaking to Darko and Kali, either," she interrupted. "I don't know how to explain it right now, but it has something to do with Calliope. I just need to get her to be quiet, and then we need to change those two back and get off this island."

A look of realization came over Andy's face. "Wait, is Calliope talking in your head? Because I think Anteros might be doing the same thing to me. Well, maybe. I'm not sure."

Zoey was too stunned to speak as she began piecing things together. What had happened to Andy—how he'd lost control of his body—Circe's magic couldn't have been the reason. Well, not the *only* reason. Maybe Circe's magic had been a trigger, but if Anteros was talking to him in his head, like Calliope was talking to Zoey, then it had to have been Anteros who'd possessed him.

That raised another question: if Anteros could take over Andy's body, did that mean Calliope could take over Zoey's, too? And what prompted Anteros to do so in the first place? For instance, had Circe's magic been the catalyst, or had the catalyst been something else? Had Calliope and Anteros been growing stronger ever since Zoey's and Andy's powers started developing? Was it only a matter of time before the gods completely took over the both of them?

Before Zoey could vocalize her revelation or any of her questions, the familiar cackle of a woman sounded from where Circe lay "dead" on the floor. Zoey turned, and her heart jumped into her throat.

Circe stood before them, very much alive, with Poseidon's Trident in hand. When had that happened? How had Zoey missed Circe regenerating? More importantly, how had Zoey missed the immortal sorceress snatching one of the objects of power she, Andy, and their friends had risked their lives stealing? "Anteros, Calliope. You're both as foolish as ever, I see," Circe hissed. "Allowing your feelings for one another to distract you, and consequently destroy you. I suppose some things never change."

Andy was not having a good day. In fact, he had not had a good day in weeks, and he wasn't sure whether he'd ever have a good day again.

Since he'd escaped the Underworld, and since he'd let go of the possibility of resurrecting his dead father, mother, sister, and best friend, Andy had only wanted to focus on one thing: stealing the rest of the Greek gods' main objects of power and defeating them.

Except it hadn't been very easy to focus on just

the one thing. While he was flying across the country on the backs of pegasi, battling monsters and demigods alike, and discovering he was the god Anteros incarnate, the feeling that he needed to confess his love for Zoey had nagged and nagged and nagged at him. Finally, he'd told her how he felt. And he didn't regret his confession one bit, though he knew he'd seriously fumbled it and needed to apologize for being so insensitive about her past.

The thing he *did* regret—what was absolutely mortifying him at this very moment—was the fact that just after Circe had worked her potions on him, everything had gone black, and then the next thing he knew, he'd been kissing Zoey.

He'd been *kissing* her. On the *lips*.

It had been his first kiss. It had ended with Zoey angrily pushing him away.

And he didn't even know how it had happened.

One minute, Circe had done something weird to him. Turned him into a pig just as she'd done to Darko and Kali, according to Zoey. But then the next minute, the oddly familiar voice of a man sounded in his head, saying he was going to "take over their body," and there'd been a flash of blinding silver light.

Andy had blacked out after that, and when he'd awoken, he was human again—thank God, because that meant there was a way to change back Darko and Kali—and he'd been making out with Zoey. A second later, Zoey shoved him off her, and he'd noticed Circe was "dead" on the floor. He'd then faded in and out of consciousness, feeling as though he had to fight to stay awake. Once he came to, guilt overcame him. *Zoey must not have wanted to kiss me*, he thought. *Crap, crap, crap. Why do I keep screwing everything up? How am I ever gonna make it up to her after all this?*

To make matters worse than ever, Circe had regenerated without them noticing, and now she stood before them with Poseidon's Trident in hand.

Yeah, Andy was not having a good day.

Circe lunged for Zoey, brandishing the Trident. At the same time, Zoey dove for the Helm of Darkness. She seized the Helm and tugged it over her head, disappearing in an instant.

Circe whistled. "My pets, come to the kitchen! I have treats for you!"

Howls and snarls sounded from the other chambers in the palace, the floor trembling as Circe's wolves and lions stampeded through the halls toward the kitchen. Darko and Kali squealed from behind Andy, and his stomach lurched. How were he and Zoey supposed to keep those two safe from Circe and her pets, steal back Poseidon's

Trident, and not get killed in the process?

Circe charged in Andy's direction, Trident at the ready, and Andy leapt to the side, furiously flapping his wings to avoid her.

"You've found yourself in quite the predicament." The voice was blabbering on in Andy's head again. Zoey said Calliope had been speaking to her; Andy had a feeling that meant the man speaking to him was Anteros.

"Anteros?" Andy asked, dodging Circe again. "Is that you?"

"We have no time for questions, boy," the voice replied. *"Relinquish some control of our body and I will save us all."*

"What?" Andy exclaimed. "No way. This is my body. You can't—you can't just—"

The voice interrupted, *"I swear I won't push your consciousness aside, as I did before. I swear we will work together this time. I was eager to gain control after sixteen years of being trapped in the shadows, and I extend my sincerest apologies for my rash behavior. But if you do not relinquish control—at least some of it—then I fear we'll all perish tonight."*

Circe jabbed the Trident at Andy, nearly grazing his biceps, and he fluttered backward toward Darko and Kali. When Circe's wolves and lions got in here, he'd have to make sure they couldn't lay a paw on his friends, so he needed to stay close. "Do you regret choosing Calliope yet?" Circe shrieked at him. "I always knew I'd receive the chance to destroy her for stealing you from me, just as I destroyed Scylla for winning the heart of my dear Glaucus."

Andy thought back to the strange dog-eel-monster he and his friends had encountered when they'd first arrived on the island, considered Circe's potions and what she could do to a person, and was hit with realization. "You—you *made* that thing?" he cried. "That—that Scylla-creature?"

She offered him the most deranged smile he'd ever seen, her fiery eyes blazing. *"Yes, she did,"* the voice in his mind said. *"In the old days, the sea god Glaucus fell in love with the beautiful nymph Scylla, but Scylla did not return his feelings. Desperate to gain Scylla's affections, Glaucus came to Circe and asked her to brew a love potion that would force Scylla to fall for him. But Circe fell in love with Glaucus instead, and when Glaucus rejected Circe, she poisoned Scylla's bathing pool, transforming the nymph into a monster."*

"How do you know all that?" Andy exclaimed at the voice.

The voice made a sound of exasperation. *"To answer your original question—yes, I am Anteros, and because I am who I am, I 'know all that.' Now, relinquish some control of our body, unless you want to be killed this evening, unless you want your friends to be fed to Circe's pets, and unless you want Calliope—or Zoey, as you know her—to be doomed to a fate such as Scylla's."*

Right as Anteros finished, a dozen of Circe's wolves and lions came barreling into the chamber. Circe whistled, gesturing at Andy, Darko, and Kali with the Trident, and the animals careered toward the trio.

There was nothing else Andy could do. "How, Anteros?" he blurted. "How can I relinquish control?"

"Close your eyes and search for me. I have been dormant here in the twisting passages of your mind, waiting for the day I might become strong enough to speak to you, anticipating the moment we finally begin our convergence." Andy had no idea what the hell Anteros was rambling on about, but he didn't have time to ask. Before Anteros even finished speaking, Andy closed his eyes and focused on searching for the god in his mind.

Finding Anteros happened far quicker than Andy had expected. Almost right after closing his eyes, Andy spotted the god. He stood at the mouth of a pitch-black cave-like structure, and he looked just as he had when Andy had seen him in those visions in Aphrodite City. He wore white robes and possessed youthful features, dark hair cut short, and feathered butterfly-shaped wings just like Andy's—or perhaps Andy's were just like his.

In his mind's eye, Andy ran toward Anteros. He wasn't sure why, but he didn't have wings here, so he couldn't fly. Anteros soared toward him. Something told him that they'd have to be touching if whatever it was Anteros intended to do was going to work.

Within seconds, they reached each other. Anteros seized Andy by the wrists, and the buzzing in Andy's chest started up again.

The sensation grew stronger, stronger, stronger. It reached a crescendo, spreading all throughout Andy's body, and in a flash of blinding silver light, he became one with Anteros.

Karter lay in bed in his room, staring up at the fabric canopy surrounding him.

Before a few demigod warriors had escorted him here, his father had told him to go straight to sleep, to rest and rejuvenate his body so that he could train further, then execute Diana in three days' time. But it seemed he was unable to even follow that simple of an order.

His mind raced, his pulse pounding in his ears, the sour scent of sweat wafting into his nostrils. He scrunched up his nose. Perhaps he should have bathed before crawling under the sheets.

Really, though, how was he supposed to sleep at all after everything that had happened these past few weeks? Syrena and Spencer were dead. Just when Karter had lost all hope of survival, he'd been told he'd be made into an immortal god so long as he executed Diana using green lightning. He'd managed to create and control green lightning. And then, and then . . .

And then I failed, he thought. *Again.*

He sighed, rubbing his eyes and rolling onto his side. The skin around his right eye, his scarred eye, felt like mottled leather beneath his fingers, and images of the night he'd taken on the punishment meant for Spencer and Syrena flashed through his mind.

Flinching, he contemplated the memories. How much longer could he go on like this? Every time he tried to protect his friends, he disgraced himself in the eyes of the Olympians. But then, every time he attempted to gain the favor of the gods, he betrayed the people he loved most in the world.

The difference is that Spencer and Syrena are dead, he reminded himself. *They're gone. I'll never see them again. But the gods aren't dead and gone. There's still a chance to please them, to find my place among them . . .*

Except I don't deserve any more chances.

Zeus should have killed me in the amphitheater. He should have put me out of my misery.

Still, there was another part of Karter that wondered if maybe, just maybe, he didn't really deserve to die. Maybe every event up until now had happened for a reason. Maybe all of it had occurred for the sole purpose of making him the god he'd always been meant to become. After all, wasn't everything supposed to be predetermined? Written by the Fates long ago? He remembered Asteria saying something about fate and destiny back in Hephaestus City—how although there were many possible outcomes to everyone's destiny, the "universe" sometimes allowed certain events to happen in order for others to take place.

If that's the case, he thought, *and if Olympus is really where I'm supposed to be, then I'm going to have to let go of Spencer and Syrena for good this time.*

No longer can I question the parts I played in their deaths, and the same goes for my mother. All their fates were decided by forces out of my control. Everything that's happened has happened for a reason: so that I can end the war on the gods and become an immortal myself.

If I can just stop fighting my destined greatness, perhaps it will finally come.

Several knocks at the door yanked Karter from his thoughts. He shot up, threw off his bedcovers, and hastened toward the door. "Who is it?"

"Take a guess," said the familiar, seductive voice of a young woman.

Karter's breath caught in his throat. The last time he and Violet had been together and he'd disgraced the gods, she'd broken his heart. Was she here to dump him again, this time for failing to execute Diana? He knew he wasn't in love with her, even if she thought he was. But he had to admit, if she intended to break things off with him tonight, it would only add insult to injury. "What do you want?" he asked, anger already brewing in his chest.

"What else would I want at this hour?"

His cheeks went hot, and he opened the door. Sure enough, Violet stood before him, staring at him flirtatiously as she twirled her golden waves between her fingers.

So, she hadn't come to break things off with him. But when he looked into her eyes, her opalescent irises flashed. Was she trying to use her Daughter of Aphrodite powers on him? *I have to be honest with her*, he thought, his stomach clenching. *If she's playing games with me, she has to know I'm not falling for them.*

"What are you waiting for?" she asked. "Aren't you going to invite me into your chambers?"

Karter moved aside, gesturing for her to step into the room. She did so, and he closed the door behind her. "Listen to me, Violet. I have to tell you the truth. You've been a great . . . distraction, these past few days. You've helped keep me from agonizing over what I must accomplish—somewhat, at least. But you need to know . . . I'm not under your spell. If everything we're doing here is just a game to you, then it needs to end before . . ." He trailed off. He wanted to say *before I actually fall in love with you again, and you break my heart once more* but refrained from doing so.

Violet's lips parted in what seemed to be genuine surprise. "Not under my spell? What are you talking about?" Her eyes went wide. "*Ohhh*, you mean my *love spell*. No, that's not what's going on here, Karter. I only use that power on my enemies. Besides, even if I *were* trying to put you under a love spell, the only way it wouldn't work is if you have feelings for someone else." She pouted. "Are you interested in some other girl? Is that why you're bringing this up?"

For several moments, Karter was at a loss for words. Of course he wasn't "interested in some other girl." Right? "No, I'm not. Stop changing the subject," he snapped, sounding far more bitter than he'd intended to. "I'm almost certain you forced me to fall for you when we were younger, and then you ended things with me because I disgraced myself to the gods, and now . . ." He trailed off again, wanting to ask her so many things: *Are you trying to make me fall in love with you again? Are you doing so because being with me is beneficial for you? Do you only want me because I'm to be made a god?* But he found he couldn't, found he was scared the answers to his questions would all be *Yes.*

She averted her gaze from his and did not reply for a long while. Finally, she spoke. "I never forced you to fall in love with me." She sounded more earnest than he'd ever heard her. "Not when we were younger, and certainly not now. As I've already told you, I only use that power against the enemy. When it will help my chances of victory. But I understand why you think I would have used the ability on you. Not only did I hurt you, but I put on quite a diabolical front, don't I?" Her lips curled up into a sad smile, and she turned around and started opening the door. "I'm sorry for that. I'm sorry for breaking your heart, too. I'll go now. I can see you don't want me here."

Karter couldn't help himself. His mind was racing with new questions that had to be answered. Otherwise, he might go mad. He lunged forward and grabbed Violet's wrist, stopping her from going any farther. "You've never used your powers on me?" he whispered. "Truly?"

"Truly." She spun around to stare him in the eye.

He released her. "Is that why it felt so real? When I fell in love with you?"

"Yes. And, just so you know—I was in love with you, too."

"Come sit, if you want." He headed over to his bed, and she followed close behind.

The moment they sat down, Violet wrapped her arms around Karter's neck and went in for a kiss. However, he pulled away, shaking his head.

Violet's brow furrowed. "What is it? I thought you—we—"

"I don't understand," he interjected, plucking her arms from his neck. "If you loved me, *truly* loved me, then why did you end things with me because of this?" He pointed at his face, at the lightning-bolt scar his father had given him. "You said, and I quote, that I was a shame to the demigods of Olympus, and that there was no point in surrounding yourself with ugly, unlovable things like scars."

She hugged her sides. "Yes, I did end things with you because of your scar. And yes, I did say those horrible words. But I didn't do any of it because I wanted to. I *had* to."

"What do you mean?" A lump formed in his throat as he asked the question. He swallowed hard, forcing it down.

"My mother . . . she didn't want me involved

with you after that happened." Violet's voice trembled. "She was worried it would cause the Olympians to distrust me, to question my loyalty to them. She said being with you could jeopardize me gaining their favor, and that I needed to cut all ties with you immediately—that I needed to thoroughly break your heart—or suffer the consequences. I always loved you, Karter. But I chose to pretend I didn't for the sake of appearances. I chose to pretend to despise you and move on so that I wouldn't forfeit my favor with Zeus. Essentially, I chose to hurt you to save myself. I don't know how I'll ever be able to make it up to you. But now . . . now that you're to be *made* a god . . . being with you wouldn't put me at risk anymore."

Karter was dumbfounded. Part of him thought this sounded like a convenient tale Violet had haphazardly spun, but another part of him believed every word. "You're lying," he responded. "You have to be. My punishment from Zeus—it destroyed me, and so did you. All I had left was Spencer and Syrena, and now they're . . . they're . . ." His eyes filled with tears.

This display of sadness didn't garner any sympathy from Violet. All the vulnerability in her demeanor quickly dissipated, morphing instantly into the cold, calculating armor Karter had witnessed her wear time and time again. She raised a hand, almost as if to strike him, but quickly lowered it. "You can't continue down this road if you ever want to become a god," she yelled, and his tears disappeared at her sudden outburst. "You can't continue to feel guilty because of Spencer's and Syrena's deaths. Those two have done nothing but hold you back, both in life and in death. Neither of them understood what it *really* takes to gain the favor of the gods. They thought they were untouchable, immune to the laws laid out for demigods because of their heritage and powers. But no one is exempt from the consequences of hubris. If you don't let go of their memory, they'll drag you down to Tartarus with them."

Karter flinched at the thought of Tartarus, at the thought of his friends being trapped there. When he'd traveled into the Underworld to save Spencer, he'd stood at the edge of its deepest pit with Zoey and Andy, and he'd nearly been sucked into the blue flames when he'd rescued Zoey from falling in. *That was enough of Tartarus for a lifetime*, he thought, shaking his head as he shoved the memories away. "What do you hope to accomplish by telling me all of this?" he asked.

"I hope to help you." Surprisingly, she sounded as if she was telling the truth. "I couldn't before, for fear of my loyalty to the gods being questioned.

But maybe I can make up for that now." She caressed his unblemished cheek, and he closed his eyes, leaning into her touch, though he didn't fully trust her yet.

He knew that most likely, she was being dishonest about their tumultuous past. She had probably used her love-powers on him, and her mother probably hadn't forced her to break up with him. For so many reasons, it was easy to believe that everything she'd just told him was a lie. After all, she could be manipulating him because he was to be made a god. Maybe she hoped to gain something from him once that happened. But maybe, just maybe, she was being honest.

At the same time, if she was being truthful, she had essentially just admitted to breaking Karter's heart so she could keep the favor of the gods.

Whether she was spinning a lie or telling the truth—well, neither scenario was ideal. *But she's here now*, he thought, *and she apologized for hurting me. If, after all my failures, I'm getting another chance, then maybe she deserves another one, too.*

With that thought, Karter closed the space between them, pressing his lips against Violet's, and she kissed him back fiercely. She tasted as sour as she had these past few days, and it made him think about what she'd said regarding Syrena and Spencer—how they'd held Karter back. For some reason, even now that he knew he had to put their memories to rest, that sentiment didn't sit right with him. After Zeus had maimed his face, Spencer and Syrena had been the only ones there for him . . .

For what felt like the millionth time that evening, Karter shoved his intrusive thoughts away. Rather than thinking of those who'd once shown him kindness, he buried his hands in Violet's golden-blonde waves and continued kissing her, focusing on how silky the strands felt when he wrapped them around his fingers.

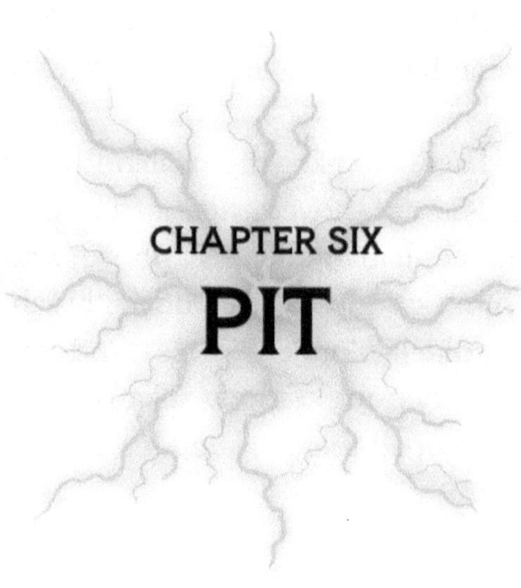

CHAPTER SIX
PIT

In a split second, several images—no, *memories*—whirled through Andy's mind.

First, Andy was flying toward the Olympian palace. Then he was sprinting through Olympus's halls in search of Zeus so he could confront the King of the Gods about what he'd done to Calliope. Andy found him in the palace garden, but he sent Andy hurtling toward Earth . . .

Anteros's voice rang in Andy's head. As the god spoke, Andy's memories liquefied and faded into the darkness like ice melting in boiling water.

"Before we think about any of that," Anteros began, *"there's something we must do."*

Involuntarily, Andy's eyes opened, and he took in the scene before him. It seemed to be unfolding in slow motion. Circe's wolves and lions charged toward him, Darko, and Kali. Against his will, he clapped his hands. In another flash of silver light, a bow and a quiver of arrows appeared in his grip.

"Holy crap!" Andy exclaimed.

"Yes, it is quite exciting," Anteros said, though the words were coming from Andy's mouth rather than sounding in his head. "Didn't I say I would save us all?"

Not of his own accord, Andy slung the quiver over his back and nocked an arrow. The first predator approached him. A massive wolf. He was forced to aim and release the arrow, and it pierced through the wolf's throat. Scarlet fluid splattered out behind the creature. It dropped to the floor, gurgling and writhing about in pain until it went still.

Next came a lion. It rushed toward Andy, fangs bared, claws extended. Just a few feet from him, it leapt into the air, prepared to pounce. Against his will, Andy launched another arrow. The projectile whizzed straight into the lion's skull. Blood and brains spewed from the predator's wound as it plummeted to the ground.

Two more animals rushed forward, a second wolf and lion. In several fluid motions, Andy was forced to shoot two arrows at them. One missile impaled the wolf in an eye, the other spiking the lion in the heart. As the lion fell lifeless, the wolf whimpered and wailed, pawing at the object lodged in its hemorrhaging organ.

One after another, the wolves and lions sped toward Andy, Darko, and Kali, but Anteros made Andy kill or incapacitate them all with arrows. Soon, none were left standing, the quiver slung across Andy's back empty. Against his will, he clapped his hands. More silver light nearly blinded him. In an instant, the bow and quiver were gone, and something else was in his hands: a heavy, solid golden club.

Andy turned to Circe not of his own accord. She shot him a fiery glare. "Go ahead, witch," Anteros said through Andy. "Call more of your pets in here, and let us see what happens. Oh, I know, why don't you summon a few of those little nymphs of yours, hmm? I'm sure they'll put up a good fight!" He let out a cruel laugh. "You must have forgotten my father is the God of War. Battle is second nature to me."

Circe raised the Trident. "I didn't want to use this in my palace. However, you've left me no choice." She started to bring it down, but her arms froze midair. She let out a shriek and jerked around as if wrestling with an invisible force for the weapon.

"That must be Calliope," Anteros said through Andy, to Andy. "Shall we help her?"

The question must have been rhetorical, because Anteros didn't give Andy a chance to reply. Not that he would have argued against helping Zoey, anyway. But suddenly his wings were flapping, and he soared forward. When he got within arm's reach of Circe, Anteros made him smash the golden club into the side of her skull.

Circe tumbled to the side, the Trident flying from her grasp. At the same time, the Helm of Darkness clattered to the floor, and Zoey appeared next to it, sprawled out upon the tiles. She groaned in pain, pressing her hand against her forehead. *No, no!* Andy thought. *Did I hurt her?* He wanted to go to her, to scoop her up in his arms and ask if she was okay. To round up Darko, Kali, and the objects of power and get out of here as fast as possible.

However, when he tried to jerk himself toward Zoey, when he tried to fly to her, he found himself soaring in the direction of the Helm of Darkness and Poseidon's Trident, and then he was snatching them up. With one hand, Anteros forced him to grip the Trident tight; with the other, the god made him slip the Helm over his head. Chills rushed through him as the object of power cloaked him with invisibility. Finally, against his will, he flew to Circe and landed before her.

Circe pressed a hand to her head, golden liquid dribbling from a fracture in her skull. Legs shaking, she climbed to her feet. "I know you're there," she said. "And I know it's the real you, Anteros. Not some cheap imitation who has the gall to call himself your reincarnation. So, now that you have the Helm and the Trident in your possession, what kind of horrible fate do you have planned for me?"

Andy wanted to say that he *was* the real him, that he was Andy Regan and there were no cheap imitations present, and that she was immortal so there really wasn't anything horrible they could do to her—not permanently, at least. But when he opened his mouth and spoke, he heard Anteros's voice and words rather than his own. "I plan to perform the Descent Spell, casting you far from here. You might be a minor goddess, but I'm sure you've heard of the enchantment before, considering your knowledge of magic." He released a volley of malicious cackles. "Funnily enough, Calliope is the one who told me about the spell in the first place, years ago."

Circe screamed. It was a high-pitched, earsplitting, hair-raising shriek, one that Andy imagined was powerful enough to shatter glass. Internally, he cringed at the sound, but externally, he stood perfectly still, as if Anteros had him frozen in place.

When she finished her screeching, she fell to her knees and clasped her hands, tears of orange fire rolling down her cheeks. "Please, Anteros. I loved you. And I know that at one time, you loved me back. Before Calliope came and ruined everyth—"

"None of that matters anymore," Anteros replied calmly, casually. "Even if I did love you once, Circe, you cannot go unpunished for this transgression." He made Andy raise the Trident. Bring it down against the floor. And then chant something—something foreign and ancient and magical sounding—that must have been the spell he was talking about. As if in response to the chant, the ground shook violently, then split open beneath Circe to reveal a black abyss so deep Andy couldn't see the bottom.

Circe screamed as she tumbled down. She clutched onto the edge, dangling over the abyss, and ribbons of bloodred smoke curled up and around her from within the pit.

Worried for Zoey's safety, Andy managed to sneak a peek out of the corner of his eye at her. She was scrambling away from the pit. Behind him, Darko and Kali were squealing in terror. *At least they're safe*, he thought. Anteros forced him to focus solely on Circe again.

"Please, my dearest Anteros!" Circe shouted. "Mercy! Have mercy!"

Anteros chuckled coldly. "Mercy? Were you planning to extend mercy to the mortals you transformed into swine? What about to my vessel? To Calliope's?"

"I thought—I thought—"

"Whatever you thought, you were wrong." Anteros chanted something else. Circe begged him to stop. He didn't listen. Instead, he made Andy ram the Trident against the floor again.

As Anteros went on incanting, the edge that Circe was holding onto began to crumble. She screamed as bits of floor and earth rained down on her head. Then she lost her grip and plunged into the pit.

Once Circe disappeared, her screams no more than echoes, the ground shook again, the earth beginning to seal itself together. When it finished, all that was left to suggest the floor had opened at all was the dirt scattered about and the remnants of the bloodred ribbons of smoke as they evaporated into thin air.

It was then that Andy realized how nervous he was right now, his heart pounding, his palms slick with sweat. The buzzing in his chest had returned, accompanied by a strange new burning sensation.

Andy dropped the golden club and pulled the Helm off his head, tossed it aside, and turned around—this time all of his own accord. He faced Zoey. "Andy?" she said, her voice hoarse. "Andy, are you okay?"

He parted his lips to reply but found he couldn't speak. *"Apologies,"* Anteros said in his head. *"I overexerted our body when I performed the spell, but it will be all right. We must take a while to rejuvenate."*

As Anteros finished speaking, the ground seemed to shift beneath Andy, and the room began to spin. "Andy!" Zoey shouted. She leapt to her feet and ran toward him.

The hot vibrations in Andy's chest grew ever stronger, his vision becoming blurry. He staggered forward, intending to go to Zoey's side, but tripped and fell face-first instead.

Distantly, Andy could hear Zoey crying out for him. Soon, however, the cries ceased, and darkness consumed him.

Zoey had no idea how Andy had done it. Had no idea how he'd opened the ground, sent Circe down into the pit he'd created, and then sealed everything back up again. Sure, she figured the phenomenon had something to do with the powers of the Helm of Darkness and Poseidon's Trident. Not only because he'd been in possession of both items when he'd done it, but also because of what Circe had said earlier about tapping into the objects' true potential. Even still, she had no idea where to begin to start understanding the logistics of what had just occurred.

The process must have also had quite an effect on him, because when he'd taken off the Helm and she could see him again, his face had been deathly pale, sweat seeping from his pores. He'd stumbled forward and fallen to the floor, and now he lay unconscious on the soil-covered tiles at her feet.

Heart racing, she knelt by his side and checked his pulse and breathing. *His heart's beating, and his breathing seems normal. That's good, right? God, what I wouldn't give to have Diana's healing powers right now.*

Several squeals interrupted her thoughts, and she looked up to see Darko and Kali—who were both still pigs—trotting toward her. *Crap. Yet another problem I'm going to have to take care of, and fast. What if more wolves and lions or even the nymphs in the palace come in here, before Andy wakes up? Before I can find an anecdote for Darko and Kali?*

"*Anteros will be fine, just as you already suspect,*"

Calliope said in Zoey's head. *"It might take a bit, but he'll wake. Even so, you need my help."*

Zoey huffed, though she was finding it rather difficult to stay frustrated considering Calliope had confirmed Andy was going to be okay, and also considering Darko and Kali had reached her side and started licking her hand and arms affectionately. In this state, they almost reminded her of her childhood dog, Daisy. "Oh, yeah?" she responded to Calliope. "And how do you propose to help me? If it's by taking over my body, like what Anteros did to Andy, you better believe it's not happening." She grimaced, trying not to imagine what Calliope would make her do with Andy if the goddess took over her body.

"As much as I would love to control our *body, I'm not sure whether I'm powerful enough to do so yet."*

"You keep saying we're the same person, but I'm not convinced." Zoey went back and forth between petting Darko and Kali behind the ears. "How did you reach that conclusion?"

"I have no time to answer such maddening philosophical questions! When Circe tells whatever gods of the Underworld who took over in Hades's absence how she arrived there, they will be in contact with Zeus immediately. We must make haste! We must change the mortal and the satyr back into their true forms and escape this island before—"

"Wait, wait, wait! Hold on a second. Did you

just say Circe is in the Underworld? Is that—is that what Andy did to her? Sent her there? Is that what the gaping hole in the palace floor was all about?"

"*You have always been quick witted. Perhaps you'll listen to reason, then, if I take a short time to explain a few things to you.*

"*Yes, Anteros sent Circe to Hades, and he used the Helm of Darkness and Poseidon's Trident coupled with the Descent Spell to open and close the portal. But if we don't escape this island as soon as possible, I can assure you his efforts will have been for nothing. Once Zeus discovers we're here, either he will send his minions for us, or he will come for us himself. And despite the resilience and strength you have demonstrated not only recently, but also over the years, you're still no match for the King of the Gods. Not yet.*"

Zoey rubbed her temple. *This is a lot to take in. I need to focus on the task at hand and try to figure out everything else later.* "Okay, for the time being, I won't ask any more questions about Circe and the Underworld. Now, how do I turn Darko and Kali back?"

"*You cannot do so by yourself. You must transform them by channeling me, by using my magic.*"

"Don't I already have magic? When I use my voice-powers and whatnot? They seemed pretty otherworldly to me, at least."

"*Yes, that is true. You already have a small bit of magic—this is what others recognize in you as your divine essence, and what you know as your powers. Anteros, as well. You see, the convergence began for Anteros after he touched his statue in Aphrodite City; this is because the statue held remnants of his old magical energy, and he absorbed some of it by coming into contact with it.*

"Your convergence began later that day when Anteros touched you after your fight with the astynomia *in Aphrodite City. When he came into contact with you, you absorbed some of the magical energy he'd absorbed earlier. You felt it happen in the form of an electric shock. But, although you've both begun your convergences—and although you grow stronger each day—you have still not reached full power. Therefore, you must channel me to save your friends."*

"Andy and I began our . . . convergences?" Zoey asked, raising a brow. "What's that supposed to mean?"

"We are running out of time. We must make haste! You must channel my magic! Please, close your eyes and find me in the labyrinth of your mind. I wait for you at the entrance, where I've been waiting for you for years. In the past, you couldn't see me, but now that the convergence is progressing and I can speak with you, I suspect you will spot me easily."

As much as Zoey didn't want to admit it, Calliope was right. They were running out of time. Once Circe explained to any god aligned with Zeus what Andy had done to her, someone would be on their way here.

So she did as the goddess said. She closed her eyes and began to search the darkness of her mind.

It happened quickly. Zoey caught sight of Calliope standing at the opening of a cave-like structure, and she was immediately struck by how much she resembled the goddess. Not that they appeared exactly alike, because they didn't. Calliope stood much taller than Zoey, her features more chiseled and more classically beautiful than Zoey's. Still, they shared several defining characteristics—they had similar tan skin, bright-blue irises, and long, curly brown hair. Calliope wore a turquoise dress that was stunning on her, and Zoey noted that turquoise was one color she also looked great in. If someone told her Calliope was her long-lost aunt or cousin, she certainly wouldn't discredit them.

Calliope must have seen Zoey, because the goddess ran toward her. Zoey ran toward Calliope as well. Something told her they'd have to be touching if whatever it was Calliope wanted to do was going to work.

Moments passed, and they reached each other. Calliope snatched Zoey by the arms, and a strange buzzing sensation began humming in Zoey's chest. The sensation grew stronger, stronger, stronger, until Zoey could hardly bear it any longer, but still she did not pull away from Calliope.

The buzzing spread throughout the rest of Zoey's body. Glowing light the color of a clear midday sky flashed, and then Zoey felt herself merge—felt herself become one—with Calliope.

The blue glow faded, and in a split second, what could only be memories flooded Zoey's mind.

First, Zoey was in her bedchamber on Olympus, concocting a speech she planned to give to the minor deities of her pantheon. The speech was meant to convince them that they needed to rebel against the Olympians. When it was over, she also intended to educate them about the Descent Spell.

Then Zeus was there with her, and he snapped her neck, and she "died." When she finished regenerating and awoke, Zeus was carrying her through the Garden of Olympus. Finally, the god sent her barreling toward Earth . . .

"Ah, yes," Calliope said, still in her mind. *"You're finally recalling bits and pieces of our past. Even so, we have no time for memories."* Compelled by an urge not her own, Zoey blinked her eyes open. Andy lay unconscious before her, Darko and Kali pacing nervously at her feet.

Suddenly, and very much unlike before, Zoey was undaunted by the task at hand. Suddenly, she felt as if she knew not only what had to be done, but also exactly how to do it.

She snapped her fingers, though she wasn't sure if she'd wanted to do so or if something else had forced her to. A flash of bright-blue light emanated from her hand, practically blinding her. Although she wanted to close her eyes, she found she could not. Something was keeping them open. She tried to cover them, but her arm wouldn't budge. Had Calliope taken over her body despite promising not to?

"Calliope!" she shouted. *At least I can still talk*, she thought, her eyes watering. "What's happening?"

"Be quiet, or else you'll break my concentration." Calliope's clear, regal voice rang all around Zoey, no longer only in her mind, but what was strange was that the words came out of her own mouth. And yet, the distinction between their two different voices was clear as day. While Zoey sounded every bit like an eighteen-year-old girl, Calliope sounded just as Zoey imagined a powerful, ancient goddess would.

Zoey pressed her lips into a thin line; even if she wanted to interrupt whatever Calliope was doing, she had a feeling she wouldn't be able to. A familiar tingling sensation started up in her throat, and she suspected Calliope had just used her own voice-powers on her.

When the blue light finally faded, Zoey blinked

hard—this time of her own accord—trying to clear her vision. There was a slight burning in her chest, different from the buzzing sensation, but it quickly subsided. *"We'll talk again soon,"* Calliope said in her head. *"But for now, I need to rest. It's been years since I last counteracted another goddess's magic, and Circe's is strong."* She released a soft, sweet sigh. Zoey's vision cleared.

As Zoey took in the sights before her, she blinked some more. She could hardly believe what she was seeing.

Andy lay unconscious on the floor and Darko and Kali stood before her still, but Darko and Kali were no longer pigs. Darko had been returned to his satyr form, and Kali was human again. They appeared just as they had before.

Kali smiled at Zoey while Darko poked and prodded at his horns, arms, and hooved legs in disbelief. "What happened?" Kali asked. "We were pigs, but then Andy wasn't and I thought I saw him kiss you, and then I'm pretty sure Circe fell down into a pit, and you were petting us, and—"

"Andy!" Darko cried, racing to Andy's side. When Kali noticed Andy lying unconscious on the floor, she raced to his side as well.

"He's okay," Zoey said. "He'll wake soon. He just—he exhausted his body, I think. From sending Circe down to the Underworld."

Darko looked up at Zoey with an incredulous expression. "Huh?"

"He did what now?" Kali asked.

Zoey briefly explained how Anteros had taken over Andy's body and, after turning Andy back into a human and defeating Circe's pets, used the Helm and Trident to open a portal to the Underworld and sent Circe there. Then how Calliope had taken over Zoey's body, and how the goddess had transformed Darko and Kali back into their normal selves by counteracting Circe's magic.

"Despite everything, Circe will be back," Zoey said. "More of her wolves and lions could come after us, too. Maybe even her servants. We have to find a way off this island, stat."

Several roars and howls came from somewhere in the palace. The sounds of paws hitting the floor followed.

"Those seem like they're coming this way," Darko said.

Zoey nodded. "They're after us." She picked up the Helm and handed it to Kali, then seized the Trident. "Kali, put on the Helm, and both of you carry Andy. Since you'll all be connected, you'll all be invisible. Meanwhile, I'll use the Trident and my voice-powers to hold off anyone who tries to stop us. I doubt Circe's pets and servants can dodge them the way she did."

Kali put on the Helm and disappeared, and Darko grabbed Andy under the armpits. Kali must have picked up Andy next, because both he and Darko disappeared with her. All the while, the roars and howls continued.

"C'mon," Zoey said, running toward the kitchen's exit. She held tight to the Trident with her hand, gesturing at the others to follow her with her handless arm. "Let's get outta here."

She passed through the door. Once she determined the hall was clear, she hurried into it, the sounds of feet falling and hooves clacking following her. She veered right, away from Circe's other pets. They came from the direction of the palace's entrance; surely it had an exit too, right? Hopefully on the opposite side?

They reached a curve in the hallway and Zoey went along with it. But when she saw what awaited her and her friends beyond the bend, she stopped dead.

What could only be four forest nymphs—Dryads, Zoey thought—and five ocean nymphs—Nereids, if she remembered correctly—blocked the group's path. The greenery-clad Dryads had long grapevines like tentacles twisting and curling all around them, while the blue-skinned Nereids had whips of water ready to strike in their nimble hands.

The one thing both types of nymphs had in common, though, was that they glared at Zoey, their narrowed eyes filled with hatred.

One of the Nereids stepped forward, snapping her water-whip against her palm. "We heard screaming. The palace was shaking horribly. And now we sense our mistress's absence."

A Dryad came up beside the Nereid. Her vines snaked around her arms. "Where has she gone, exactly?"

Something bumped into Zoey from behind, knocking her forward a few feet, and Kali cursed under her breath. "Stop, stop, stop," Darko whispered frantically.

The nymphs cocked their heads. "What was that?" another one of the Nereids asked.

Zoey cleared her throat and thought about what she could say to convince these nymphs that Circe was fine, that their mistress wasn't gone, and that they should let Zoey and her friends pass. She focused on her voice-powers, focused on the tingling in her throat that would inevitably come . . .

Except it didn't.

She closed her eyes and focused on her voice-powers again, harder this time, but still the familiar tingling sensation did not come.

"Umm," she started, and not very eloquently, for a supposed goddess of eloquence, "not to worry, my . . . friends. Circe is just, uh, out."

The nymphs shot her disbelieving scowls, and she thought, *Calliope! What's happening? Are my powers stalled because you turned Darko and Kali back to normal or something?* The goddess didn't respond.

The Nereid who'd initially stepped up drew closer to Zoey. "What have you done with our mistress?"

Zoey backed away, gripping the Trident so tight her knuckles went pale. What was she supposed to do? To say? If her voice-powers weren't working, and if the nymphs already suspected something was up and the rest of Circe's pets were after her and her friends, how were they supposed to get out of the palace? Not to mention off the island?

Could she perform the spell Anteros had done on Circe? The Descent Spell or whatever he'd called it? Could she send Circe's pets and servants down to the Underworld to buy herself some time?

She knew the spell must involve the Helm and Trident, but didn't magic like that require words too? When the Fates had cast their cloaking enchantment, they'd definitely incanted *something*, though Zoey couldn't remember what. So, what were the words Anteros had used when he'd done the Descent Spell?

She racked her brain, trying to recall what he'd said, but it had sounded so strange. So ancient and otherworldly and—

Wait a second, she thought as an idea struck her. *Maybe Prometheus could help us out of this if he escaped the Labyrinth and avoided getting caught. How did Spencer and Diana say a god can be summoned, again?*

"Tomorrow we'll gather some berries and build a small fire as a sacrifice to summon her," Spencer had said. That was when they'd initially called on Persephone for help into the Underworld so they could steal Hades's Helm of Darkness.

Gods and demigods are also strongest when they're near something that gives them power, Zoey remembered. *Prometheus is a Titan god of fire, so if we made one and offered a sacrifice in his name, maybe he could muster the strength to help us!*

More of the nymphs stepped forward, brandishing their water and vines like weapons. "Well, mortal?" barked a Dryad. "Are you going to answer the question, or do we have to torture you to get you to talk?"

"Kali, Darko!" Zoey yelled over her shoulder. "My voice-powers aren't working. Take Andy and run back to the kitchen as fast as you can, then make a fire and grab some food to sacrifice. I'm right behind you!" All she heard in response were Kali's feet and Darko's hooves striking the floor as they hastened away.

The first Nereid practically growled, lunging toward Zoey and snapping her water-whip. Zoey darted to the side, but she wasn't fast enough. The whip grazed her shoulder, hot pain searing the impacted flesh. She cried out. Almost lost grip of the Trident.

A Dryad came forward next. With a vine, she slapped Zoey off her feet. Zoey landed hard on her spine. The Trident tumbled out of her hand and slid a few yards away.

Another Nereid charged toward Zoey, water-whip ready. As the nymph brought down her weapon, Zoey rolled sideways toward the Trident. The water smacked a tile uselessly. The Nereid shrieked in contempt, rushing after Zoey. Two Dryads ran up behind the Nereid to help her, vines ready.

As the Nereid brought down her water-whip a second time, Zoey snatched the Trident. She propelled herself into a crouched position, then thrust the Trident's prongs into the Nereid's stomach.

The other nymphs halted in their tracks, gasping as scarlet liquid trickled from the Nereid's wound and mouth. Her water-whip de-solidified and splashed to the floor, and she fell limp.

The nymphs stared in wide-eyed shock at their

lifeless companion, and Zoey ripped the Trident from the Nereid's body. Mustering all her strength, she slammed the object of power against the tiles before her feet.

Tremors arced through the floor from the point of collision. The nymphs screamed, quakes tossing them backward.

Zoey didn't waste any time. She had to take advantage of the disorientation. She swung around and bolted back toward the kitchen.

Moments before she reached the chamber, several lions and wolves barreled out of another room at the end of the long hallway. When the predators spotted her, they roared and howled, hurtling toward her.

To make matters worse, the shouts of young women echoed behind her. She chanced a glance over her shoulder; the nymphs must have recovered quickly, because they were chasing her now, and they were catching up fast.

Heart racing, Zoey spun around to face the nymphs. She rammed the Trident against the floor again. The vibrations sent them spiraling through the air.

Pivoting toward the wolves and lions, she brought the Trident down a third time. The convulsions took a bit longer to reach the animals than they had the nymphs, but they still did the trick. The creatures went flying backward, yelping and yowling all the while.

Zoey hurried into the kitchen and quickly assessed her surroundings. For the most part, it looked just as she'd left it, except Darko and Kali worked at a stove in a frenzy as they tried to build a fire. They'd piled a bunch of fruits and vegetables on the counter beside them, and the Helm and a still-unconscious Andy lay at their feet.

Using the Trident, Zoey yanked several racks of jars of food and glowing goo in front of the doorway. The jars shattered, their insides and loads of broken glass spreading across the floor. Hopefully, that would keep Circe's pets and servants busy for as long as it would take Zoey to summon Prometheus.

"Oh, good," Kali started, her voice laced with sarcasm and panic. "You made it back. Care to explain what exactly we're doing here?"

As Zoey ran to them, Darko did something over the stove, and orange flames crackled into existence. Kali backed up while he tossed their pile of food into the fire. "We're making a sacrifice to summon Prometheus so he can help us get out of here," he said.

Zoey stopped at Darko's side and leaned on the counter, trying to catch her breath. "Exactly," she replied.

"Aren't Prometheus's godly abilities limited?" Kali asked. "Because of Hephaestus's chains?"

"Yeah," Darko answered. "But I bet he can still make it. He has to. Because unless Zoey can get her voice-powers to work on these guys, we're dead."

The smells of smoke and burning fruits and vegetables filled Zoey's nostrils, and she thought back to what Spencer had said to summon Persephone. *"Persephone, it's your one and only stepson, Spencer. Please accept my sacrifice and make yourself present to me. I need your guidance."*

Zoey stood up straight and closed her eyes. "Prometheus, it's me. Zoey. It's also Andy and Darko and Kali. Anyway, please accept our sacrifice and make yourself present to us. We really, really need your help. Seriously, if you don't show—"

She never finished her sentence, a volley of animalistic snarls sounding behind them. She swung around and saw the wolves and lions scrambling over the fallen racks, trying to make their way into the kitchen.

"Shit!" she shrieked, turning back to the fire. "Prometheus, please! Help us!"

Several more seconds passed. Nothing.

"Okay, he's obviously not coming," Kali said. "He's not strong enough, because I'm sure if he could, he would. What about someone else?"

"Who else is there?" Darko cried. "The Fates said they aren't going to help us anymore, Apollo was captured by the other gods, and—"

There was a loud *crash* as a few of the wolves and lions knocked racks aside to get into the kitchen. They careered toward Zoey, Darko, and Kali, but they couldn't run more than a few feet. They slipped and slid on broken glass and glowing goo.

Kali snapped her fingers. "The goddess who visited Andy in his dream when he was passed out and his wings were growing!"

Darko snatched more fruits and vegetables. "That's it, that's it! She can help us! Prometheus said she's a goddess of prophecy, right? But what was her name? There are so many deities who deal with prophecy!"

"Asteria," Zoey replied. "I think her name's Asteria."

A lion and two wolves gained their footing. They snarled and bounded for the group.

Darko chucked the food into the fire. "Asteria, great goddess of prophecy, please accept our sacrifice and *get us out of here!*"

Zoey wasn't sure whether Asteria would come. She wasn't even sure whether that was the goddess's name; it had just been a best guess.

The fact of the matter was, Zoey couldn't count on anyone else to save them now. If no one made it here, it was up to her.

After all, she was a Chosen One.

She spun around and leapt in front of her friends. *I'll protect them, no matter what.* She raised the Trident.

The predators were thirty, twenty, ten feet away.

Zoey brought down the Trident.

Just as the prongs rammed into the floor, something strange happened. Something she'd never expected.

Thousands of shimmering miniature stars materialized in front of her. They encircled her, ensnared her and her friends and all their possessions. Then there was a flash of blinding light, and next thing Zoey knew, they were all soaring across the night sky.

CHAPTER SEVEN
STARS

The morning sun shone brightly into Karter's bedchamber, straight through his burgundy canopy and into his eyelids. He let out a soft groan, wrestling with himself to stay asleep.

Eventually, he gave in. He opened his eyes and looked over. Violet lay beside him in bed, and he nearly jumped in surprise at the sight. Her golden waves were fanned out around her perfect face as she slept, her chest rising and falling peacefully.

The previous night's events rushed back to him. Their arrival at Olympus. The grandchildren-of-

Hephaestus being struck by Zeus with lightning. Diana's failed execution. Violet coming to Karter's room.

Karter sighed. As much as he wanted Violet's story to be true—and not because he was desperately in love with her or anything, but because it would mean there were people on Olympus who genuinely cared about him—he still couldn't be sure whether she was telling the truth.

Still, he reminded himself, *if Zeus is willing to give me all these extra chances, then perhaps it wouldn't hurt to give her another one, too.*

I suppose I'll find out whether she's telling the truth soon enough.

He reached over to stroke a few wayward strands of her golden hair, and his touch seemed to wake her. She yawned, her opalescent eyes fluttering open. She rolled over and offered him a coy smirk. "Last night was incredible."

Karter's heart skipped a beat, but he focused on staying suave. In the past, he'd allowed himself to be giddy around Violet, to open up to her, and this time he wanted to remain closed off until he knew for sure what her true motivations were. "You think so?" he asked. In response, she grabbed his face and kissed him. Closing his eyes, he kissed her back.

Several booming knocks sounded at Karter's

bedchamber door. Someone tried to push it open, but Karter had locked it last night, so it didn't budge. Karter pulled away from Violet, and they both turned toward the door. "Who is it?" Karter called.

"Your father, the King of the Gods and owner of this palace," Zeus replied. He sounded profoundly irritated. "You would do well to unlock this door before I knock it down."

Karter didn't need to hear another word. He leapt into the air and drew the canopy around his bed to hide Violet, then flew toward the door and unlocked and opened it as quickly as possible, before Zeus did something rash. And there he was, the King of the Gods, his hugely muscular arms crossed over his broad chest as he glared down at his son.

Karter swallowed hard, his lightning scar throbbing with the memory of old pain. He stepped aside so his father could pass. "Please, come in."

Zeus did just that, striding inside with all the authority that a King of the Gods should possess. "Violet, Daughter of Aphrodite," the god began, "I know you're here, canoodling about with my son. Please leave. *Now.*" Violet didn't hesitate to heed the order. She threw back the canopy and scurried past Karter and Zeus out of the room.

Zeus leered at her figure as she hastened down the hall, the thin fabric of her robes revealing the curves beneath, and Karter cleared his throat, trying to suppress the agitation rising within him as he witnessed his father's infamous shamelessness firsthand. "What can I do for you, Father?" he asked, hiding his frustration as best he could. "I'm eager to please."

The King of the Gods chuckled. "Yes, you are, my son. Yes, you are. The Daughter of Aphrodite's affections for you are evidence enough of that."

Karter's cheeks grew hot. "Sorry, I—"

"No need to apologize," Zeus boomed, clapping Karter on the back. Surprisingly, though, it didn't feel like a stern action. It felt jovial. "I see now that you take after me more than I once believed." Karter flinched, unsure of whether he liked hearing that in this context.

"Father, if I may ask," he started, trying to change the subject, "why are you here this morning? It's rare for you to visit me like this."

"Ah, of course. My arrival must come as a surprise to you." Zeus glided toward Karter's bed, sat down, and patted the space beside himself. "Sit down and relax while I explain."

Karter raised a brow but didn't ask any more questions, walking over and sitting next to his father. The action felt strange, awkward.

Zeus clapped Karter on the back again, chortling. "You seem so tense. I said *relax*." Karter forced a smile and allowed his shoulders to fall slightly. "Now, as to the reason I'm here," Zeus continued. "I believe I might know why you could not follow through with the Daughter of Apollo's execution last night."

Every muscle in Karter's body went taut. "You do?"

"Yes. I thought about it all night, and I concluded that you simply need more support to help you harden your heart for this task."

"How did you come to that conclusion?"

"Because at one time I, too, had to harden my heart to gain power, and I know it is no easy feat."

"You really had to do that?"

"Of course." Zeus gently patted Karter on the shoulder. "I know how much you cared for the Daughter of Poseidon and the Son of Hades. I know that executing someone they called a friend is difficult. But you are capable of it."

Karter put his face in his hands. "Father, I don't . . . I don't understand. None of this should be difficult. If I'm to be made a god, I must let go and for—"

"Stop," Zeus interrupted. "There is no 'if.' Becoming an immortal among the rest is your destiny. Even so, a spectacular fate is never easy."

"What do you mean by that?" He looked up at his father. "What do you mean, 'a spectacular fate is never easy'?"

Zeus considered this for a while before replying. "The gods make difficult decisions each day. There are certain acts I have committed in the past. Acts I did not wish to commit. I had to harden my heart and carry them out. Otherwise, I would not be where I am today. I would not be as powerful, respected, and feared."

"Wait, there are things you *didn't* want to do?" Karter asked, genuinely curious. He'd never heard anything like this from Zeus before. "And you made yourself anyway?"

"Yes. Why would I lie about such a thing?"

"With all due respect," Karter began, running a trembling hand through his hair and averting his gaze from Zeus's penetrating stare, "it's surprising to hear you say such a thing. I didn't realize that at one time you also had . . . weaknesses, for lack of a better word. Since I arrived on New Mount Olympus, I've been trained so that I can carry out your wishes without allowing my mortal frailties to get in the way. However, even with years of training, I'm affected by them still." His scar was throbbing now, but he continued. "Although I'm sure all you've said is true, it's difficult to believe that at one time you had to 'harden your heart,' as you put it."

Karter braced himself as the words finished spilling from his lips. He chanced a glance up at Zeus, preparing for a cruel retaliation to his words, but all he received from the King of the Gods was an almost warm, almost affectionate expression.

Karter raised a brow. Zeus never acted this way. What was going on?

Stop, Karter thought. *Stop reading into these things so much.*

"Allow me to tell you about my first wife," Zeus said. "About the horrid way I had to betray her to remain all-powerful."

"I heard about your first wife during our history lessons with Apollo. Metis was her name, wasn't it? And she was an oceanid and a Titan."

"Yes, all of that is correct. In any case, destroying Metis was one of the most difficult things I've ever had to do."

"I didn't realize that."

"Let me explain." Zeus stroked his beard thoughtfully. "I suppose I should start from the beginning."

"Before you defeated my grandfather, Kronos, right?"

"Correct. Kronos ate my siblings. It was an attempt to keep us from overthrowing him. But my mother, Rhea, saved me, and I was raised knowing that my destiny was to free my brothers and sisters so that, together, we could one day vanquish Kronos."

"Yes, I remember," Karter said. "Apollo told us about that, too. You had to force Kronos to regurgitate the gods who had been devoured?"

"Correct, and that is where dear Metis made herself useful. She concocted the potion that made my father vomit up his children. After that, I fell in love with her and married her, and it was a happy union. However, a prophecy soon emerged, one that said Metis would bear me two children. It was said that our first child would be a daughter. Our second would be a son powerful enough to overthrow me."

The memories of Apollo's lessons surged through Karter's mind. "I think I recall the rest of what happened now. Metis became pregnant, and you had to . . . to . . ."

"I had to trick her," Zeus finished for him. "I convinced her to turn herself into a fly, and then I swallowed her."

"That's how Athena was born from your head," Karter added. "She was your and Metis's child, and Metis gave birth to her from inside of you. Then she grew, and you thought your head was going to explode from the pressure. You cracked your skull open, and Athena burst out from it."

"I can see how much you have learned from Apollo over the years," Zeus remarked. "It is a shame, then, that I must put him in Tartarus. Perhaps you can take over his job of educating the youth from now on."

"Perhaps," Karter replied, thinking over everything Zeus had told him. "I do have one question regarding something Apollo never addressed in his lessons. How do you know Metis didn't escape your body when you ejected Athena from it?"

Zeus stared down at Karter with a blank expression for almost a minute before bursting into a fit of boisterous laughter.

What's so funny? Karter wondered. *I thought it was a fair question.* "Father?" he asked. "How do you know for sure that Metis hasn't escaped you?"

Zeus tried stifling his giggles. "Oh, my dear son, you amuse me so. I am *King of the Gods.*" He wiped some tears of laughter before continuing. "Nothing escapes me, and even if Metis ever manages to, I will never allow her to trick me into impregnating her a second time."

Although Karter wasn't entirely convinced by Zeus's logic, he decided to drop the subject. "Do you ever miss Metis?" he asked. "Do you ever regret what you had to do to her to remain King of the Gods?"

A dark shadow came over Zeus's face, and he pressed his lips into a thin line. Karter wondered if perhaps he shouldn't have asked such a question, shrinking back. Finally, Zeus replied, "On occasion, yes, I do regret betraying her. It has been millennia since I did so, and although I have not only remarried, but also taken many lovers, no one can replace her."

No one can replace her. The words struck Karter. They echoed in his thoughts, and as they did, the faces of his mother and Spencer and Syrena, of Diana and Asteria, and even of Zoey and Andy, flashed through his mind.

"And that is why," Zeus said, "I must continually remind myself of the reason I chose to dispose of her. It helped me remain King of the Gods." He patted Karter on the back. "Remember this, my son: True love is strong. Eternal, even. And that is the *problem* with it. Because if you allow it to control you, it becomes your greatest weakness—your Achilles's heel. If I had allowed my love for Metis to control me, I would not be the god I am today."

Zeus stood and walked over to the bedchamber door. He paused at the entryway. "I know you are trying to forget those you have lost, but I cannot lie to you. You must know, you will never forget them. Although your grief for them will lessen with time, their memories could very well stain your psyche forever. But that does not mean you must give in to weakness. That does not mean you must act as many mortals do and allow your frailties to control you. You can still kill the Daughter of Apollo and achieve your destined greatness. You can still rise and become like the gods.

"Now get up, prepare for the day, and come to the courtyard. You have training to do." With that, Zeus exited the chamber, leaving Karter alone with his thoughts.

Zoey had never been happier to step onto solid land.

Granted, back in her life in the Before Time, she hadn't flown in a plane or sailed in a boat or anything like that, so she guessed she didn't have many experiences to compare this one to. The most excitement she'd ever had as far as transportation went was flying on the backs of pegasi and steering Troy and Marina's Pocket-Sized Submarine through the Atlantic. Now she supposed she could add "soaring across the night sky by way of thousands of little stars" to the list.

Even still, as the sun began its ascent and the stars lowered Zoey and her friends onto a beach that she assumed was part of the mainland, she couldn't help but plop down onto the brown-and-blue shore, even if she could only lie there for a minute or two. "Thank you so much, Asteria—er, at least, I think you're Asteria." She dug her fingers and toes into the cool, wet sand and closed her eyes, listening to the sounds of wind and ocean waves. "Whoever you are, thanks for saving us."

"My pleasure," the unfamiliar voice of a woman said from behind her. "Also, welcome back to the mainland." Zoey shot up and swung around to see whoever it was.

A pale, pretty woman turned out to be the owner of the voice. Her curly red hair spilled over her shoulders, both her silver irises and her dark, star-dotted dress twinkling even in the dim light. "Greetings, Chosen One." She offered Zoey a small smile as she stared down at her. "I suppose you look like her, yes. Similar hair, similar eyes. But it appears your mortal body has some differences from your immortal one, much like Anteros's."

"So, *are* you Asteria?" Kali asked, kneeling in the sand next to Andy, who was still unconscious, and Darko, who stared at Asteria in shock.

"You've gotta be her, right?" Zoey added. "I'm guessing you're not just a goddess of prophecy, but also one of stars, considering . . . well, you know."

Confusion flittered across the woman's face. It disappeared in an instant, and she chuckled, shaking her head. "I suppose you wouldn't remember me. Not yet. I only appeared to Anteros before now."

Zoey raised a brow at the woman. She must have met Calliope before, and she was probably mixing Zoey and Calliope up. *Well, she's in for a surprise,* Zoey thought. *Because I've decided I'm definitely not Calliope.*

Back when we were fighting Poseidon and Triton, I thought maybe I was. But then the real Calliope showed up in my head and started telling me I was in love with Andy—when I'm so not.

"To answer your question," the woman went on, "yes, I am Asteria. Pleased to meet you all." She curtsied. "I suppose you must be quite hungry and thirsty after the perilous journeying you've been up to. Stay here and guard Anteros while I find fresh water and food." She started off toward the thick green tree line in the distance.

"Wait!" Kali shouted after Asteria. The goddess paused and turned around. "Do you know . . . do you know if Diana is all right? The Daughter of Apollo—has she been killed?"

"The Daughter of Apollo is alive," Asteria answered. "Thankfully, Karter, Son of Zeus, could not execute her last night. His failure bought us some time. The Daughter of Apollo's new execution date is in three days' time. You will be happy to hear that the grandchildren-of-Hephaestus are still alive as well. But if we are to save them, you all need your strength, which is why I must find you food and water. We can discuss everything else when I get back." She hurried away, her dress billowing out behind her in the wind.

Kali sighed in relief and let herself fall onto the sand. "We still have time to save our princess."

Darko curled up in the space between her and Andy. "Thank goodness."

A twinge of anxiety made Zoey's pulse quicken. She was happy Asteria brought them to the mainland, and super grateful Diana and Troy and Marina were alive. But that didn't necessarily mean they were okay. What if the gods were hurting them? Torturing them?

What's more, Zoey's stomach sank at the mention of Karter. *If it weren't for him turning on us, we wouldn't have to save anyone in the first place.* She hugged her knees to her chest, burying her face in the fabric of her skirts as she tried to forget about that stupid, scar-faced demigod.

Pretty soon Darko and Kali started snoring. Zoey glanced over, and sure enough, they were deep in slumber, Kali on her stomach and Darko on his side facing Andy.

Zoey smiled and rolled her eyes. If Diana were here, she'd probably do the same. *"Typical,"* she'd say, and Zoey would laugh and agree.

Andy suddenly groaned, which was weird because he hadn't made any noise since he'd passed out. He knit his brow, his eyes moving rapidly behind their lids.

What are you dreaming of? Zoey wondered. She scooted closer to him and brushed his cheek with the back of her hand. Electric tingles danced across her skin, memories of the make-out session they'd shared flooding her mind, and her cheeks went hot. She yanked her hand away from him, shoving the thoughts away.

He cried out in his sleep and rolled to one side, then the other, a distressed expression on his face.

"Andy?" Zoey whispered, poking his shoulder. "Are you okay?"

He continued thrashing around, but he did not wake.

"Andy," Zoey said, louder this time. "Hey, wake up already. You've been asleep long enough. Get up, lazy butt."

He seized Zoey by the arm and opened his eyes. However, he didn't look like himself. Not at all.

Luminosity overtook his eyes—the whites, the irises, the pupils, everything. The organs glowed a haunting, all-consuming silver.

Zoey gasped as borderline-painful electricity crackled through her arm where he held onto her. She tried to pull away from him, but found she couldn't move—she was frozen in place. Electricity hummed through her, up her arm, then along the rest of her limbs and the whole of her body.

What the hell is going on?

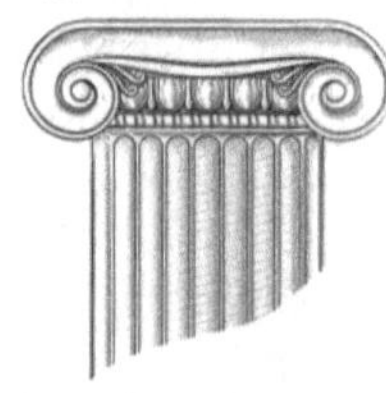

Andy was in the garden once more: the garden he'd seen in his visions in Aphrodite City, when he'd touched the statue of Anteros, and when he'd been dreaming several days ago. This was not only where he'd seen Anteros and Calliope under a gazebo, but also where he'd "met" Asteria, Titan goddess of stars, prophetic dreams, and necromancy.

Cypress trees, marble fountains, golden paths, and bushes of flowers surrounded him on all sides, planets and stars looming over him, hovering so closely it appeared as though he could reach up and pluck them from the night sky. All of it would have been a beautiful sight if he could stop and admire it. But he couldn't stop and admire anything.

Because he had to run for his life.

He didn't know what—or who—was stalking him

through the vegetation, but he knew that if he slowed his sprint for even a second, it would gain on him. And if it caught him, he'd be done for.

Sweat seeped from his pores, his muscles screaming at the effort of maintaining speed. How long had he been running? It felt like forever. Maybe I should try flying? *he wondered. However, when he leapt into the air and focused on flapping his wings, nothing happened.*

As he continued his dash, he reached back and found the space where his wings had once been empty. That's weird. *Remembering that after he'd touched the statue of Anteros and had those weird visions in Aphrodite City his eyesight had improved, he lifted a hand to his face and discovered he was wearing his glasses again.* What's happening?

"Stop!" a man boomed from behind him. Was that Anteros or someone else? *Andy couldn't be sure. "Stop, child! I'm trying to help you! To help us!"*

Must be Anteros, *Andy thought, and despite the god's words, he dared not stop. Something told him that if he did—if he allowed Anteros to "help" him—he would lose himself forever.*

Somewhere up ahead, voices echoed through the air. Achingly familiar ones. Though they were muffled by trees, the sounds of them sent twinges of pain through Andy's chest. His eyes welled with tears.

"Andy!" a little girl called for him in a singsong way. "Andy! Big brother, where are you?" Mel-Mel.

A boy around Andy's age yelled out next, "Dude, get

your ass over here!" Mark.

"I think what Mark meant to say," a woman began, *"is that we're eager to see you, sweetie, because we've missed you dearly."* Mom.

"And because we need to discuss a few things with you," a young man with a deep, gloomy voice said. Spencer? Is that you?

An older man added, *"A few very important things."* When Andy heard the older man's voice—when he realized who it belonged to—his breath hitched. Dad!

Almost forgetting about Anteros chasing him, Andy ripped through the vegetation with new vigor and raced toward the voices. Who cared about some crazy god when his family and best friend and possibly even Spencer were waiting to see him? Losing Dad to cancer, Mom and Mel-Mel and Mark to the Storm, and then Spencer to Persephone's revenge had all been harder than anything else he'd gone through.

He hadn't realized it until he'd heard their voices, but enduring their deaths had proven to be more difficult than battling monsters and immortal deities. More grueling than knowing that the fate of the world rested in his hands.

Soon Andy reached a clearing. The edge of the garden, he thought, though he wasn't sure how he knew that.

A few paces more and he stopped in his tracks, standing at the edge of a jagged cliff. However, rather than overlooking land, it appeared to be towering above space itself. Far below, colorful planets orbited the blazing sun, stars of the galaxy twinkling.

"Stop!" Anteros screamed from somewhere behind him. "Don't jump off the edge! We must complete the convergence before it's too late!"

What did Anteros mean when he said "complete the convergence"? Was he trying to take over Andy's body again? Or was there something else at play here?

Andy shook his head, gazing out over the edge of the cliff. It didn't matter what Anteros meant—Andy knew no good would come from whatever the god wanted.

In truth, Andy was sick of the nonsensical dystopian land the Greek pantheon had created. Since the world's end, he had experienced loss after loss after loss. Couldn't he just have the Master Lightning Bolt in hand, torch Zeus with it, and be done with this war on the gods? At least then he could rest. One day reunite with those he loved.

"Sweetie, jump!" his mom yelled. It sounded as if her voice was coming from far beyond the cliff, somewhere in the radiant galaxy. He could hear her loud and clear, but as he peered through comets and constellations, he couldn't see her anywhere. It was as if she were a disembodied voice rather than his mother in the flesh.

Mark was next to shout, and Andy couldn't see him, either. "She means off the cliff, you idiot. Let's go." Andy glanced between the trees behind him and the galaxy before him, heart in his throat, his palms growing slippery with sweat.

"*Big brother,*" Mel-Mel's voice started, "*you need to come here.*"

Spencer added, "*Yes, you do. Before it's too late.*"

"*Before what's too late?*" Andy questioned them. "*What are all of you talking about?*"

"*Jump, son,*" his dad replied. "*I promise we'll catch you. We won't let you fall too far. Just enough to escape him.*"

The trees behind Andy rustled, and he chanced a glimpse over his shoulder to make sure it wasn't Anteros. Still in the clear, thank God. "*Why can't you come up here?*" Andy asked.

"*We would if we could,*" his dad answered matter-of-factly. "*But we can't. You're just gonna have to trust me on this one, kiddo.*"

Another rustle in the trees behind Andy. He looked back. Spotted Anteros soaring toward him.

The sight of Anteros, the words of Andy's loved ones, and the fear of what was to come—those were enough.

He leapt off the edge of the cliff, and then he was tumbling, tumbling, tumbling down into space.

Up above, Anteros wailed in fury, but Andy didn't look back. After all, why would he? The farther he fell, the more he could see them.

Spencer.

Mark.

Mel-Mel.

Mom.

Dad.

Their misty blue outlines beckoned to him from far below, vague yet unmistakable, their phantom-like arms reaching out as if to catch him.

Andy opened his own arms, ready to embrace them all.

However, he never got the chance.

A sea of silver stars glinted into existence, surrounding him. In the blink of an eye, they swallowed him whole.

CHAPTER EIGHT

DISCUSSION

As Karter trained in the courtyard alongside two of his godly half-siblings and his father, Zeus's statements from earlier this morning echoed in his head. *I know you are trying to forget those you have lost, but I cannot lie to you. You must know, you will never forget them.*

"Focus on the sky's energy as it courses through you," Zeus boomed, his words crashing through Karter's thoughts. Peridot electricity crackled at the king's fingertips, some silver strands of hair sticking to his skin with sweat. "You only have three days to finish learning the art of green lightning. I'd like to see you concentrating harder."

"Apologies." Karter focused on improving his stance and looked up at Zeus. "How did you say I should start, again?" Zeus's eyebrows knit together furiously, and Karter's scar throbbed with the memory of old pain. *That was the wrong thing to ask.*

As quickly as Zeus grew angry, he forced a bright smile. His lips did twitch at the corners, though, as if he was struggling to maintain his happy expression. "Oh, my son, you amuse me so. Here, I will start over once more." He began rattling off a list of things Karter must do to create and control green lightning, but with each passing moment his voice grew more distant. All Karter could think of were his words from earlier this morning . . .

"Although your grief for them will lessen with time, their memories could very well stain your psyche forever. But that does not mean you must give in to weakness. That does not mean you must act as many mortals do and allow your frailties to control you. You can still kill the Daughter of Apollo and achieve your destined greatness; you can still rise up and become like the gods."

And live for the rest of eternity suffering from the loss of Spencer? Syrena? Mother? he wondered. *Never to forget how I had to betray Zoey and kill Diana? Never to move on from any of them, as I once thought I could?*

Something whacked Karter on the side of the head, yanking him back to reality. He glanced over to see that a long, twisting grapevine had hit him, and one of his half-siblings strolled into view: Dionysus, God of Wine, Fertility, and Insanity. "What troubles you, child?" Dionysus asked. He drew the vine back to his side, to where the others spiraled and coiled at his feet, and swiped the fiery red curls out of his green eyes. "In all the times I've helped train you, I have never seen you so distracted."

"I have to agree with Dionysus," Karter's other present half-sibling added, his voice as deep and thunderous as Zeus's. Heracles—God of Strength, Gatekeeper of Olympus, and Protector of Humanity—stepped toward Karter. According to several of the Olympians, when Heracles had been a mortal, he'd been just as hugely tall and muscular as he was now. Karter found it hard to believe that any person could be so large, even if they had the King of the Gods' divine blood running through their veins. "I have trained you many times over the years," Heracles went on, "and you have never struggled quite like this."

Zeus sighed in frustration, allowing his peridot bolt to fizzle out. He turned to Heracles. "Before the rest of the Olympians leave for their mission, I want to make sure they fully understand what I expect from them. I need you to . . ." He glanced between Karter and Dionysus, then offered Heracles an exaggerated wink. "I need you to take care of what we discussed earlier."

"Of course, Father," Heracles replied. Without saying anything else, Zeus hastened toward the archway leading back into the palace.

Once Zeus disappeared, Karter raised a brow at Heracles, his stomach churning. "What did Father mean by all that?"

Heracles offered a stern look. "Now, Karter. You know you're not supposed to pry. Whatever you are meant to know, we'll tell you."

Karter was about to apologize when Dionysus blurted out, "Well, *I'd* like to know what Father meant, thank you very much. I mean, I already know the other Olympians are leaving for their mission to banish Apollo to Tartarus, but—" He clamped his hands over his mouth, as if realizing his mistake and stopping himself before he could say more.

Karter couldn't mask his astonishment. "What? But I thought—I thought Father was going to wait until *after* Diana's execution to banish Apollo? Also, why would they have to leave Olympus to do it? Why not just open a portal to Tartarus and be done with it?"

Heracles shot Dionysus a glare and pinched the bridge of his nose. "And to think, some of the gods believe *I* am an imbecile." Dionysus slapped Heracles's calf with a vine, but Heracles didn't even flinch. He turned toward Karter and said, "I suppose, considering you are to be made a god, it would not hurt to tell you the truth. Besides, Father instructed me to help you conquer a . . . *personal* trial you have yet to overcome, anyway." The hulking god started back for the palace, gesturing for Karter to follow. "Come. We have much to discuss."

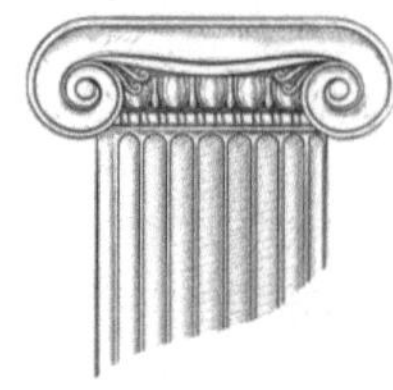

Whole minutes ticked by, and Andy would not release his grip on Zoey, his still-silver eyes unblinking. For as long as he kept his hold on her, she couldn't move, couldn't speak, electricity arcing through her body. *Stay calm*, she thought. *This'll all be over once he wakes up, or once Asteria comes back. Let's just hope there aren't any monsters around to find us . . .*

In her peripheral, she could see Darko and Kali asleep on the sand. She wasn't sure if it was a good or bad thing they hadn't woken up yet.

Andy released a pained groan. His grasp on Zoey tightened. "No," he croaked. "Mom. Dad. Spencer . . ." He mumbled a few other things after that, but she couldn't decipher anything after "Spencer."

Was Andy dreaming about the late Son of Hades? If he was, why was it happening at a time like this, when his eyes were consumed with a silver glow? When touching him sent electricity whizzing through Zoey's body and kept her frozen stiff?

Zoey hadn't been able to see Spencer in Hades through the Helm of Darkness, but that didn't mean his soul wasn't out there, somewhere. Was he visiting Andy, or—

"Forget about that dreadful Son of Hades," Calliope said, interrupting Zoey's train of thought.

Oh, so now you decide to show up, Zoey thought at Calliope. *I could have used your help or our powers back in Circe's palace, just so you know. Thanks for bailing on me.*

"I was weakened after counteracting Circe's enchantments for your companions," Calliope explained. *"I had to rest. There was nothing left in me to give."*

Zoey mulled this over, thinking about how Calliope had shown up after Andy kissed her—

when he'd electrocuted her, really—and then how the goddess had shown up again after Zoey touched him again—and he'd electrocuted her a second time. *I think I understand.*

"*You do?*"

Something magical is happening inside of Andy, Zoey thought. *It started after he came into contact with the statue of Anteros in Aphrodite City. When he touched me after that, there was this weird electric shock. Then, after Circe turned him into a pig and he transformed himself back and kissed me, it happened again, then a third time just now when I brushed his cheek and he grabbed me. I think . . . I think that whenever Anteros, or the magic, or whatever it is gets stronger in Andy, the shift in energy affects me, too, effectively feeding* you.

That must be how my powers started to develop, and why you can talk to me now. When Anteros grows inside Andy, and when Andy touches me, you grow inside of me, too.

"*You truly are clever,*" Calliope remarked. "*I think I agree with your theory. All the more reason for you to believe me when I say we are one and the same. When we finish our convergence, we will be a force to be reckoned with.*"

Zoey swallowed hard, a knot forming in her stomach. *What do you mean when you say "finish our convergence"? What's happening to us, exactly? When did it start, and when will it end?*

Right then, thousands of miniature stars materialized all around Andy, circling his head in a shimmering, spiraling dance. Slowly, the silver glow began to fade from his eyes. He blinked hard, releasing his grip on Zoey's wrist. Finally, she could move again, the electricity dissipating from her body.

Breathing a sigh of relief, she scooted back to give him and the swirling stars space. "Andy? Are you back?"

He coughed a few times, looked at her, and smiled. "Hey."

The stars spinning around him dissolved into the air, and Asteria manifested behind him. Sweat had formed at her brow, her hands trembling. "Anteros, are you quite all right? You almost— almost—"

"Wait a second." He shot into a seated position. He paused, holding his face in his hands for a few seconds, then turned sharply to Asteria. "Are you—are you the one who woke me up?"

Darko and Kali yawned, blinking and sitting up. "What's all the commotion about?" Kali asked.

Zoey scowled at them. "Remind me to never let you guys watch for monsters again," she snapped. "Less than five minutes into guarding Andy and you were both out cold!" They offered her sheepish looks.

Asteria gazed between them, one by one, before focusing solely on Andy. "I am the one who awoke you, Anteros," she said. "I also transported you and your companions from Circe's island to the mainland. You hadn't awoken since opening the portal to Hades, and although I was out looking for food and water for you and your companions, I made sure to keep a close eye on your mind. I am a goddess of prophetic dreams, you see, and when I saw what you dreamt of mere moments ago, I grew quite worried."

"You know about the portal to Hades?" Andy blurted.

"Why were you worried about Andy?" Zoey asked at the same time.

Andy faced Zoey, his irises flashing between gray and silver. His mouth drew down into a frown. "About that, yeah. It was really, really weird. I was running from Anteros. He—he wanted something with me. I'm not sure what, but I knew it wasn't good, that if he caught me, something— something terrible would happen. And then I started hearing voices—my parents, my baby sister, my best friend, Spencer . . ."

"Spencer?" Zoey asked, breath catching in her throat.

"I thought I told you to forget about the Son of Hades," Calliope piped up in her head. Zoey resisted the

urge to roll her eyes, trying to stay focused on what Andy was saying.

"Yes," Andy replied, his frown deepening. "Everyone I care about who—who's dead. They were calling out for me. They said they had something important to tell me, and—"

"I suspect they do not have your best interests at heart," Asteria interrupted. "What's more, I do not believe the voices you heard even belong to your loved ones lost. No, they surely belong to dream and nightmare gods, and those deities intend to keep you from realizing your destined greatness. From saving the world."

Andy gave Asteria an incredulous look. "Wait, what? I never said my family and friends were actually there. I thought . . . Well, I don't know. Once I woke up, I thought it was all just a dream."

Before Asteria could respond, Zoey spoke up. "Besides, how would those gods have access to Andy when the Fates cast a spell on us to keep us hidden from any deities we don't expressly reveal ourselves to?"

Asteria pursed her lips, thinking about Zoey's response.

The goddess eventually opened her mouth to speak, but Andy beat her to it. "Uhh, guys?" he started, glancing at the beach around them.

"Where are we? I mean, I know we're on the mainland, but, like, *where* on the mainland?"

"We are south of New Mount Olympus," Asteria said. "Half a day's walk north would place us beneath the boulder holding Zeus's palace."

"Um, it would've been nice if you'd have mentioned how close we are to Olympus earlier," Zoey remarked. "That's absolutely terrifying to think about."

Someone's stomach growled. "You didn't happen to find any food and water while you were gone, did you?" Kali asked Asteria.

The goddess clapped her hands, and a few canteens and drawstring sacks appeared from thin air, falling to the sand before the group. "Help yourselves," she said. "Then we talk. And walk, I suppose, considering we must find Prometheus and the nymphs as soon as possible."

Everyone dug in, yanking open the sacks of food and gulping down the water in the canteens. Until Zoey took her first bite, she hadn't realized just how thirsty and hungry she'd been. Her body ached for nourishment, and she didn't hesitate to satiate it.

After Zoey drank so much water and ate so many roots and berries that her stomach felt stuffed, she asked, "Why did you say we were going to be walking after this? Earlier, I mean. Wouldn't it be faster if we just flew wherever we needed to go? Like how you flew us over the remainder of the Atlantic?"

"We can fly at nightfall," Asteria responded. "I am strongest at night, when most are sleeping and the stars are bright in the sky. Flying the four of you for such a great distance drained me, as did keeping an eye on Anteros's mind, even despite your delicious sacrifice. I must take the day to rejuvenate. Still, we can start toward Prometheus and the nymphs before then if we go on foot. After we join forces with them, we'll travel to Olympus to rescue the Daughter of Apollo and the grandchildren-of-Hephaestus—and then, all together, steal the Master Lightning Bolt."

Andy stopped chewing, his mouth full of berries. His eyes went wide, his jaw dropping. "Wait, *what?*"

"You want us to steal the Master Lightning Bolt while we're also trying to save Diana and the twins?" Zoey cried, blinking hard. Asteria raised a brow and nodded slowly. "How in the world do you expect us to pull that off?"

"No offense, lady," Kali started. "But we had enough trouble stealing Poseidon's Trident, and we didn't have captives to rescue then."

Darko nodded. "We also weren't up against a lot of members of the pantheon and all the demigod warriors, and on New Mount Olympus we will be. It'll be hard enough to save Diana and the twins—there's no way we can manage to steal the Master Lightning Bolt while we're there, too. We'll be lucky to escape with our lives, let alone the gods' most powerful magical object."

Asteria's lips curled up in a devious smile. "Not true. When you were in Poseidon's palace, you did not have an army of Dryads and Naiads and two Titan gods to aid you on your quest. But when you are on New Mount Olympus, you will have the nymphs and Prometheus and me. I chose not to meddle in your affairs before, as there was a chance of unfairly swaying your destinies. However, the war on the gods is about to begin, and when it does, all of our fates will hang in the balance. It is now that mortals and deities alike must choose a side to fight on. I picked whom I would battle for long ago, as did Prometheus, even if he did not realize it until recently."

Zoey's head spun. Sure, with help from Asteria, Prometheus, and the nymphs, she and her friends had a better chance of succeeding, but Darko's point still stood. Not to mention a bunch of demigod warriors lived there. Zoey had no idea how many demigods there were, but even if there were only a few, and even if those few were half as powerful as Spencer, Diana, or Karter, they'd still be hard to fight.

Before Zoey could express her concerns, noises came from the tree line. Voices. Asteria swung around, hands raised and ready to fight. "Who goes there?"

In response, an arrow soared through the air above her head and splashed into the ocean.

Zoey's breath caught in her throat. *Someone's found us.*

Asteria pivoted toward Zoey and Andy, an expression of pure desperation on her face. "Zeus sent Artemis and her Huntresses after you, and they must have tracked us here. Grab the objects of power and flee. I will hold her off for as long as I can. Now go, run for your lives!"

CHAPTER NINE

IMAGINE

Heracles led Karter through an empty hall in Zeus's palace, sunlight glaring in at them through the arched windows lining the walls. "And so you see," the god went on, "initially, Father's plan was to wait until after you executed Diana to banish Apollo—he was under the assumption that you would kill her last night. But since you didn't, and since the Chosen Two evaded your capture, Father decided he'd go ahead with banishing Apollo today anyway. The logic behind that decision was only reinforced when he considered that the Chosen Two have stolen Poseidon's

Trident, on top of already having the Helm of Darkness.

"Father is sending Poseidon, Demeter, Athena, Ares, Hephaestus, and Hermes on a mission to the Underworld. They have six days to banish Apollo to Tartarus. At the same time, Artemis and her Huntresses are tracking the Chosen Two, while Father, Hera, Aphrodite, and Hestia will watch over Olympus and the primary cities."

Karter nodded, though he was still shocked that Zoey and Andy had managed to storm Poseidon's palace, steal the sea god's Trident, and live to tell the tale. Not to mention they'd done all of it without his, Diana's, or Spencer's help, as they'd had when they'd invaded Hades. Karter knew they were strong and determined, but to battle Poseidon and Triton themselves? To manipulate the Trojan Cetus into devouring its own master? They were truly more than they appeared.

Then again, Karter thought, *that should come as no surprise. Spencer believed in them enough to betray the gods and help them on their quest, and Syrena believed in the idea of them enough to sacrifice herself so they could be brought back to life.* "I understand," he finally said to Heracles. "If Apollo somehow escaped and joined forces with the Chosen Two, they would become even more formidable."

"Exactly." Heracles paused in front of a

window revealing another one of the training grounds on New Mount Olympus. Outside, his daughter Iro sparred with her teammates. "Even so, I don't believe there's anything to worry about. Apollo will be in Tartarus before the six days are up. Not only that, but in a couple of days' time, you will kill the Daughter of Apollo and end this war on the gods, just as Father saw in his visions. That is the destiny foretold for you, and so shall it be."

At the mention of Diana's execution, Karter gulped. Eager to change the subject, he said, "All of that makes sense. I still have one question, though."

"What is it?"

"I . . . thought the gods simply opened a portal to Tartarus whenever they needed to banish someone there. I suppose what I'm wondering is, why are they *traveling* to the Underworld to exile Apollo? Wouldn't it be easier to open a gateway to Tartarus itself and send him there that way?"

Heracles let out a long sigh, and Karter looked up at him. As Karter studied the god's profile, he realized that he could have closely resembled Heracles if he'd grown up to be taller and broader, and if he had never been struck in the face with one of Zeus's gold lightning bolts. When he'd been younger, many had even asserted that he resembled Heracles, that one day he would appear exactly as the older demigod did. He guessed it was because the two of them had similar facial structures and the same shade and texture of hair. Before Karter's irises had changed from his punishment, they'd even been the same color brown as Heracles's.

The God of Strength turned, his dark eyes boring into Karter. "I can't tell you why the gods must travel to the Underworld rather than simply create a portal to Tartarus. Father strictly forbade me from explaining it to you, and I refuse to disrespect his wishes. Not only that, but *you will not* breathe a word of the information I've shared with you to *anyone*. I don't want rumors started. We don't need any of the demigods or minor deities panicking about nothing. Do you understand?"

A bead of sweat trickled down Karter's temple. "Yes, yes, of course. I won't say anything. Not to anyone."

"Good." Heracles headed toward a forked hallway and took the left passage. "Now come. We need to go someplace private for this next part, considering what we might have to discuss. Follow me." Karter had no idea what they "might have to discuss" that needed privacy, but he did as Heracles requested.

Soon they reached Heracles and his wife, Hebe's, bedchambers, images of the Stymphalian

Birds, Lernaean Hydra, Nemean Lion, and other monsters Heracles conquered in his mortal life carved into the wood of the door. Heracles threw it open, and they stepped inside.

It didn't surprise Karter that the chambers were large and lavish. The polished white-and-gold columns, walls, and ceiling gleamed in the light, the marble furniture and deep-purple cushions and blankets in pristine condition. There was even a staircase leading down into a bubbling pool of water at one end of the room, a balcony on the other, similar to the setup in Zeus and Hera's bedchambers.

Not only did Heracles have this position on Olympus, but he also had his own city on the other side of the ocean, located somewhere on the continent called Europe. For as long as Karter remembered, the god had visited his city and Olympus in intervals, since Zeus didn't have need for a true gatekeeper often.

Still, rooms on Olympus and a city full of worshippers? Heracles truly led a charmed existence. *He hasn't always had it easy, though*, Karter thought, recalling the events of his half-brother's mortal life. How Hera had tormented him so.

"Onto the balcony, little brother," Heracles said, walking in that direction. "It's time for the real training to begin."

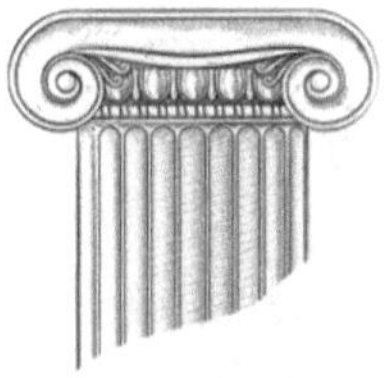

Andy didn't waste any time. Didn't question whether someone had really tracked their location and was chasing after them. When Asteria said to grab their things and run for their lives, he leapt to his feet and seized Poseidon's Trident. At the same time, Zoey snatched the Helm of Darkness out of their pack and tossed it to Kali.

"Put it on!" Zoey shouted. "Hold hands with Andy and Darko. I'll touch one of them so we'll all be invisible!"

Kali didn't hesitate to follow Zoey's instructions. One moment she was there, the next she wasn't. Then she was grabbing Andy's free hand, and Darko's too. They disappeared along with her. Darko must have taken Zoey's remaining hand in his because she turned invisible next.

Together, the four of them barreled across the beach in the shallowest of shallows, where the coming waves would hopefully wash away their footprints, but the gritty sand and frigid water made it difficult to travel as quickly as usual. Behind them, Asteria shouted, "If you want the Chosen Two, you'll have to destroy me first, Moon

Goddess." A female voice replied, but the words were muffled. Andy couldn't make out what was said.

Asteria yelled something else, and Andy picked up his pace, still holding tight to Kali. "C'mon, guys," he said, heart racing. "We gotta go faster!"

Out of the corner of his eye, he caught sight of someone stepping out from the tree line. A colossal, muscular someone. Was that Artemis, as Asteria had initially suspected? Or some other Huntress?

He glanced over to get a better look. The figure looked classically masculine, with dark-olive skin and curly black hair. Could that be . . .?

"Anteros, Calliope, *stop*! I was mistaken!" Asteria cried from behind them. The group stumbled to a halt and turned around, still not letting go of one another. Three young women stood next to Asteria, though Andy couldn't make out many of their discernable features from here. "I apologize for frightening you so," the goddess continued. "But Artemis and her Huntresses did not find us. It's the nymphs and—"

"Prometheus!" Zoey shrieked with glee. She reappeared, hurtling up the beach toward the massive figure. Kali let go of Andy, and she and Darko became visible as she released the satyr and took off the Helm. She slipped the object under her arm and ran after Zoey.

Andy peered toward the tree line, Darko at his side, and sure enough, he spotted the Titan. Prometheus jogged toward Zoey and Kali, his wrists and ankles still bound with what was left of the chains forged by Hephaestus, his torn white robes covered in grime and dried blood.

Relief flooded Andy. *It was a false alarm*. He and Darko shared grins. He hopped into the air and soared toward Prometheus, and Darko galloped behind him.

"I see you're finally putting those wings to good use, Bird-Boy," Prometheus said with a laugh as he scooped up Zoey and Kali, one with each burly arm, and hugged them to his chest. Andy landed beside them, and Prometheus set Zoey and Kali down. The Titan eyed Poseidon's Trident in Andy's hand. "Nice pitchfork," he said.

Andy dropped the Trident right as Darko reached Prometheus as well, and then Prometheus picked up Andy and Darko just as he had Zoey and Kali and hugged them so tightly Andy thought his eyes might pop out of his head. "You did it," the Titan said, swaying side to side. "You got the Trident and made it back to the mainland. Ol' Zeus is in for the surprise of his eternal life!"

He set them down, and Andy and Darko coughed, hitting their chests a few times. "Yeah, he probably is," Andy remarked.

The neighs of horses sounded from deeper within the trees, and Kali gasped. "Is that—"

"Ajax, Aladdin, and Luna?" Prometheus finished for her. "As a matter of fact, it is."

Sure enough, two pegasi with chestnut-colored coats, dark manes and feathered wings, and amber eyes trotted out from the trees toward the group, followed by another pegasus with a black coat and mane and striking green eyes. The three nickered at the sight of the group, and Andy could have sworn they were smiling.

Zoey and Kali squealed, scampering toward the pegasi, and together the girls threw their arms around each of the creatures' necks, one by one. Andy and Darko shared more smiles, stepping up after them to do the same.

After everyone finished reuniting with the pegasi, Kali hugged them a second time. They nuzzled her neck and hands and licked her cheeks. "I can't believe it," she said, her eyes growing watery. "I was so scared I'd never see you three again."

"And *we* were scared we'd never find the Chosen Two in these unending woods," a sweet-sounding feminine voice said from the right. "Just yesterday, we began searching the beaches." Andy turned to find three short, familiar nymphs wearing wildflowers for jewelry and flowing forest-green dresses, bows in each of their hands, quivers of arrows slung over their backs. *They must have been the ones shooting at us*, Andy realized as Asteria strolled up next to the Dryads.

Zoey bounced with excitement. "Eugenia, Narcissa, Harmony! You made it!"

Eugenia smiled, which made her adorably plump cheeks even chubbier. "Of course we did. After all, we intend to assist you in saving the Daughter of Apollo."

"And in leading a war on the gods," Narcissa added matter-of-factly, her thin eyes narrowing as her gaze rested on Andy's wings. He tried to curl them in on himself, uncomfortable under her scrutinizing stare.

Harmony hopped to Darko's side, grabbed his hands, and spun him around with her. "But best of all, there are a ton more nymphs back at our camp," she said, her coiled locks bobbing as she jumped and twirled. "All of them want to help!"

Darko's cheeks flushed, and Kali shot him a knowing smirk. "I'm just glad you guys managed to find Prometheus and my pegasi for us," she said.

"Don't give them all the credit," Prometheus snapped. He crossed his arms, his chains clanking. "After I regenerated and followed the thread out of the Labyrinth, I traveled toward Olympus for a few days and stumbled on the pegasi all by myself."

Asteria gave Prometheus the side-eye. "The details of our assembly aren't significant. What matters is that we're all together now." Prometheus stuck his tongue out at her. Rather than responding to the gesture, she turned to Andy and Zoey. "The Dryads explained that they caught sight of my hair—which is similar in color to Artemis's—and, assuming I was the Moon Goddess, shot at me from afar. However, we must stay vigilant, as Artemis still intends on capturing you two. She and her Huntresses could be lurking at any corner."

For some reason, talking about Artemis sent shivers down Andy's spine. An image of a fierce, beautiful young woman with frizzy red ringlets framing her pale face flashed at the back of his mind. "Artemis . . ." he started, silver light suddenly obscuring his vision. He closed his eyes, willing the glow to go away. He had no idea where it was coming from, and it was giving him a headache. Despite his best efforts, it didn't subside. Worst of all, a booming voice much unlike his own escaped his lips. "Yes, I know Artemis, Goddess of the Moon, the Hunt, and Chastity. She is Daughter of Zeus and Leto. She is also Apollo's twin sister, and a powerful Olympian."

As the words finished spilling from Andy's mouth, the silver light overtaking his vision vanished. His headache subsided, and he raised his head to look at his companions. All but Asteria wore shocked expressions. Harmony stopped dancing with Darko, and even the pegasi seemed surprised.

"Does that . . . happen often?" Harmony asked.

Darko gently pulled his hands from hers and made his way toward Andy. "Not until recently," he said. "Andy, what's going on with you?"

Before Andy could explain how he suspected it had something to do with Anteros swirling about in his head, Asteria spoke up. "It is part of the convergence," she said. "You see, now that it's begun, Anteros and Calliope will soon transform into their most powerful selves—the truth revealed." She turned to Andy and Zoey. "Facing the truth will prove to be your greatest challenge yet. You cannot fight it, Chosen Two. You cannot question it. If you do, you will be at war with yourselves, with each other, and you will not defeat the gods."

Trying to understand what Asteria meant by all this brought Andy's headache back. "Uhhh, what?"

"'Uhhh, what' is right," Zoey said, facing Asteria. She sounded fearful, a slight tremor in her voice. "What do you mean, we'll 'transform' into our 'most powerful selves,' and that it will be the 'truth revealed'? Also, you do realize we're not Calliope and Anteros, right? We're Zoey and Andy. Sure, those two might be parts of us, but this convergence thing just sounds silly, and quite frankly I'm starting to think it's all bullsh—"

"Whoa, whoa, whoa," Prometheus interjected, throwing his still-shackled arms in the air. "Hold your pegasi, kiddo." He turned to Asteria. "What is all this nonsense about Anteros and Calliope and a convergence, now?" Asteria sighed tiredly.

Andy patted Prometheus's arm. "We still aren't one hundred percent sure what the convergence stuff is all about, but we'll catch you up on what we know."

"You'll have to explain yourselves while we travel back to camp," Narcissa said bluntly. "We must leave and gather with our recruits so we can find another spot to stay tonight."

Eugenia threw her long auburn braid over her shoulder. "Yes, the longer we remain in one place, the better chance Artemis and her Huntresses have at finding us. We must avoid them at all costs."

"That's very true," Harmony added, and for the first time since Andy had met the young-looking Dryad, her bubbly voice had grown solemn. "Even if we defeated them in a fight, they'd surely take the lives of hundreds of our friends, and we need all the help we can get when it's time to invade

New Mount Olympus."

"How many nymphs did you guys manage to draft for this, exactly?" Kali asked.

"Last time I took a head count," Eugenia said, "our number of recruits was 3,396, including us." She gestured at Narcissa, Harmony, and herself.

Andy's jaw dropped. "You guys have gotta be joking. There's no way."

"I specifically remember telling you we could gather thousands of nymphs to help you save Diana and stage future attacks against the gods," Narcissa snapped. "Do not act so surprised."

Harmony playfully tapped Narcissa on the shoulder. "Narcissa, be nice. He's going to free the world from Zeus, you know." Narcissa crossed her arms, and Harmony offered Andy an apologetic smile. "Don't mind her. She gets like this when she's hungry."

"Let us leave at once," Asteria said, glancing over her shoulder as if she was worried someone was behind them.

Eugenia smiled, turned toward the tree line, and started hiking in that direction. "Everyone, follow me."

Sweat seeped from Karter's pores, the scent of incinerated flesh assaulting his nostrils. As the minutes ticked by at an agonizingly slow pace, a familiar burning sensation began to spread through his chest like a plague. *Heracles is working me to the bone*, he thought. *I might not live to the day of Diana's execution if he keeps this up.*

"Go on," Heracles said. He stood down below on his bedchamber balcony, his arms extended toward Karter, toward the early-evening sky, the skin that stretched over his hulking muscles black with lightning scorch marks. "Your warm-up is over. Harness the power of the sky and strike me down with a green bolt now. You've thrown enough red and gold ones at me. I want to see green."

Intending to follow Heracles's orders, Karter soared even higher. *I need to allow the energy of the sky to flow through me, as Father suggested.* He looked up, narrowing his eyes at the fluffy clouds above him, so close he felt he could reach out and pull them apart.

When he decided he'd flown high enough, he stopped to steady his labored breathing and concentrated on the sky—his source of power, as Zeus had called it. He focused on the sky's energy, inviting it to course through him, to revitalize him. Hot energy throbbed in his chest and spread to his limbs. *Now centralize that power into a green bolt*, he thought.

Karter suddenly felt as if thousands of needles were pricking his skin, just like last night when he'd first conjured peridot lightning. Heart skipping a beat, he opened his eyes. Green electricity vibrated in his palms, up his arms.

Down below, Heracles yipped and whooped, punching the air with his fists. "Now, pretend I'm the Daughter of Apollo and beat me down," he yelled. "Just like we practiced with the red and gold lightning bolts. Only this time, the strike will be lethal. Well, temporarily, of course."

Karter sucked in a deep breath, focusing on maintaining his peridot electricity as he looked down at Heracles. At first, imagining the god as Diana had been difficult. In appearance alone, Heracles was almost the opposite of her. It had taken Karter several attempts before he'd succeeded, but it had grown easier with each try. And, thankfully, now it seemed as though he'd mastered the skill. He floated down toward the god, peridot electricity humming in his hands.

When Karter landed on the balcony, he stared at Heracles, but all he could see was Diana, just as she had looked last night. Soaked from head to toe, blonde hair plastered against her scalp, her freckled skin the whitest he'd ever seen it. She held her head high, and once more Karter was reminded of Syrena on the night of the Daughter of Poseidon's execution.

Karter's green bolt fizzled out.

Frustration brewing in his chest, exhaustion overtaking his body, Karter released a scream of indignation, falling to his knees. *I've failed again. Can't I get anything right?*

"What was *that?*" Heracles asked. He didn't sound angry, didn't even sound irritated. Just confused.

Karter put his face in his hands. "I can't do it. I can't kill Diana."

"Why not?"

"Because of Syrena. Because of Spencer. Their deaths were my fault, and she was their friend. When I imagine killing her, I feel like I'm killing them all over again." He sucked in a shaky breath. "I don't know if I can end the war and become a god. Not if I have to do it this way."

Heracles didn't speak for a long while, and Karter braced himself for the moment when the god would leave to tell Zeus what Karter had said. After that, Zeus would inevitably come here and kill Karter for his weakness.

However, none of that happened.

Instead, Heracles spoke to Karter, his tone soft and caring. "I thought this might happen, which is why I brought you here. To tell you the truth, I understand your guilt."

"You do?" Karter asked, slowly looking up at his brother.

"I do. I murdered Megara and our children, you know. I loved them more than anything, yet I'm the reason their lives were cut short."

Karter nodded; the demigods learned about this in their history lessons. When Heracles had still been a mortal in the old days, Hera sent him into a temporary fit of madness. In his crazed state, he murdered his first wife and their children. When the madness passed, and when he realized what he had done, he made it his life's mission to atone for their deaths and became a servant of King Eurystheus, who assigned him the Twelve Labors.

"I can only imagine how difficult this is for you," Heracles went on. "If I were forced to execute someone and doing so reminded me of my sins, it would be grueling. However, that doesn't mean I couldn't do it. And it doesn't mean you can't, either."

Karter leapt to his feet and began pacing. "How do you expect me to pull it off, exactly?" he cried. "I couldn't do it last night. Couldn't even do it during training. It's hopeless. I—I'm hopeless."

"You're far from hopeless," Heracles replied with a chuckle, and Karter had to hold himself back from punching the god. Did he think this was amusing?

Instead of resorting to violence, Karter asked, "Why do you say that?"

"Because you're not alone. You have my help." Heracles walked to Karter and rested a hand on the demigod's shoulder. "Father told me of your struggles, and he knows I understand them better than anyone. After all, I have to put up with the goddess who tried to kill me while I was a mortal, and who sent me into a fit of madness that caused me to murder my family. Not only that, but she's Queen of the Gods and the mother of my wife, so I have to treat her with respect. Respect, of all things!" He winked. Laughed, even.

Karter shifted uncomfortably. He had no idea how Heracles could treat a situation like this with such levity. "How is it you intend to help me?"

"Let me ask you something. Do you ever grow angry?"

Those words struck Karter. Did he ever grow angry? What kind of a question was that? Had Heracles not seen his reaction to losing the green lightning only a few moments ago? "Of course," he answered, trying to maintain a respectful tone. "Doesn't everyone?"

Heracles smirked down at him. It wasn't an amused expression, nor was it a knowing one. It looked malicious, almost. A twinge of fear passed through him. "What is it that makes you angry? Your mother's death? How about the Daughter of Poseidon's? The Son of Hades's?"

A lump formed in Karter's throat. What was this? Was Heracles mocking him?

"And whose fault is it that all of them are gone?" Heracles added.

Karter's chest grew tight. Hot tears welled in his eyes, but he held them back. He couldn't do this. Not here. "It's—it's my fault. If I had just reached Spencer sooner. If I had just protected Syrena. If I had just . . . never been born."

"You're sure it's your fault?"

Of course I am! he wanted to scream in Heracles's face, but refrained. *Be respectful*, he thought. *Think about the question. He says he's here to help. So, there must be a reason he's asking this.* Karter contemplated the inquiry, picking through his memories carefully. Was there anyone else who could share the blame for their demises?

"Let me ask you this," Heracles said. "You already know that I blame myself for my first family's murders. But who is it that tampered with my mind that day? Who is it that sent me into a temporary madness, causing me to kill them?"

"I suppose it was Hera who did so," Karter stated, a bitter taste on his tongue as he said his stepmother's name.

Heracles threw his head back, holding his stomach as he burst into a fit of laughter. "Yes, precisely! It was Hera who toyed with my sanity. Although I'm technically the one who murdered my wife and children, could you say that Hera forced my hand? Could you say that the Olympians forced my hand, since they didn't stop Hera from influencing me? And, if so, could you say that, in a way, the gods also influenced how your life and losses have unfolded?"

"Yes, I suppose you could look at my situation that way," Karter said. "But it still doesn't change things. If I—if I had never been born, my mother, Spencer, and Syrena . . . they would still be here. Hera killed my mother because of me. I couldn't stop Spencer and Syrena from betraying the gods, nor could I stop the gods from destroying Spencer and Syrena. In the end, I'm still responsible for it all."

"You're only partially responsible for some of those things. You said it yourself: Hera killed your mother. She did so when you were a small child. How could you be at fault for that? Yes, perhaps there was more you could have done for your friends. Kept a closer eye on them, maybe, or talked them through their struggles more often. But wasn't it Father who struck the Daughter of

Poseidon with a green lightning bolt? Wasn't it Persephone who stabbed the Son of Hades in the gut?"

Karter mulled over Heracles's words before responding. "What do you hope to accomplish by telling me this?"

"I hope to make you angry." The words spilled rapidly from Heracles's lips, as if the god had been waiting to say this all day. "Furious, even. For too long you've wasted your potential. Moping about. Feeling sorry for yourself. It's time you channel your feelings into something worthwhile."

"How?"

Heracles began to circle him. "Embrace your feelings. Embrace the losses you've endured. They make you who you are. They prepared you to become a god among the rest." He paused, stroking his chin. "The world is not so simple, Karter. Not so black and white. You can allow yourself to be angry at Hera, at Persephone, and even at our father for killing those you love most. At the same time, you don't have to betray the gods. In fact, you can disagree with their choices and *still join them.*"

Karter clenched his jaw. "All my life, I've been told to respect the gods no matter what. To never challenge them aloud. In the few instances I've disobeyed, I've been punished for it. Why would this time be any different?"

"Because this time, as much as they might not care to admit it, you're no longer just a pawn in their game," Heracles said. "Father saw one vision in which the war on the gods ends quickly and easily, and it involved you executing Diana with a green lightning bolt. In a way, you determine what happens next. You decide whether this war on the gods ends or continues."

"Are you saying I have a choice?" Karter asked, his heart skipping as he asked the question. "That I don't have to kill Diana?"

"Of course you have a choice. That's what destiny is, anyway. The result of a series of decisions we make throughout our lives, along the journey from when our life threads—our threads of fate—are first spun, all the way to when they're finally cut." He playfully elbowed Karter in the side. "Although, in our cases, our threads of fate never are cut."

In response, Karter only chuckled nervously. When he'd first found out he was to be made an immortal god, he hadn't believed he had a choice in any of this. Zeus said he was meant to kill Diana, and so he'd accepted the destiny at face value. But after the events of last night, after learning everything he had today about how he would never forget his loved ones lost . . .

Heracles clapped him on the back just as Zeus had this morning, in an almost affectionate manner. "Now that you understand it's all right to be upset with the gods for what they've let happen to you," Heracles began, "I have a new proposition for you. Hopefully, it will help you succeed at the execution."

"What is it?"

"Rather than imagining me as the Daughter of Apollo, imagine me as Hera. As Persephone. As Father. Imagine you are saving your mother, the Son of Hades, the Daughter of Poseidon, from all of them. Use your feelings—your sadness, your anger—and shoot me with a green bolt."

Karter looked away from his half-brother. "You think that will work? You think it will help me achieve my . . . my destined greatness?"

"I do."

Heart in his throat, Karter shot into the air again, toward the clouds. When he determined he'd flown high enough, he stopped and focused on the sky, his source of power. He concentrated, concentrated on allowing the sky's energy to flow through him, to rejuvenate him. Hot energy pulsed in his chest, through his limbs.

He centralized the power, and once again he felt as though hundreds of needles were pricking his skin, peridot electricity arcing in his palms, along his arms.

Far below, Heracles cheered him on, and Karter focused on what he must do next. *Imagine he's Hera, sending Ladon to kill Mother*, he thought. *Imagine he's Persephone, stabbing Spencer in the gut.*

Imagine he's Zeus, striking Syrena with a green lightning bolt.

Pain and rage coursed through Karter's veins. A few tears trickled down his cheeks, but he couldn't allow his emotions to overcome him this time. After condensing his peridot electricity into a solid bolt, he reared back and launched the attack at Heracles.

In the end, his aim proved true.

When the lightning struck Heracles, the god screamed and convulsed.

Soon the bolt disintegrated. As the life faded from Heracles's eyes, he fell onto his back, his chest a cavity of ash. The smells of smoke and burnt flesh filled the air, and Karter thought, *I've done it. I've really, finally done it.*

CHAPTER TEN
TOAST

Several hours passed before Andy and his companions finally made it to the Dryads' camp, the afternoon sun shining high in the sky, hot rays of light piercing through the thick trees of the forest. There had to be thousands of nymphs, just as Eugenia and Narcissa had insisted there would be, all as pretty as the other nymphs Andy had seen thus far. Thankfully, they'd packed up camp (which, to Andy's surprise, consisted mostly of armor and weaponry) and were already prepared for travel to avoid Artemis. They'd just been waiting on Eugenia, Narcissa, Harmony, Prometheus, and the pegasi to return before leaving.

The nymph recruits were overjoyed to see that their Dryad leaders had stumbled upon Andy and Zoey and co in their search, cheering and clapping with enthusiasm once they found out who the newcomers were. Narcissa insisted that Andy and Zoey were not to be pestered by anyone, as they were "very important," and that they needed to "focus on the task at hand, not on any of you." Harmony, on the other hand, argued that it was all right if Andy and Zoey wanted to "make friends" and "get to know" the nymphs they'd be leading into battle.

In the end, Eugenia put a stop to the debate and asked the nymphs to simply keep to themselves for the time being, then told everyone to have a quick drink and snack before they left to find another camping spot. "Once we settle down somewhere," she said, "we'll begin formulating a plan to infiltrate Olympus." Eugenia's gentle orders sobered the nymphs up. They did as she said without protest, and then everyone was off, hiking through the trees once again. Just in case Artemis and her Huntresses attacked, Eugenia placed Andy, Zoey, Darko, Kali, and the pegasi in the center of the nymph army, keeping them protected on all sides.

The trip was a bit awkward because Andy didn't know any of the Dryads and Naiads surrounding him and his companions, and he wasn't in the mood to make new friends just yet. Also because he had some questions for Asteria regarding what she thought was going on with him and Anteros and Zoey and Calliope (since she hadn't really talked on their initial hike to the nymphs' first camp). However, Asteria pulled Prometheus to the back of the horde so they could discuss a few things, which meant chatting with the Titan gods was off the table for now. Andy suspected this also disturbed Zoey, as she barely spoke during the whole journey, a strained, far-off expression on her face.

By the end of the day, when the sun began to set, the nymphs decided to stop and make camp.

"Is there anything we can help with?" Andy asked.

"No, not really," a Naiad dripping with water replied.

Within minutes Andy saw why the nymphs didn't need his and his friends' help setting up camp. Rather than pitching tents and the like, the Dryads used their powers to erect thirty-foot-tall walls of logs and greenery—presumably to keep out monsters, but maybe they were for some other sort of protection, too. All the while, the Naiads went off to gather and wash provisions for dinner.

Kali let out a low whistle. "Wow."

"That's no kidding," Andy said, watching the construction in awe.

As the nymphs kept working around the group, Eugenia, Narcissa, and Harmony approached them. "Come," Eugenia said, gesturing at them to follow. "Let us determine our plan to storm Olympus."

The group followed the Dryads through the trees, and after about ten minutes they reached a sort of cabin. It looked like the walls surrounding camp, and Andy knew right away that the nymphs had made it for him and his friends to sleep in tonight, as he remembered the nymphs saying nature was their true home and they didn't need houses. Eugenia opened the big entryway doors, and the distinctive smell of lush green grass filled Andy's nostrils.

Similar to the dwellings the nymphs constructed for satyrs back west, the cabin looked like someplace a fairy would live. Sunlight spilled in through the windows, vines and wildflowers poking out and twisting up and around the log walls and ceilings.

Prometheus and Asteria stood in a corner, hunched over and whispering to one another. When the group stepped into the cabin alongside the nymphs, the gods turned, going quiet.

Prometheus and Andy made eye contact briefly. Andy thought he saw a hint of sadness in the Titan's gaze, but if he did, it was there and gone in an instant. Prometheus looked away.

Eugenia shut the doors and gestured at the soft grass floor. "Please, everyone, sit. Rest your tired feet."

They did as she said. Prometheus clasped his hands in his lap, keeping his head down. "If we're going to break into Olympus, we need a solid plan."

Asteria nodded. "I think the best course of action would be to sneak in with the aristocrats the gods invite to Diana's execution." She gestured at Andy and his friends. "You all will need disguises, of course, and several baths. You don't exactly blend in as you are now." She faced the nymphs next. "Dryads are generally present at these events as well, but they are the ones who already live on Olympus, so you must conceal your true natures until the battle begins."

"I can disguise everyone," Prometheus said. "That way no one has to go into one of the cities and find clothes for this. We can just start straight away for Olympus."

"No, you cannot disguise everyone," Asteria replied. "Those chains weaken your power. You must limit using it prematurely as much as possible. Disguise everyone's magical nature, not their physical appearances as well, for you will need all your strength at the battle of the amphitheater."

Andy shivered. "What about you?" he asked Asteria. "Can't you and Prometheus share the burden of hiding all of us?"

"Technically, we could," Asteria answered. "But visions of the future have shown me I will be arriving late to the execution. I am afraid you will be sneaking in without me."

"If 'visions of the future' show you you'll be arriving late," Zoey started, "then can't you just, like, change the course of events leading up to the execution—change the choices you make until it happens—so we don't have to sneak into Olympus without you?"

Asteria shrugged. "I can try. Even so, that does not mean fate will favor us. It is best if everyone who needs clothes goes into a city to get them— just in case."

"What did you mean when you said that fate might not favor us?" Kali asked.

"There are many possible outcomes to every situation. Our choices do affect our individual destinies, and the people and events around us, but sometimes the universe allows certain things to happen in order for others to take place."

"Ohhhh-kay," Andy replied, his head spinning from all she'd just said. Almost nothing made sense these days. "So, is that it? Is that our plan? We sneak into Olympus with the aristocrats invited to the execution? Oh, and we maybe do it in fancy clothes, I guess. How do people even get there, anyway? I thought they weren't allowed to leave the cities."

"If they're invited to an event on Olympus, they can leave," Darko said. "I think their invitations are enchanted by the gods to keep monsters away, or something like that. I don't know how they get up onto Olympus, though. They're favored by the gods because of the massive number of sacrifices they make, but no human is favored enough to be gifted a pegasus."

Asteria tucked a few red curls behind her ears. "For large gatherings such as an execution as important as this one, Heracles, the Gatekeeper of Olympus, is asked to usher guests into the amphitheater. He checks the guests' invitations, then transports them to their seats."

"He checks the guests' invitations?" Zoey said. "We won't have invitations. We aren't invited. Or did you forget that tiny but very important detail?"

Prometheus waggled his eyebrows at Zoey. "Did *you* forget that I'm a trickster god? With a bit of magic, I can just make us invitations for a short time. And once we're in our seats, I won't have to keep up the façade, so it shouldn't take up too much power. The gods won't suspect a thing."

Zoey offered Prometheus a stern expression. "Really? You think the literal Gatekeeper of Olympus won't notice you doctored some invites?"

"Did the portal leading into Poseidon's palace notice the four of you weren't Poseidon?" Prometheus countered.

Zoey thought over the Titan's point for a second. "Okay, fair enough. I hadn't considered that."

Andy chewed the tip of his thumbnail. "Where're we gonna get new clothes from? Which city will we have to sneak into this time?" Memories of stealing garments from Aphrodite City, and especially of fighting the *astynomia* there, swirled through his thoughts. A knot formed in his stomach.

"I recommend Artemis City," Prometheus said.

"*What?*" Asteria cried, narrowing her eyes at the other Titan. "Have you gone mad? Artemis is hunting the Chosen Two. If they are discovered in her *polis*, they—"

"Think about it," Prometheus interrupted her. "Apollo's was just destroyed. The citizens who weren't killed were left to their own devices and ordered to emigrate to another city. They're practically refugees now. They've been left unprotected—even the rich government officials who used to make lots of pretty sacrifices aren't being defended, since they primarily worshipped Apollo. Now, don't you think those people are probably desperate to find a new home? And don't you think desperate people looking for a new home would travel to the nearest piece of civilization? Tell me, what's the closest city to Apollo's, hmm?"

"Artemis City," Darko answered. "The closest city to Apollo's is Artemis's, because they're twins."

Zoey cupped her chin. "I see what you're saying, Prometheus. Because of the number of refugees flooding Artemis City, if we go there, it'll be difficult for us to be detected. In fact, no one will bat an eye at our arrival. They probably won't even think twice about how dirty we are. I'll bet everyone who's shown up is filthy after the hell they've gone through to get there."

Prometheus grinned. "Precisely . . . *Zoey*." For some reason, he put emphasis on her name. Asteria gave him a confused look, but he seemed to make it a point to avoid the goddess's gaze.

"What about once—once we're actually on Olympus?" Andy asked. "What happens then?

How do we rescue Diana and the twins and steal the Master Lightning Bolt?"

"I imagine at first you'll be somewhere in the crowd, far from the Daughter of Apollo, her executioner, the grandchildren-of-Hephaestus, and the gods," Harmony piped up. "Since, you know, Heracles transports guests straight to their seats. If all the excitement is taking place in the middle of the amphitheater, you'll need a way to get down."

"Well, Andy could fly down with someone," Kali suggested. "Probably Zoey. I don't think he'd have a chance to come back for the rest of us, though. We'd have to find our own way without being hindered by the crowd. Unless Andy and Zoey used the Helm of Darkness to stay out of sight, some people would probably figure out it's an attack and alert everyone else, which would cause panic and chaos." She snapped her fingers. "Hey, I know! Dryads are coming with us, right?"

Narcissa leaned forward. "Of course. A few Naiads, too."

"They could build a bridge over the crowd into the amphitheater," Kali went on. "Using those handy plant-powers."

"That could work," Eugenia remarked. "Dryads cannot conjure plants, though. We can only manipulate them and make them grow, so whoever came with you would have to carry them in. Still, what a clever idea."

Harmony bounced in excitement. "It really is!" Darko stuck out a hand for Kali, and she gave him a high five.

Prometheus clapped his hands against his thighs. "Once we're all together in the amphitheater, the hardest part will be fighting the gods."

"It will be quite difficult, even though we do not intend to win the war in this single battle," Asteria said. "Thankfully, it is not impossible if we utilize enough manpower. We will also have the element of surprise on our side—and two of the gods' main objects of power."

Zoey hugged her sides, a sour expression on her face. "Don't forget about the demigods, though. They're the three who captured us in Hephaestus City, and . . . well, you know."

"The Son of Zeus?" Asteria asked. Zoey nodded, her expression darkening even more. Asteria tilted her head at the girl, and Andy did the same. He'd practically forgotten about Karter at this point, and he hadn't expected Zoey to be so bitter about the guy. Yeah, it would have been nice to have the demigod on their team, and it sucked he'd chosen to side with the bad guys, but it was over and done with. There wasn't anything they could do about it now, so there was no use in dwelling on it.

Prometheus burst into a fit of boisterous laughter. "There're way more demigods on Olympus than those four. Oh, yes there are. Trust me on that one." He chuckled a few more times, then composed himself. "Anyway, most of 'em will probably be trapped in the crowd after the fight begins and everyone starts to panic, but yes, we'll need to watch out for several, the Son of Zeus included." He pointed at Zoey. "I'll personally kick him into the next century for ya. Okay, kiddo?" She forced a smile.

"What happens if we manage to incapacitate the gods and demigods?" Darko asked. "What do we do next?"

"After that we'll have to be quick," Prometheus answered. "We'll steal the Master Lightning Bolt from Zeus—he always keeps that stupid thing tucked away in his robes—then free Diana and the twins and get off'a that hunk'a rock as fast as we can." He looked to Asteria. "Think you can fly us down once we're all finished up?"

"Yes, but I believe we should have a second plan in place as well, just in case something happens to me." Andy hoped it wouldn't come to that, but he agreed. They needed a backup escape route.

"Maybe the nymphs can make another bridge or staircase back down to the ground?" Darko suggested. "Or, if there are a lot of pegasi on Olympus, Diana can take us to the stables, and we can ride some away?"

"Most of us don't know how to direct pegasi," Narcissa replied flatly. "There isn't enough time for all of us to learn well, anyway. We are friends, not handlers, of nature and her creations."

Darko puffed out a breath, and Andy said, "Okay, bridge or staircase it is. Pegasi would probably be faster, but we can't split up. We can't leave anyone behind."

"Well, I think that settles things," Eugenia chirped, standing up. "We rest here for the night. Tomorrow, the Chosen Two, their companions, and a group of nymphs will go to Artemis City. Then, once they come back, we'll all leave for Olympus at once."

"Wait," Andy began, "how long will it take us to get from here to Artemis City?"

"If I fly you," Asteria said, "only a few hours."

Zoey climbed to her feet. "Why don't we just go now?" She turned to Asteria. "This morning you said there's only three days before Diana's new execution date, and we spent almost an entire day walking already. If it takes hours to fly to Artemis City, and then we have to sneak in, get clothes, sneak out, and fly back—it could take up a whole other day. That's not even considering the fact that something could go wrong and hold us up. We need a head start."

Kali stood as well. "I agree. We can't waste any time."

"What you need right now is a night of good sleep," Asteria asserted. "You have been either fighting or at sea for days, and you have not properly rested. You must do so tonight, to keep up your strength, and if you wake early tomorrow, there will be plenty of time to complete all your tasks and make it to the Daughter of Apollo's execution on time."

Harmony hopped up next. "Asteria's right, you know. About needing rest. You guys look *exhausted*. Get some beauty sleep!"

"Beauty has nothing to do with it, Harmony," Narcissa scolded, pinching the bridge of her nose.

Harmony made a shooing motion at Narcissa. "Oh, lighten up. You know what I meant."

Andy turned to Asteria. "You really think we'll have enough time to save Diana, even if we take tonight to rest?"

The goddess nodded, and after a bit more coaxing on everyone's part, the group finally agreed to sleep and head toward Artemis City early in the morning. The nymphs brought some dinner to the cabin, and by the time the sky went dark, the group was left alone to crash.

Once Darko's and Kali's heads hit the grass-pillows the nymphs had made for the group, and once they wrapped themselves up in the vine-and-flower blankets the nymphs had also made for them, Andy could hear them snoring. He and Zoey lay down as well, not beside each other but not far apart either. As they enveloped themselves in their separate beds, Andy could tell something was bothering Zoey. Something was bothering him, too.

To be honest, he couldn't stop thinking about what Anteros—and now what Zoey and Asteria—had been saying about this whole Andy/Anteros and Zoey/Calliope debacle.

At first, when Anteros had called Andy's body "our body," as if it were the god's body, too, and not just Andy's, Andy hadn't given it much thought. He hadn't given Anteros saying *"In time, you'll come to understand that we are the same being"* much thought, either. His focus had been on saving his friends and getting off Circe's island, and Anteros had helped him do that.

However, after today's events—and *especially* after Asteria kept calling him and Zoey Anteros and Calliope—well, Andy was confused. More confused than he ever thought he could be.

Were Andy and Zoey their own people?

Or were they Anteros and Calliope?

He looked over at Zoey, barely able to see her under the dim light of the stars sparkling in through the windows. She had her back turned to him, her curly hair splayed out behind her. She didn't seem to be asleep yet. Remembering their kiss back at Circe's palace, he cringed. *I still can't believe that happened. I really, really need to apologize to her again. Not just for the kiss, but for how I totally screwed up confessing my feelings for her, too . . .*

"Yes, you really, really do need to apologize for that specifically," Anteros said in his head.

Andy flinched. *You're back.*

"But the kiss?" Anteros went on. *"No, you don't need to apologize for that. It was my doing. I'm sorry if it caused either of you distress. Ever since I first saw her—through your eyes, of course—I knew she was Calliope, and I desperately wanted to reunite with her. I know the Calliope part of her wanted to reunite with me, too."*

Andy ignored the god's explanation. Even if it was true, Anteros shouldn't have done what he did. Although he'd helped Andy and his friends, forcing Andy on Zoey was not okay, and Andy wasn't sure he could be trusted. *Gee, thanks for clarifying. Means a lot,* Andy thought sarcastically.

"Of course. Anyway, apologies for my long absence. I needed time to regenerate after performing that spell on Circe,

and after chasing you through our mind. Which reminds me: why didn't you stop and listen to me when I told you I was trying to help us? You're making this far more difficult than it needs to be, boy."

Wait, that was real? That wasn't just a dream?

"Of course it was real," Anteros snapped. *"So next time listen to me, unless you intend to ruin our chances of completing the convergence."*

If Andy hadn't trusted Anteros before, this short conversation made him trust the god even less. Asteria had said something about a convergence, about how Anteros and Calliope would "soon transform into their most powerful selves." Not only that, but if the dream he'd had was real—if his loved ones lost had really been in his head, trying to contact him—that made Anteros even less reliable. Andy's loved ones hadn't seemed to want Anteros to catch him.

Asteria said she believed the voices in his dream had to have been nightmare gods, but Andy didn't believe that for a second, either. The logic simply didn't hold up; Zoey had proven that in her argument regarding the Fates' spell over the group and their allies.

If the dream was real, Andy knew the voices had to have been his loved ones. Despite the fact that Asteria had rescued him and his friends from Circe's island, he wasn't sure yet whether she had his best interests at heart, but he knew his loved ones did. He knew he could trust them completely.

You're trying to take over my body for good, Andy thought hard at Anteros, narrowing his eyes as if the god were standing before him now. *Calliope's trying to do the same to Zoey. That's why she got so flustered when Asteria mentioned the convergence stuff.*

We're not you guys reincarnated at all, are we? You're both just—trapped inside of us, somehow. And now you wanna use us for your own personal gain.

Anteros sighed. *"That is not true in the slightest. The truth is that you and I are the same being, just as Zoey and Calliope are the same being. If you would like to believe we are only using you both, then go ahead. Just know it will not stop the convergence. Resistance will only prolong the inevitable, making this harder than it needs to be for all parties involved."*

Andy snorted, rolling his eyes. That's exactly what he would say if he were a god trying to take over the mortal's body he was trapped in.

Anteros said something else, but Andy tuned him out, focusing on Zoey's hair once more. Now that they were on the mainland again, things felt as if they were unfolding faster than ever. *This might be one of my last chances to apologize to Zoey before things spiral out of control again*, he thought. *Darko and Kali are asleep, so maybe if I'm quiet enough about it . . .*

Andy took a deep breath, trying to calm his

frantic heartbeat. *This is it. It's time to say sorry. For everything.*

He pushed his blanket away, scooted over to Zoey, and tapped her on the shoulder. "Um, hey . . . you," he whispered. "You still up?"

"Yeah," she whispered back, an anxious quiver in her voice. She rolled over to look at him. "What's up?"

"Can I talk to you about something?"

The way Andy was looking at Zoey, the way his wings curled in nervously on themselves, made her stomach do a flip. The last time he'd been acting like this and had asked to talk to her, he'd ended up confessing that he thought he was in love with her. What did he plan on telling her this time?

"Whatever it is, be kind to him," Calliope hissed in her head. *"Just because you don't believe you have feelings for him does not mean that is the case. If you break his heart, you will regret it later. This I promise you."*

You're right that if I hurt him, I'll regret it, Zoey thought at the goddess. *But not for the reasons you think.* She glanced over her shoulder to make sure Darko and Kali were still sleeping. Once she determined they were, she answered his question. "Yeah, sure. What is it?"

"It's about yesterday," he whispered. "When I kissed you— I'm so sorry. I promise, I wasn't in control of that. Anteros took over my body and—"

"I know. Seriously. You don't have to beat yourself up about it. I'll admit, I was mad at you initially, but once I realized it was Anteros who did it, I understood. Calliope's messing with me too, remember?"

Andy nibbled on his thumbnail. "Y-yeah. I do. But that's—that's not—"

"That's not what?"

"That's not everything."

This was what Zoey had been afraid of. Her stomach twisted and turned. She sat up and looked away from him. Couldn't bear to face him any longer. "What do you mean?" she asked, fiddling with a curl that framed her face.

He was quiet for a long time. It seemed he was just as afraid to utter these next words as she was afraid for him to. "The other day, when I told you I'm in love with you—"

"You don't have to say sorry for that. It's how you feel, and I'm glad you can be honest with me."

"Sure, but I . . . I . . . Listen, Zoey. Lemme just spit it out. I don't wanna say sorry for telling you how I feel." She faced him again. They locked eyes. "I'm not sorry for loving you, and I never will be. What I am sorry for is how I treated you when you came clean to me about all the stuff people used to say about you at school, back in the Before Time."

Suddenly she couldn't breathe. She couldn't believe they were discussing this right now. Couldn't believe he was *apologizing* to her for how he'd acted before.

"It was seriously uncool," he went on. "I was being an insensitive jerk. I don't care about your past. What I care about is you, all of you. Even if I don't understand some of the stuff you've done, just . . . No matter what, the past doesn't change anything. It doesn't change how I feel about you. You're perfect. Amazing. Kind, and strong, and . . ."

He trailed off, and she looked away again, tears welling in her eyes. If she faced him right now, she might burst into tears. "Okay," she said.

"I don't need an answer from you right away," he added. "An answer about how you feel about me, I mean. I'm sure it seems like I'm trying to get one out of you by bringing this up again. You can just tell me whenever you figure it out or whenever you're ready."

She swallowed hard. "I—I really appreciate your apology. No matter what, we're good. We're friends. Everything's okay."

"Awesome," he replied, and he sounded genuinely relieved, as if a weight had been lifted from his shoulders. "I just . . . I had to make sure that you knew I knew I was being an ass before. Y'know?"

Despite the tears in her eyes, despite the fear she had of bursting into a fit of sobs if she let herself look at him, Zoey couldn't help but do just that. And, when she did, her lips turned up in a small smile. "I do know. Thanks, Andy."

He smiled back at her. The sight made her heart ache. *I hope you're right, Calliope,* she thought at the goddess. *I hope you're right that I'm actually in love with him and haven't realized it yet.*

Because I don't know how I'm ever going to tell him otherwise.

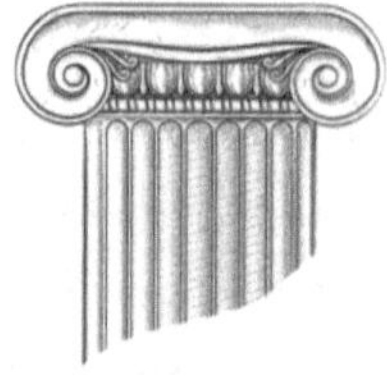

Karter hovered outside the main dining hall of Zeus's palace on New Mount Olympus, swallowing hard as he watched the hundreds of smiling gods, demigods, and nymphs chatting within. Some sat at the rectangular food-and-drink-filled tables lining the golden tiled floors, while others stood by or leaned on the tall, vine-wrapped columns. Lanterns hung from the curved ceiling, bathing the chamber in soft, warm light.

He ran his hands through his hair and shifted uncomfortably on his feet. A day of training—of successfully conjuring and controlling a green lightning bolt, and consequently "killing" Heracles with it, and all by harnessing his emotions rather than burying them—had rendered him thoroughly exhausted and sore. More exhausted and sore than he'd ever been after a day of training.

Even still, Zeus insisted that after Karter's "long and perilous" journey, and after all Karter "endured and accomplished" in such a short time, he should "have some fun" tonight. *You need to recharge,* " his father had said. *"Replenish yourself before Diana's execution in a couple of days. That way, when the time comes, you'll have no excuse to falter."*

And so Karter had gone to his bedchamber, stripped down, washed, put on a clean set of his finest robes, and mentally prepared himself for the party Zeus had planned this evening. Gatherings on Olympus were held often, and this one wasn't for any special occasion, but Karter's heart still skipped with anxiety at the prospect of attending. He usually loved parties like this because attending them meant carousing with Spencer and Syrena, but those two were gone. Not only that, but the last time he'd been present for a celebration was the most recent summer solstice party, and that was the night Syrena and Diana fled Olympus to betray the gods and revive Zoey and Andy.

Karter took a deep breath, trying his best to calm his nerves, and stepped toward the dining hall.

As he wandered inside, those around him went quiet. Many watched him with wide eyes. Some began whispering among their companions. Karter heard bits and pieces of a few of their conversations as he passed them.

"Think he'll be able to execute the Daughter of Apollo next time?" a Dryad asked the minor gods around her.

"Of course," they said, not quite in unison. "It's his destiny."

"Uck," another nymph muttered. "Hopefully, immortality will fix that awful scar of his."

The goddess beside her replied, "Agreed. It ruined his good looks."

Stomach churning, Karter pushed his shaggy black hair over the right side of his face.

Finally, he spotted Violet and Iro. He hurried toward the young women, soon discovering they sat at a table with Layla, Xander, Corinna, and Liam. As always, Violet was a vision of beauty, her golden hair piled atop her head in an elegant updo.

Layla, Iro, and Corinna looked great, too; all three wore their hair in a similar style to Violet's.

With a pang of grief, Karter wondered whether the girls had coordinated their looks for the evening. Back when Karter, Spencer, and Syrena had still been a team, and when Diana, Layla, and Pearl had still been a team as well, Syrena used to invite the other three girls to her room before parties so they could do their hair and makeup together. They would usually attend gatherings on Olympus with matching or complementary styles—they'd even dab themselves with the same perfumes—all-smiles and giggle-y as they entered the main dining hall for the festivities.

When Violet spotted Karter, she patted the seat next to her. "You're just in time." She winked. "Come, sit by me."

He made his way over to Violet and sat down at her side, she and Iro smiling at him as he did so. Xander glared daggers at him, while Corinna and Liam remained engrossed in their own conversation. Layla stared blankly off at nothing.

"My father has already spread word throughout the palace about how well your training went today," Iro said. "I can't believe you're almost an *immortal god.*"

"Uhhh, neither can I," he replied. "Today has been . . . surreal."

Violet seized his hand and placed it on her thigh, then grabbed the unblemished side of his face and made him look at her. A sweet, fruity-floral scent wafted from her skin, tickling Karter's nostrils. "Finally, after all these years, we can be open about our feelings for one another."

Across the table, Xander snorted and mumbled something under his breath, though Karter couldn't hear what. Karter shot the Son of Hermes a quick scowl and turned back to Violet. "Finally, indeed." He gave her a quick peck on the lips.

Soon the Olympians who hadn't gone on the mission to the Underworld strutted into the dining hall. They started toward the head table, which was located on the dais at the end of the room.

First came Hestia, who shared many of the same features as Hera, such as the Queen of the Gods' long brown hair. Hestia wore a flaming dress—literally, crackling fire made up the fabric. Karter assumed it was a representation of Hestia's Goddess of the Hearth status.

Next came Aphrodite, Goddess of Love and Beauty herself. She wore a grape-purple silk gown that almost touched the floor, and she was the spitting image of Violet—or, rather, Violet was the spitting image of *her*. Aside from their dramatic height difference, of course. Violet was the same height as Karter, while Aphrodite stood a few feet taller than them both.

Last came Zeus and Hera. Arm in arm the pair entered the chamber with as much grace and authority as one would expect from the King and Queen of the Gods. They'd donned matching blue outfits, and Hera wore peacock feathers for earrings. Gold circlets had been placed atop their heads, shimmering jewelry adorning their necks and wrists and fingers.

As the four immortals marched through the crowd, nymphs, demigods, and minor gods alike *ooohh*ed and *aaahh*ed at their beauty and attire.

"Where are the rest of the Olympians?" Liam whispered to Corinna. In appearance he mostly took after his godly father, Dionysus, with his red hair and green eyes. "Besides Apollo and Artemis, I mean."

Corinna swiped a few stray coils from her dark cheeks. "Mother told me they had business to attend to in the cities." *Well, Corinna, Demeter lied to you,* Karter thought, biting his tongue. *They're banishing Apollo to Tartarus as we speak.*

"You don't seriously believe that, do you?" Layla snapped at Corinna. "We're days away from Diana's execution, Prometheus is on the loose, the Chosen Two have yet to be captured—I could go on and on. The gods are up to something. I think they might be hiding information from us."

"Why would they do that?" Iro piped up, resting her forearms on the table. "What would they gain from it? We're their warriors."

"Maybe it's something . . . bad," Layla replied. "Maybe they don't want us to—to panic." Karter tensed. He couldn't believe how close to the truth Layla's prediction was. How had she thought of it?

Not only that, but he'd never known Layla to question the gods. She'd always just followed orders. Even when her teammate Pearl had been killed and the gods refused to bring Pearl back to life, she hadn't argued with the decision. Where was this coming from?

Violet waved a dismissive hand at Layla. "Oh, hush up. You're never any fun, and it's only gotten worse since we captured the Daughter of Apollo. Can't you just enjoy the evening, or at least pretend to? I'm tired of your attitude."

Layla narrowed her eyes at Violet, her brown skin and irises shifting into an angry red. Her gaze flickered over to Karter, then back to Violet. She parted her lips, surely intending to snap back, but before she could utter a word, Zeus's voice boomed across the chamber.

At first, the King of the Gods said the same things he always did at these get-togethers—thank you for being here tonight, let's have a grand old time, et cetera et cetera—but then he said something Karter never expected. "Now, before we feast, let us toast one of the most powerful demigods the world has ever seen, the one destined to end this war on the gods: my son Karter!"

Karter froze as almost everyone in the dining hall began to clap and cheer for him. After all his failures, and especially after that flop of an execution last night, he certainly had not anticipated for something like *this* to happen.

"Please stand, Karter," Hera said. For once, the tone in her voice was warm. Compassionate, almost. He did as she asked and slowly turned toward the head table. Sure enough, she stared down at him from the dais with the most kindhearted expression he'd ever seen her wear. She raised her cup to him. "Thank you for everything you've done and will do for the gods. I wholeheartedly believe you will earn a place in the pantheon. Perhaps one day, you will even earn a place in my heart—as my son."

The crowd *aaaww*ed at Hera's words, but Karter found he couldn't muster the strength to even pretend to feel honored. Maybe if the Queen of the Gods had said such a thing years ago he could have, but not after Asteria forced him to recall every gory detail of his mother's murder, and certainly not after his discussion with Heracles today. *Just remember what Heracles told you*, he thought. *You can disagree with the gods' choices and still join them. The world is not so black and white.*

It took everything in Karter to offer Hera a curt nod, his jaw clenched, his fists balled at his sides.

Aphrodite spoke next. "Young man, you are truly the savior of us all."

"The very definition of a hero," Hestia added. "An example of what all Warriors of the Gods should strive to be."

Zeus raised his chalice. "To my beloved son. A hero, savior, and soon-to-be god!" Everyone clapped and cheered and drank to that, but Karter found he felt no joy or appreciation for it. Instead, a cold emptiness spread through his chest. Since when had the Olympians considered him a savior or hero? Since when had Hera treated him with anything but disdain? Since when had Zeus referred to him as the god's "beloved" son?

Before he could contemplate these things further, someone snatched him by the wrist and yanked him back into his seat. He looked over to find it was Violet. "They're already worshipping you, love," she said, a dazzling smile on her lips. She kissed him before turning to the others at the table.

Iro giggled girlishly, facing Corinna and Liam. "Can you imagine how everyone will treat us after tonight? After seeing us sitting with Karter, Son of

Zeus himself?"

Layla rested her chin in her hands and stared off at nothing again. Xander muttered something else under his breath and poked at his meal. Violet, Iro, Corinna, and Liam chatted excitedly, then started in on their food and drinks.

For some reason, though, even after the day he'd had, Karter found he wasn't hungry. Found he didn't care to participate in the revelry tonight. He forced himself to eat, but even his favorite dishes were flavorless and hard to swallow.

After dinner, and after Violet made him dance with her some, Karter slipped out of the dining hall. He headed back to his bedchamber, where he could sleep and, hopefully, push away the intrusive thoughts that wouldn't leave him be.

CHAPTER ELEVEN
CLOTHES

Shortly after Zoey and Andy's talk in the cabin, they'd crept to their respective spots and gone to bed. The next morning came quickly, and Zoey couldn't have been more grateful for that. Sure, the night of sleep had been nothing short of magical, and she was sure her friends felt the same. But they needed to reach Artemis City, and they needed to do it fast.

A group of five unfamiliar nymphs prepared breakfast for Zoey and the rest of the group in the cabin. Once they finished eating, a Dryad who'd been referred to by others as Chloe and was very similar in appearance to Narcissa led them outside, where seven other nymphs awaited them. Zoey only knew three of the seven new nymphs: Eugenia, Harmony, and Narcissa.

Eugenia smiled serenely and offered a big bag of all sorts of extra weapons to the group. Apparently, the nymphs had scavenged the tools in their travels. Remembering that no citizens were allowed to carry weapons in the gods' cities, Zoey and the others selected daggers because the blades could be easily concealed within their clothing. They were also bringing the Helm of Darkness and Poseidon's Trident, as they didn't think it would be a smart idea to leave such valuable items back at camp, and surely Prometheus could use some trickster magic to conceal the items for as long as they were in Artemis City.

Soon Prometheus and Asteria joined Zoey and her companions, and the five nymphs who'd cooked breakfast for the group and the seven who'd approached them outside then led them all toward the outer rim of camp. As they walked, they ran into Ajax, Aladdin, and Luna. Kali made sure to hug the three pegasi before they left. "Stay here, inside the camp, until we get back," she told the creatures, wagging a stern finger at their noses. They whinnied happily in response.

Once the group—which now consisted of Zoey, her companions, and the twelve nymphs—exited camp through the tall gates made of logs and vegetation, Asteria transformed herself into thousands of little stars and carried everyone off into the sky. It wasn't much different from riding pegasi, mostly because they were just flying crazy fast while high up in the air, and everyone was pretty chill for the duration of the trip.

At the beginning of the flight, Zoey watched Andy, Darko, and Kali play what looked like thumb-war. They'd asked Zoey if she wanted to join in the fun, calling their game "Sword Fight," but she wasn't in the mood for activities like that right now. She was too worried about rescuing Diana and the twins, and fighting the gods, and facing Karter, and getting more unsolicited dating advice from Calliope.

After about a half hour passed, Zoey couldn't help but notice Harmony scooching away from the other nymphs, closer and closer to Darko. Darko seemed to notice it, too. He kept stealing glances at the pretty Dryad. Andy elbowed Darko in the side and whispered something to the satyr, and then Darko made a show of losing a couple of rounds of his game with Andy and Kali. They proceeded to pretend-kick him out of their "championship"—Zoey could tell they were faking it—and then Darko scooted over to sit next to Harmony. The two talked and laughed and played "Sword Fight" all on their own, and whenever Andy and Kali would peek over at the pair, they'd high-five.

The exchanges warmed Zoey's heart. She only wished Diana and Spencer were here to see them. *Then again*, she thought, *Spencer was always more of a get-down-to-business kind of guy, probably because he was grieving Syrena. Maybe he wouldn't find it as cute as Diana would.* She sighed sadly. *Guess I'll never know.*

"Get that horrible Son of Hades out of your head," Calliope snapped at Zoey. *"Stop thinking of what-ifs and focus on the boy right in front of you."*

Zoey didn't respond. She just looked up at the fluffy clouds, at the blue sky. She was tired of telling Calliope she didn't return Andy's feelings, so she ignored the goddess.

About two hours later, Asteria carried them over a massive clearing filled with something that looked like the ruins of a city. However, it couldn't have been a city from the Before Time. What was left of the smashed buildings looked like the pillared ones they'd seen in Aphrodite City, the cobblestone paths and stone houses winding throughout fractured beyond repair. Hundreds upon hundreds of graying human limbs protruded from the debris.

A sweet, putrid stench—something like spoiled meat and overripe fruit rotting in the sun—wafted up into Zoey's nostrils. Sour bile rose in her throat, and she had to cover her nose and mouth so she didn't vomit. Andy, Darko, Kali, and the nymphs must have smelled it too, because they also covered their noses and mouths, their faces turning various shades of green.

"Apollo City," Prometheus said sadly, gesturing at the destruction. "Those must be the citizens who didn't make it out in time. So many victims of the gods' wrath."

No one said a word the rest of the way to Artemis City, and thankfully, it didn't take much longer to get there. Zoey soon spotted it beyond rolling hills and trees, its layout pretty much the same as all the others she'd seen thus far. It had acres of farmland, neighborhoods, marketplaces, and temples. It still looked much different from the pristine gold-and-ivory Aphrodite City, the soot-covered bronze Hephaestus City, and the oceanside blue-green Poseidon City, though.

Vegetation wrapped up and around the stone-and-wood houses and the larger, white-pillared buildings, while trees as tall as the ones in the forest grew between them. Deer, dogs, boars, goats, and all manner of other woodland critters roamed the paved paths and streets in numbers as great as those of the people traversing them. If someone told Zoey Artemis City was actually an ancient-Greek-themed wildlife sanctuary, she would have believed them for sure.

"Whoa," Andy remarked. "It's—"

"Beautiful," Harmony finished for him.

"It also . . . makes sense," Darko added. "From what I remember about Artemis, the wild is sacred to her. No one can tame her, not even Zeus. Out of all the Olympians, she was one of the most honored and feared in the old days."

Prometheus chuckled. "She's still feared *these* days. By everyone—including me."

Zoey gulped. She really hoped Artemis and her Huntresses didn't track them down anytime soon.

Asteria dropped into the trees below, not too close to Artemis City but close enough so they didn't have to walk a long way to get there. Once everyone was safely on the ground, the Titan goddess transformed into her regular form. Then they all stretched their stiff limbs and started up the hill. "So, where're we gonna find clothes that blend in with the aristocrats'?" Andy asked. "I'm guessing the stuff we can snag off laundry lines won't cut it this time."

"Correct," Asteria said. "You'll have to go into the *Agora*, into the nicest shop you see, and buy something there."

Kali paused. "Buy something? Don't you mean steal? Last time I checked, none of us have money."

Asteria snapped her fingers, and in a flash of light two drawstring sacks appeared in her palms. She handed one to Zoey and one to Andy. "There you are. Gold coins and silver drachmas—lots of them. That should cover everything you may need."

With that, everyone but Asteria started toward the city. The Titan goddess claimed she needed to stay behind, to rest and rejuvenate after the long distance she'd flown them so that she could do it again when they returned. The nymphs left their bows and arrows with her for the time being, and Prometheus added that for now he'd have enough power to disguise Andy's, Darko's, the nymphs', and his own appearance by himself. He said he could also conceal the Trident's true nature, since they didn't have a bag to hold it in like they did the Helm.

The Titan god shrank himself down, turned his chains into jewelry, and reshaped the Trident into a cane, which he used as he pretended to limp. He hid Andy's wings, then altered the nymphs so that they seemed like regular young women, and Darko so that the satyr seemed like a regular young man. The change in Darko proved to be especially jarring. Zoey had never even tried to imagine what he'd look like without his horns and furry goat legs.

"All of you, stay close to me," Prometheus ordered as he walked through the trees. "The farther away you are from me, the more difficult it is to maintain all these disguises."

They did as Prometheus said, never straying too far from him. Soon they approached the outskirts of the city. They consisted of wheat farmland, with people in loose brown clothing harvesting the fields, just like in Aphrodite City.

Rather than hiding in the tall grass as they crept through the fields, everyone stood upright, pretending to be exhausted as they traversed the farmland. An old man and woman spotted them, and the man asked, "Are you from Apollo City?"

"Yes, we barely escaped the disaster," one of the nymphs replied tiredly.

The woman pointed at the neighborhoods of stone-and-wood houses far ahead. "Keep going. If you managed to get out of your *polis* with the ability to work, or with even a small bit of money, there should be help for you in the *Agora*. Our patron goddess had inns erected in preparation for new citizens who won't be able to buy a house right away. Maybe there's room for you in one of them." They thanked the couple and hurried off.

Before Zoey knew it, they exited the fields and

started into some neighborhoods. Here, adults and children worked away—again, just like in Aphrodite City, except for the fact that the buildings were covered in and surrounded by vegetation, and wild animals roamed the streets. Thankfully, the creatures seemed docile enough, not doing much more than sniffing as the group walked by. The people didn't blink an eye at their arrival, either. *Prometheus was right*, Zoey thought, relieved. *They've hardly noticed us.* A few more hours of walking into the city passed, and Zoey guessed about half the day had gone by, the sun high in the sky.

Eventually, they reached what had to be the *Agora*. Rows of pillared shops separated by trees lined the area for miles, citizens in dresses and tunics with handbaskets full of goods scuttling in and out of stores. There were even more animals here, and the sounds of laughter and chatter and sandals clacking against greenery-infested cobblestone paths filled the air.

"Now to find a clothing shop fit for aristocrats," Zoey whispered.

"What exactly does that look like?" Andy whispered back.

"Lots of color," Prometheus answered. "Or fine fabrics with patterns and jewels embedded into them."

Narcissa eyed their surroundings. "Yes, regular citizens cannot afford such luxuries."

For a long while they wandered the *Agora*, window-shopping for a store that fit Prometheus's specifications. They even passed a tall marble statue similar to the one of Aphrodite in Aphrodite City—although this one was obviously of Artemis rather than of the Goddess of Love.

The statue of Artemis was fierce yet beautiful, her untamed curls swelling around her face and shoulders. She wore a billowing dress that stopped at the knees, one hand on the bow and arrow slung over her back, the other gently resting on the head of a stag at her side. Like Aphrodite's statue, the one of Artemis stood inside a fountain, water spouting all about her. As people passed the fountain, they tossed coins into the water and muttered prayers under their breath.

Zoey couldn't help but stop before the statue, staring up at it in wonder. "So that's supposed to be the goddess who's tracking us," she whispered in disbelief.

"She's being surprisingly nice to that deer," Andy remarked in a hushed voice beside Zoey. "You know, considering she's a goddess of the hunt and all. It looks like they might even be friends."

Prometheus stopped on Zoey's other side.

"Stags are sacred to Artemis, among other animals. She might be a hunter, but she loves nature and everything in it, too. Now c'mon, let's keep goin'."

After what felt like forever, they found a shop on the opposite side of the *Agora* that seemed promising. It was void of customers and filled with colorful, embellished garments fit for royalty. It was also small, no larger than Zoey and her mother's old apartment in the Before Time, with robes and dresses hanging on the walls and along the metal racks. Its golden tiled floors shimmered beneath the afternoon sun, its tall columns supporting the high ceiling, which was covered in intricately detailed paintings of who could only be Artemis. In one picture, the redheaded goddess launched arrows across a night sky. In another, she ran through a forest alongside a pack of dogs. In a third, she cradled the head of a handsome, brown-bearded man in her lap, tears streaming down her cheeks as she kissed his lips.

"Who's that?" Zoey whispered to Darko and Harmony, who stood beside her. She pointed up at the bearded man in the painting.

Darko peered at the picture for several moments, but Harmony was the one to answer the question. "That's Orion," she said. "He was a giant and hunter who Artemis fell in love with in the old days. Since she's a virgin goddess and took a vow of eternal chastity, they couldn't be together. They spent a lot of time together, though, and Apollo, trying to prevent his sister from breaking her vow, tricked her into shooting Orion from afar. When Artemis realized what she'd done, she was overcome with grief. I think that's the moment this picture depicts."

Andy and Kali walked up beside them. "Hey, I think I've heard that story before," Andy said. "Orion—he was made into a constellation. Artemis placed his body in the stars, right?"

"Yes," the nymph named Chloe said from behind Zoey, her tone wistful. "She immortalized him, in a way."

Zoey huffed, hugging her arms to her chest. "Well, that wasn't very nice of Apollo. If Artemis wanted to break her vow, he shouldn't have stopped her. She can make her own decisions. She's her own person. Er, goddess, I guess." Zoey stared up at the painting some more, her chest growing tight as she took in the anguish permanently plastered on Artemis's features.

If this portrayal of the goddess and her late "lover" was accurate, then Zoey almost felt sorry for her because it meant she'd really, truly, *deeply* loved Orion. Sure, most of the gods were evil and committed unforgivable acts on the regular. However, the grief on Artemis's face was palpable.

Zoey had felt heartbreak before, but she couldn't imagine loving someone so much—and for them to love her back—only for them to be stolen away by tragedy.

"Artemis's vow of chastity has always been very important to her," Eugenia piped up from off to the right. "Although Apollo has carried out various questionable acts, as all gods have, I believe he only wanted to protect his sister in this instance. It is said they love each other very much." Zoey was skeptical of Eugenia's words, but she didn't press the issue further.

"Hello?" Prometheus called into the shop. "Anyone here? We'd like to buy some stuff, if it's not too much to ask." He sounded annoyed, and Zoey couldn't blame him. This place was empty, and they didn't have a lot of time. Was anyone working? If not, why had the doors been unlocked? Weren't the shopkeepers worried about people stealing?

A clatter sounded from somewhere deep within the building, and a few seconds later a scrawny young man with medium-brown skin and a shock of messy black hair scrambled out into the main section of the shop. He wore a wrinkled indigo tunic with golden geometric swirls for trimming, a shiny matching belt loosely tied around his waist.

As the young man stumbled toward them, Zoey

took in his dark, puffy under eyes and overall disheveled appearance. Frankly, he looked bone tired, and the sight reminded her of her own worn-out appearance most days in the Before Time. At least three days a week, she used to attend school all day, flip burgers all evening, then catch up on homework for a few hours before going to bed. She rarely (if ever) had even gotten weekends off. Usually, she'd pick up eight- or nine-hour shifts on Saturdays and Sundays to ensure she had enough money to cover the rent and bills, since her mother often missed payments.

To be fair, though, she probably looked exhausted even now. Because now, instead of worrying about school and work and money and college and her mother and the kids at school, she had to deal with the stress of being a Chosen One in a prophecy that determined the fate of the world and the future of humanity. Still, she'd take that kind of pressure over her life in the Before Time any day.

"Welcome to Zephyrine's Wardrobe Emporium," the young man said, doing his best to suppress a yawn. "My name is Sebastian, and I'll be your host today. How can I help you?" He stopped a few feet ahead of them, hands clasped behind his back. He stood several inches shorter than Zoey, couldn't have weighed more than 110 pounds, and had to be around fifteen, give or take a year.

Zoey stepped forward and focused on what she could say so as to not raise suspicions with Sebastian and, like clockwork, her throat started tingling. *I guess having Calliope in my head has its advantages here and there*, she thought, then said, "We were part of the aristocracy in Apollo City. Of course, because of its destruction, we decided to move to Artemis City."

"Of course," he repeated after her, forcing down another yawn.

"Despite the circumstances, the gods still graciously invited us to Diana, Daughter of Apollo's execution." At this, Sebastian's tired eyes snapped wide open. Zoey went on, "The problem is, most of our belongings were lost in the destruction of Apollo City, and we need something nice to wear to the event. Do you have any recommendations?"

"Uh, uh, um." He pointed at something behind him. "Let me just, umm, find you some styles from the back. Styles we haven't put on the floor yet. You need something—something *special*. If you'll be going to Olympus, I mean. Which you are. Obviously!" He spun around and ran toward the back of the shop, disappearing within the throngs of clothes.

Andy crossed his arms. "What's his deal?"

"I think he's just tired," Zoey replied. "Maybe he's overworking himself, like Jasmine has to to make ends meet." She refrained from saying, *Honestly, I can relate.*

Prometheus's gaze darkened at the mention of his great-great-granddaughter, and Zoey regretted bringing Jasmine up at all. She didn't want to upset Prometheus. Yet, at the same time, Jasmine's situation seemed to be the reality for far too many of the citizens under the gods' rule. Zoey felt as though that fact needed to be acknowledged whenever it was relevant.

Within minutes Sebastian returned with so many articles of clothing draped over his arms and shoulders he looked as if he were drowning in fabric. The garments consisted of every shade under the sun, their embellishments extravagant and complex.

The nymphs were first to pore over the robes and dresses, giggling and whispering as they brushed their fingers over the fine detailing. In the end, Harmony chose a lemon-yellow frock with flower-shaped jewels sewn into the neck and hemline, Eugenia picked a glittery rose-pink gown that cinched at the waist, Narcissa selected a hunter-green tunic with swirling silver embroidery stitched throughout, and the others went for many other styles in a variety of vibrant hues.

Andy, Darko, and Prometheus looked over the clothes next. Apparently, Sebastian's stock from the back was "a bit too fancy" for their taste, so they opted for some pristinely white chitons, which hung at the front of the shop.

When it finally came time for Zoey and Kali to check out their options, Zoey couldn't help but feel overwhelmed about it all. She'd never had the money for such beautiful clothing, nor had she ever attended an event that would require it. She stared down at the garments, speechless.

As Kali picked up a set of robes the color of amethyst, she asked Zoey, "What's wrong?"

Zoey was silent for a moment before responding, carefully considering her words. "Oh, you know me. I'm just . . . not sure what will look good. I never know what to wear to these things."

"And you know me, too," Kali said, winking.

"I do?"

"Oh, yes. You do." Kali swept up a second garment: a flowing bright-blue gown with gold accents. She held the dress out to Zoey. "Why do you think you keep me around? I *always* know what to wear to these things."

Zoey grinned and accepted the offering. "Thanks, Kali."

Kali returned the smile. "You're welcome."

Before Zoey and Andy paid Sebastian for the

clothes, he suggested everyone pick out some sandals. They did just that, then gave him what they owed for their finds, packed everything up in bags, and hurried out onto the streets of Artemis City once more.

"Looks like the sun will be setting here in a couple of hours," Prometheus said, looking up at the sky. "Flying and finding that place took up most of our day."

Darko nodded. "Which means we won't make it out before curfew."

Andy shifted his weight from one foot to another. "We don't have time to stay in the city for the night. Besides, we don't want a repeat of our fight with the *astynomia* in Aphrodite City. We'll have to use the Helm of Darkness to conceal ourselves and escape."

For a while they walked back from where they'd come, but as the sun began to set and the citizens began to disperse, they found an empty alleyway to hide in. Andy put on the Helm of Darkness, and everyone held hands so that they all disappeared.

Cloaked with invisibility, they crept toward the outskirts of Artemis City. They bumped into a few *astynomia* on their way out, and it took until well after the sun had set for them to escape, but nonetheless they did it.

Once they reached Asteria waiting for them in

the forest, they separated, and Andy removed the Helm of Darkness so Asteria could see all of them. She offered them some food and water, which they gratefully ate and drank, and after they finished, the Titan goddess transformed into thousands of little stars and whisked them into the sky back toward camp.

For several hours, Zoey dozed off and on, as did her companions. "We should reach the others soon," Narcissa said, yawning. "I'm afraid we'll need to find a new camping spot right away, though. We can't have Artemis and her Huntresses finding us."

Darko cocked his head to the side. "Did anyone else hear that?"

"Hear what?" Prometheus said.

"The yells," Eugenia answered for Darko. "I hear them, too."

Everyone went deathly quiet. Zoey raised her head, holding her breath as she listened for whatever it was Darko and Eugenia had heard.

One second ticked by. Two, three.

That was when Zoey heard the sounds.

They were hard to make out, as they seemed far away, muffled by distance and wind and trees. But there was no mistaking what they were.

Screams.

Harmony and Narcissa shared a panicked look.

"It's the others!" Harmony cried. "Asteria, please hurry!" Despite how exhausted Zoey knew Asteria was, the goddess picked up the pace. They flew even faster now, Zoey's hair whipping backward in the gales.

"Could a monster have found camp?" Andy asked. "Or do you think it's Artemis?"

Eugenia turned to face him, surely to respond to his question. However, she never got the chance.

A shining silver arrow whizzed toward Eugenia from the right and pierced the Dryad straight through her throat. She slumped down onto her spine. The rest of the nymphs screamed her name. Narcissa and Harmony scrambled to her side.

Before Zoey had time to react, a shimmering chariot drawn by four massive flying stags careened into view from where the arrow had come from. In the chariot stood a tall, pretty woman with a frizzy mop of curly red hair. She wore a tattered white dress, a bow in hand and a quiver of silver arrows slung across her back. Zoey knew who she was right away. *Artemis*.

Scarlet fluid rocketed from Eugenia's wound. Eyes wide, she pressed her palms against her neck. Harmony was already wailing, tears spilling down her cheeks. She gripped Eugenia's shoulders tight. Narcissa cradled Eugenia's head in her lap, her pale face turning ashen with terror as gurgling noises sounded from Eugenia's bleeding throat.

Artemis smirked at Zoey and Andy. Shivers shot up Zoey's spine. "Wipe the shocked expressions from your faces, Chosen Ones. I have never lost a hunt before, and I have no intention of losing one tonight."

CHAPTER TWELVE

ARTEMIS

"Do not make any sudden movements," Calliope ordered in Zoey's head as Asteria darted them every which way. Artemis's flying stags zipped her chariot alongside the group with masterful precision. *"And do not speak without choosing your words carefully. Artemis has found us, so we must proceed with great caution."*

Prometheus clambered in front of everyone. "Stay behind me!" He spread out his arms, his chains, as if to shield them from Artemis, but even with how large he was, he couldn't cover them all.

"I suggest you leave us be, Moon Goddess, or you're about to be in a world of hurt." Artemis only tilted her head in response.

Eugenia trembled and choked as Harmony and Narcissa held her. The other nymphs crowded around the trio of Dryads, most of them sobbing. "Somebody do something!" Harmony shrieked. "Please, save her!"

"Nothing can be done," Narcissa replied, her voice calm, save for a slight tremor. "None of us have power over healing. She cannot be saved. I— I am so sorry, Eugenia. I will always treasure the friendship we shared."

Artemis's smirk intensified. "Do not mourn the insolent traitor, nymphs. You'll be joining her soon anyway."

Eugenia suddenly stopped shaking. Her body seized up. Her hands, which had once gripped her neck, fell slack. The bubbling sounds in her throat ceased. The light faded from her unblinking eyes, the rest of her going still.

Several of the nymphs cried out her name, their voices cracking. A pit formed in Zoey's stomach. Tears threatened to cloud her vision.

There was no doubt about it.

Eugenia was dead.

"Eugenia, *please*," Harmony croaked. "Please, please, wake up. We can't do this without you!"

Narcissa sniffled, wiping a few tears from her eyes with the back of her hand. "Harmony, stop. She's—she's gone."

"It's a pity I cannot kill the Chosen Two, as I have killed the Dryad," Artemis said with a sigh. She whipped her stags, and they lifted her chariot up above everyone. Asteria darted from side to side, surely trying to shake Artemis off them, but the stags ensured Artemis stayed close.

The Moon Goddess looked down, narrowing her eyes at Zoey and Andy. "Destroying you would bring me infinite amounts of joy. You're the reason my dearest brother is being thrown into Tartarus." She nocked an arrow and pointed it in Kali's direction. "At least I can slaughter your companions before taking you to my father."

She loosed her arrow. Zoey, Andy, and Darko screamed Kali's name. At the same time, Prometheus hurtled back and threw himself on top of the girl. The arrow pierced straight through Prometheus's chest.

The Titan god moaned and rolled to the side, revealing an unharmed Kali. He clutched his heart as golden liquid leaked out from between his fingers. His jaw fell slack, his eyes going as wide and lifeless as Eugenia's.

Asteria plunged downward. She fluttered faster than ever into the trees, away from Artemis. Her voice echoed in the air around Zoey and her companions. "Even as the stars shine brightly, I have grown too weak to carry all of you. When we reach the ground, you must don the Helm of Darkness and run. Under no circumstances can you be captured, so you must not try to save the other nymphs. Some will escape and live to fight another day, but many will not. I'm sorry, but if any of the Huntresses capture you, all hope will be lost. I beg you to retreat. I beg you, *don't* let the lives lost tonight be in vain."

Once they hovered only a few feet above the forest floor, Asteria hurled them onto it, then swirled back into the sky toward Artemis.

Andy, Darko, Kali, and most of the nymphs didn't hesitate to do as Asteria said. Right away, they bolted farther into the trees. Harmony held onto Eugenia's body a moment longer, but as Narcissa urged her on, she finally relented and dashed after everyone else.

However, Zoey found she couldn't run. Not that she wanted to; she hated the idea of leaving behind people who needed help, especially ones who were in this mess because of her and Andy, but she also understood Asteria's logic. She and Andy were leading the war on the gods. They couldn't be captured tonight, no matter what. The best way to avenge those who'd lost their lives already would be to escape now and fight later.

Zoey focused on moving her feet, and something twitched in the back of her mind. They wouldn't move. She remained rooted in place.

"Retreating will accomplish nothing," Calliope said in her head. *"Artemis and her Huntresses cannot be outrun, nor can they be defeated with brute force. What's more, they will track and find you even if you're wearing the Helm of Darkness.*

"Deep down, you know all of this to be true. Deep down, you know you must stop them from kidnapping you and killing your companions by joining with me."

A bead of sweat rolled down the side of Zoey's face. She clenched her hand at her side. *By joining with you?* she thought at Calliope. *Does that mean using my voice-powers?*

"Zoey, what're you doing?" Andy yelped from up ahead. "We have to go!"

"Perhaps," Calliope responded. *"Let us find out together. Channel me. Channel my power, and we will do all we can to stop them."*

I bet you'd love if I listened to you, and you got some control over my body again, Zoey thought back at Calliope. *Yeah, no thanks. Andy and I survived a battle against Persephone at the edge of the pit of Tartarus, and we fought Poseidon on the surface of a storming Atlantic. I think we can figure this one out on our own.*

Calliope snorted. *"Perhaps you're not as clever as I*

thought. You're a fool if you believe you accomplished those feats on your own. Without the Son of Zeus's help in the Underworld, the flames of the pit of Tartarus would have swallowed you whole. And without my and Anteros's powers during your confrontation with Poseidon, the Trojan Cetus would have done the same.

"*Face it, little girl. You need me as much as I need you. Let me help you. If you don't, I fear Artemis and her Huntresses will capture you within the hour.*"

Zoey gulped, recalling how Anteros had forced Andy to kiss her when he'd taken over the boy's body. She didn't want to risk having another incident like that, but what other choice did she have? What if the only way to beat Artemis and her Huntresses was by relinquishing control to Calliope?

She glanced over at Andy, Darko, and Kali. The three of them had halted, waiting for her next move. Ahead of them, Harmony and Narcissa paused as well. Then the rest of the nymphs who'd gone with them to Artemis City did, too.

Zoey looked up at Asteria and Artemis next. Asteria whirled around Artemis in the form of stars, trying to disorient the Moon Goddess. It seemed to be working for now, but considering Artemis's reputation, Zoey didn't think it would take long for her to get past Asteria.

All the while, the howls of the nymphs back at

camp grew louder. *We're running out of time*, Zoey thought, and surprisingly, Calliope didn't offer an unsolicited response.

One second ticked by—then two, then three, before Zoey gave Calliope an answer. *Fine. I'll channel your power again. But you have to win this fight. Promise me, for the brave nymphs who agreed to fight for us, and especially for Eugenia.*

"*I cannot promise we'll rise victorious, even with my power,*" Calliope said. "*However, I can assure you of something else: this is everyone's best chance at victory. Now, close your eyes and search for me, as you did the first time.*"

Zoey followed the goddess's instructions. She clamped her eyes shut and searched the dark, twisting labyrinth of her mind.

Like before, it happened quickly. Zoey spotted Calliope standing at the entrance of a cave-like structure. Calliope ran toward Zoey. Zoey ran toward Calliope.

Soon they reached each other. Calliope seized Zoey by the arms, and that same strange buzzing feeling hummed in Zoey's chest. The sensation grew stronger and stronger, but even when Zoey couldn't bear it any longer, she didn't pull away from Calliope.

The sensation spread throughout the rest of Zoey's body. Only then did light the color of a clear midday sky flash.

Zoey screamed as she merged with Calliope once more.

Andy had never been so scared in his life. Not when he'd faced off with monsters, not when he'd fought demigods, not even when he'd battled the immortals themselves.

As Asteria fought Artemis in the sky, as the rest of the nymphs screamed in the distance, Zoey was pretty much having a full-on seizure on the ground before him. She shook and writhed and spasmed, her head twitching from side to side. Her blue irises began to glow, and then the luminous color melted into her pupils and the whites of her eyes until she hardly even looked like Zoey anymore.

"Zoey!" Andy shouted, racing toward her. Darko, Kali, and the nymphs followed close behind.

When they reached her, Andy took her hand in one of his own, and Kali grabbed her by the shoulders, surely trying to steady her. "What's going on with her?" Kali asked.

"Something similar happened to Andy while we were at Circe's palace, remember?" Darko said.

"He was thrashing around and—"

"That's gotta be it!" Andy interjected, releasing Zoey's hand. "She's letting Calliope take over her body so we won't have to abandon the nymphs. I'll bet Anteros will want me to . . ."

He trailed off, and Anteros said, *"You are correct. If you relinquish some control of our body, we can help Calliope. If I know her as well as I think I do, I might already know what she's planning."*

Andy bit his lip. As much as he didn't want Anteros to prance him around like a puppet, it sounded as though the nymphs back at camp were getting totally owned, and Asteria probably couldn't hold off Artemis much longer. He had to do *something*.

"Fine," he said to Anteros, out loud this time.

Darko raised a brow at him. "Fine what?"

"Don't sweat it, I'm talking to Anteros," Andy replied, shaking his head. He returned his attention to the god in his mind. "I'll give you some control of my body. But you have to promise to save the nymphs and defeat Artemis."

At first, Anteros didn't respond. Instead, that familiar buzzing feeling started up in Andy's chest, moved through the rest of his body. Brilliant silver light flashed in his eyes and faded as quickly as it came.

Andy shuddered. He opened his mouth

involuntarily and, in a voice that was not his own, said, "I can promise nothing but the fact that this is everyone's best chance for survival." *No way*, he thought, unable to say it. *How'd you take over so easily this time?* The god didn't answer his question.

Someone grasped one of his hands and squeezed it tight. He turned—not of his own accord—and saw it was Zoey. She was standing, no longer convulsing, and her irises glowed bright blue. Did his glow silver? "It's time, Anteros," she said, but she didn't sound like Zoey. No, she sounded like a great, powerful goddess. "Time for us to face Artemis. Whatever happens, you must know I love you more than life itself. I always have."

"And I you, Calliope," Anteros replied. "I have waited five hundred and eighteen years to reunite with you, and I would sooner be thrown into Tartarus than part with you again." Calliope forced Zoey to press her lips against Andy's, and Anteros made him close his eyes and kiss her back. *Not again*, Andy thought, little sparks of electricity dancing along his lips from where they touched Zoey's. *God, please let Zoey be unconscious for this. Especially if she doesn't wanna kiss me . . .*

Their kiss deepened, and the back of Andy's neck prickled with anger, his cheeks going hot. He wanted to yell at Anteros, to tell him just how messed up all of this was, but he found he couldn't stop making out with Zoey. It seemed Anteros was in control for now. *How did he take over so easily this time?* Andy wondered. *Before, it happened when Circe turned me into a pig, which is justified because I was in a weakened state at that point. The second time, I had to close my eyes and look for him and touch him. But this time . . .*

Finally, Anteros and Calliope had Andy and Zoey pull away from one another, and Anteros said in Andy's head, *"Stop worrying yourself over the process. This is simply part of our convergence—yet another step in the two becoming one."*

Somewhere behind Andy, Prometheus groaned—he must have regenerated. Anteros turned Andy around to look at the Titan god. Sure enough, Prometheus's arrow wound was completely healed. His eyes blinked open. He sat up and took in their surroundings. "What happened?"

Anteros forced Andy to hurry over to Prometheus, offer him a hand, and help him to his feet. "Ready yourself, Titan. We're about to face one of the fiercest goddesses to ever exist."

Prometheus leaned down, peering hard at Andy. "Bird-Boy, is that you talking? Or is it Anteros?" When Anteros didn't have Andy reply, Prometheus appeared panicked. "No, no. Andy. You can't let this happen, kid. Asteria told me about all this convergence stuff yesterday, but I don't think it has to be this way. Don't let him take—"

"Silence, Titan," Calliope said through Zoey. She must have been using her voice-powers, because Prometheus pressed his lips into a thin line and said nothing else. "We shall speak no more of this. It is not the time for discussion. We must prepare for our opponent. All of you, ready yourselves to shoot her down. Get her on the ground, and I'll take care of the rest!"

Andy wanted to ask Prometheus what he was talking about and what Asteria had told him about the convergence, but he was forced to remain quiet and clap his hands. In a flash of light, a bow and quiver of arrows appeared in his possession, just like at Circe's palace. Calliope made Zoey retrieve the Helm of Darkness and put it on; the object cloaked her with invisibility. She must have picked up Poseidon's Trident as well because it disappeared too.

At the same time, Darko, Harmony, and Narcissa fetched their bows and quivers of arrows, Kali seized her spear, and Prometheus readied his chains. The other Dryads present manipulated the vines around them into whips while the Naiads did the same with the freshwater from their pouches.

Artemis conducted her stags in the direction of

the group, and this time Asteria couldn't stop her. The flying deer launched themselves past Asteria's stars, diving toward the forest floor.

Narcissa, Harmony, and Darko nocked arrows. Anteros forced Andy to follow their lead. "Recruits," Narcissa bellowed, "*attack!*"

The nymphs behind Andy released a volley of fearsome battle cries he hadn't realized they were capable of. Using their vegetation, the Dryads propelled themselves and the Naiads at Artemis.

Simultaneously, Darko, Narcissa, and Harmony loosed their missiles. Anteros made Andy do the same. Artemis narrowly dodged Harmony's and Darko's assaults, but Narcissa's scuffed the goddess's arm. Andy's ricocheted off one of the stags' antlers, and the deer bleated in indignation, rearing back and colliding with the other stags.

The commotion among the deer caused Artemis's chariot to totter backward. Even still, she managed to shoot arrow after arrow after arrow at the Dryads and Naiads who now lashed at her with their plant- and water-whips. Her projectiles missed some of them, but others pierced three of the nymphs through their hearts. The recruits fell dead, their bodies tumbling toward the forest floor.

"Ari!" Harmony shrieked. "Katerina! Elena!" She, Narcissa, Darko, and Andy launched several more projectiles in rapid succession.

One by one, Artemis dodged their attacks with relative ease. She even shot three more nymphs in the process: one in the shoulder and two in the stomach. The wounded nymphs wailed in pain, temporarily withdrawing from the fight.

An expression of furious resolve came over Harmony's face. She and Narcissa shared a knowing look. They tossed their bows aside and waved their arms. Vegetation curled and twisted around their feet. Then they propelled themselves up, up, up toward Artemis alongside the other nymphs.

Anteros forced Andy to clap his hands again. His bow and arrows disappeared, replaced with the same heavy golden club from before. Against his will he soared after Narcissa and Harmony.

Andy and the remaining nymphs swarmed Artemis's chariot. The goddess whipped her stags, and they halted midair, trapped. The Naiads lashed the goddess and her deer with their water-whips, while the Dryads did the same with their greenery.

Artemis readied her bow and arrows to shoot more nymphs. Harmony waved her hands, and her vines lurched her into Artemis's chariot. Despite her tiny size, Harmony seized the Moon Goddess by her red curls and yanked her backward. Artemis loosed her arrows, but they didn't hit anyone. They shot uselessly into the sky.

Artemis sneered. She pivoted, backhanding Harmony across the face. The Dryad staggered to the side. She toppled out of the chariot.

As Harmony tumbled through the air, Darko cried her name from down below. Andy tried to flap toward the nymph, to save her, but found he couldn't. Anteros wouldn't allow it. *We're supposed to be helping the nymphs!* Andy thought desperately at Anteros. *Not letting them fall to their deaths!*

"She will be fine," Anteros replied. *"Didn't you see what kind of power she possesses?"* Just as Anteros suggested, Harmony ended up being okay. She caught herself with some trees, then used them to fling herself back into the fray.

Despite the nymphs' attacks, Artemis managed to wound more of them with her arrows. They yelped, clutching their injuries and falling back slightly. An opening appeared among the swarm. Artemis whipped her stags. The deer hurtled through the gap, hauling her and the chariot along with them. She directed them toward Andy's friends below.

Anteros sent Andy darting through the air after Artemis. He quickly intercepted her, and Anteros made him club one of her stags in the skull. Chunks of bone and brains splattered everywhere. The god forced him to clobber the deer behind the first one next. In half a second the other's head was reduced to nothing but antlers and scarlet pulp.

As the two deceased stags slumped lifelessly, the others cried out in distress, rearing back as they struggled to hold up the chariot and deadweight.

Artemis released a feral growl. "How *dare* you," she snarled. "How dare you harm sacred creatures of the wild." She nocked an arrow and aimed for Andy. "I don't care if my father wants you alive. You'll be slaughtered for this transgression!"

She launched the projectile. Andy threw up the golden club against his will. The arrow bounced off the weapon and plummeted toward the forest floor.

Artemis's jaw dropped, her eyes going wide as she looked at Andy. "How did you—how did you do that? A regular mortal would not be able to evade one of my arrows. Who are you?" She paused, gaping at his wings before adding, "*What* are you?"

"I am Anteros." The words spilled from Andy's lips, though they were not his own. "Son of Aphrodite and Ares, God of Requited Love, Avenger of the Unrequited."

"It cannot be," Artemis mumbled under her breath. She stared in shock at him for a bit longer, her stags still struggling.

Thousands of miniature stars suddenly flocked

all around the floundering deer. They twinkled and sparkled and flashed in the animals' eyes. The creatures bleated fearfully, plunging toward the ground at high speed, taking their dead peers, Artemis, and the chariot with them.

Artemis crashed to the forest floor. The seat of the chariot landed on top of her, concealing her from view. The stags slammed into the ground nearby. The live ones cried in agony and terror as they writhed in the grass, their legs twisted at odd angles.

Anteros made Andy fly down and land beside his friends, the club still in his grasp. The nymphs began their descent as well.

Asteria manifested in front of Andy. Sweat seeped from her pores, and she gasped for breath. Something that looked like steam rolled off her skin. She collapsed onto her side. "F-f-fight, Anteros. F-fight, C-Calliope," she whispered. "You m-must n-n-not succumb to Artemis, and you m-must c-converge." She let out a final ragged breath. Her eyes rolled into the back of her head, and she went still.

What's going on? Andy thought at Anteros, his heart racing. *Is Asteria okay?*

"I imagine she's not been worshipped in many years," Anteros answered. *"She has not had time to replenish herself, and she must have burned herself up by using too*

much power. When that happens to a god, it is usually a sign they're in the process of fading away from existence. Asteria will not wake for a while."

The nymphs landed behind Andy, and Darko, Kali, and Prometheus made their way to his side. "Is it over?" Kali asked.

"Did you kill Artemis?" Darko added. "You know, temporarily?"

Calliope spoke through Zoey, though she must have still been wearing the Helm, because Andy couldn't see her. "No," she said. "Artemis would never go down so easily. She and her Huntresses cannot be defeated using brute force alone. Weakened, perhaps, but not beaten."

A low, sinister cackle sounded from beneath the overturned chariot. "You're right." The chariot rolled to the side, revealing Artemis. She turned to Andy. "Prepare to face your punishment, you wretched, lying demon."

The Moon Goddess climbed to her feet. She snatched a dagger from her belt and stalked toward Andy. Darko drew a dagger, Kali brandished her spear, and Prometheus raised his chains.

Before anyone could attack, Calliope had Zoey shove the Trident into Andy's free hand. She reappeared, tearing the Helm off of her head, and tucked it under her arm. She boldly stepped in front of Andy.

Artemis knit her brow, stopping in her tracks. "Calliope?" she called tentatively. "Sister, is that . . . is that you?"

"Yes, Artemis. It is I, your sister. Calliope." Calliope forced Zoey to gesture back at Andy. "And my lover, Anteros. He is no liar, nor is he any demon. He is a god. We both are."

"But"—Artemis shot a fearful glance at Andy—"but Father said—"

"What did Father say? That Anteros and I faded away? That we died and stayed dead from lack of worship because no mortals remembered our names? Our great deeds?" Artemis's mouth opened and closed in shock, but she didn't reply.

A scornful laugh escaped Zoey's lips. "Yes, I thought Father would weave such a story. That's not what happened to Anteros and me, sister. In fact, it was Father who forced us into these mortal vessels. He did so without first seeking counsel, without telling anyone of his plans, so we could not rebel against him and so no one else would, either. Little did he know we wouldn't die with these mortals in the Storm. No, the universe had other plans for us."

"And what do those plans consist of?" Artemis snapped. "Destroying the gods? Giving humanity back their free will, so they can forget about us or reduce us to nothing more than a bedtime story? If that is what the universe has planned, I shall fight it until I fade away into nothingness."

"Then you are betraying the natural order," Calliope retorted through Zoey.

Artemis stomped a foot. "If you're truly my sister, then you are betraying your own family!"

Calliope made Zoey hold her head high and her shoulders back. "My 'family' already betrayed me. Why not return the favor? When Father realized that I had discovered the Olympians' secrets, and that I intended to inform the other minor gods of them so we could save humanity, he hurled me off the edge of Olympus. He forced me to merge with this mortal girl, and now we're one."

"It cannot be true," Artemis spat, shaking her head. "I have never heard something so absurd. You must only resemble Calliope. You cannot be her."

The Moon Goddess bared her teeth, brandishing her dagger and lunging for Zoey. Anteros had Andy toss aside the club, dart out in front of Zoey, and ram the Trident against the forest floor. A tremor erupted within the earth. Artemis staggered to the side. "You winged abomination," she shrieked, regaining her balance. "I will kill you! Both of you!"

Prometheus sprang toward Artemis, chains clanking. He swung them for her. One wrapped around her wrist, the other around her neck. Narcissa and Harmony darted forward next. They curled their vines around Artemis's arms and legs. Together, the three of them wrenched the goddess face-first to the ground.

"Calliope," Anteros said through Andy, forcing him to offer Poseidon's Trident to her. "Perform the Descent Spell. Once Artemis is taken care of, I'll perform it on her Huntresses." Calliope made Zoey nod. She slipped on the Helm again, disappearing, and took the Trident from him. It turned invisible along with her. She began to chant in an unfamiliar, ancient-sounding language.

"No!" Artemis screamed, wrestling against her bindings. "You cannot perform the Descent! You are not a god!" She ripped herself free of the vines, sending Harmony and Narcissa stumbling back, but the other Dryads were already bolting forward to help. They replaced the torn vines with their own. Darko and Kali and the Naiads ran up to Artemis too. Kali plunged her spear into the exposed parts of the goddess's body repeatedly, while Darko shot her with his projectiles and the Naiads whipped her with their water. Golden liquid trickled from the goddess's new wounds, arrows sticking out from various places in her pale flesh. Harmony and Narcissa recovered, wrapping more vegetation around her.

Artemis grappled against her bindings. "You insolent worms! You will die slowly and horribly!"

"Oh really?" Kali responded. "From here, it looks like you're the one losing the battle."

Artemis suddenly went stiff, a calm expression passing over her face. She looked to the sky, to the moonlight as it peeked in at them between the trees. "You must know very little of the gods," she said, closing her eyes. A moment later she opened them, her irises glowing silver. She sucked in a long, satisfied breath. "Or perhaps it's just me you know very little of. For the moon shines brightly tonight, and she gives me strength."

The Moon Goddess heaved her arms and legs inward, splitting apart the Dryads' vines and yanking Prometheus toward her by the chain he had around her wrist.

Prometheus nose-dived into the grass. Artemis plucked away the chains he'd trapped her with, leapt several feet into the air, and landed on his back. Andy's pulse quickened at the sight, but there was nothing he could do. Anteros wouldn't let him move. *Anteros, do something!* Andy thought. Anteros only had Andy retrieve the golden club he'd tossed aside.

Artemis ripped her dagger down the length of Prometheus's spine. He howled in pain, trying to roll over, but she placed one foot on the ground and the other on his head, keeping him locked in place.

Golden liquid stopped dripping from Artemis's wounds. Her injured skin knit itself back together, ejecting the arrows from her body. Even as Darko and Kali and the Naiads charged toward her, she didn't flinch.

"Retreat, my companions." Calliope's regal voice echoed all around them, so loud it was as if it were being blasted through outdoor speakers. "This spell is meant for none but Artemis." Darko, Kali, and all the nymphs started backing away.

Artemis laughed. It was a harsh, cruel sound. "Oh, you're still raving on about that? I'd love to see you try it. Your attempts will be most humorous, I'm sure."

Calliope had Zoey chant some more. Then there was a *boom*. The ground shook violently and split open beneath Artemis and Prometheus, revealing a black pit so deep Andy couldn't see the bottom. Anteros made Andy fly backward, away from the abyss. His companions staggered back from it as well.

Artemis and Prometheus screamed. They tumbled down into the pit. Andy's stomach clenched. He twitched, trying to fly after the Titan. Anteros didn't allow it. *Prometheus, no!*

Narcissa and Harmony waved their arms,

sending a set of vines speeding in Prometheus's direction. He latched onto the plants. They stopped his fall. The Dryads directed the vegetation to pull Prometheus upward.

Artemis reached for Prometheus as she plunged down past him. Her fingers brushed the dangling links of his chains, but she couldn't grab onto him.

Narcissa and Harmony finished conducting Prometheus to safety. He grasped the edge of the pit and clambered onto solid ground.

There was a flash of silver light from within the abyss, and Artemis materialized inches in front of Andy. She panted. A single bead of sweat rolled down her face.

The Moon Goddess growled and swiped her dagger at Andy. Heart in his throat, he swung the golden club with all his might. This time he wasn't sure whether he'd done it or Anteros had.

The club collided with Artemis's skull. She moaned, clutching her head and dropping her blade as she stumbled to the side.

Anteros forced Andy to leap into the air. Against his will, Andy raised the club like a bat. He swung the weapon at Artemis once, twice. It struck her in the face both times, battering her backward onto the forest floor, toward the edge of the pit.

As Artemis lay on the ground, Anteros had Andy give her a mighty clobber. With a few vicious strikes, he pummeled her head into a mess of ginger curls, fragmented bone, and golden mash. Then, not of his own accord—though he would have done this anyway—Andy kicked what remained of the goddess over the edge of the pit. This time, she didn't transport herself out. She disappeared into the abyss, ribbons of bloodred smoke spiraling out in her wake.

Calliope forced Zoey to chant some more. There was another *boom*, and once more the earth quaked. It began to mend itself back together, just as it had in Circe's palace when Anteros performed the same spell. When the earth finished closing, all that remained were evaporating tendrils of smoke.

Off to Andy's right, Poseidon's Trident appeared. It fell to the grass. Zoey was next to come into view. She tossed the Helm of Darkness aside, staggering to her knees. Her irises no longer glowed.

The golden club in Andy's hands disintegrated, and Anteros had him walk toward Zoey and kneel at her side. Sweat poured from her skin, her chest heaving with labored breaths. She gazed at Andy with the most tender expression he thought she'd ever given him, extending her trembling hand toward his face until she brushed his cheek with her fingers. His heart skipped at her touch. "S-Sp—"

She never finished what she was going to say. Her eyes rolled up into her head and she dropped forward. Anteros forced Andy to reach out and catch her before she could hit the ground. "Nymphs," Anteros said through Andy, making him set her down gently, "stay here and ensure Calliope's vessel is safe until I return. Everyone else, follow me. We're going to banish Artemis's Huntresses to the Underworld and save as many recruits as we can." The nymphs—even the ones who'd been injured—huddled around Zoey, and Anteros forced Andy to retrieve the Helm and Trident, then to jump into the air and soar toward the yells still sounding back at camp.

Soon he arrived, finding the recruits as they battled what had to be around twenty blue- and green-skinned young women clad in robes just like Artemis's. They were equipped with silver daggers, bows, and arrows. *The Huntresses*, Andy thought. *Are they nymphs, too? They kind of look like the Naiads.*

"Yes, many of Artemis's maiden-attendants are nymphs," Anteros replied. *"Though they are more Huntress than nymph, now, after so many years. It appears for this hunt she's brought the core members of her assembly—her twenty Naiads, the ones who have hunted at her side for millennia. She has many other Huntresses, mostly consisting of oceanids and other types of nature beings, but I don't see them tonight."*

Wait, these Huntresses have been with her for millennia? Did she make them immortal or something?

"They are somewhat immortal, and they have a bit of magic like all nymphs do, but they do not possess divine essences. So long as they hunt beside Artemis and abide by her rules, and so long as she does not fade away, they can only be killed temporarily, similarly to the gods."

Despite how many more recruits there were than Huntresses, the Huntresses seemed to be winning the battle. Some of the recruits fought the Huntresses with regular weapons such as swords, spears, axes, and bows and arrows, but the others used magical means to do so. Dryads made greenery grow high, manipulating plants to wrap around some of the Huntresses' limbs and necks, while Naiads trapped others in giant balls of floating freshwater.

However, the Huntresses were too nimble and strong to be killed or stay imprisoned so easily. They slashed through the vegetation and liquid with their blades and advanced on their adversaries. It appeared hundreds of nymphs had fallen already, no matter the method with which they fought, their paling faces staring blankly at the sky.

Fury bubbled in Andy's gut; he was more than ready to take Artemis's attendants down. Or, at least, to allow Anteros to do so using his body. To his surprise, though, the events that transpired next were somewhat of a blur.

One moment, Andy was awake, present, his body abruptly humming with intense heat and electricity. The next, he was in the garden he'd seen in his visions in Aphrodite City, in the garden in his dreams, Anteros chasing after him through the trees.

Anteros made him land at the outskirts of the conflict, the *he bolted past cypress trees, marble fountains, golden paths, and bushes of flowers* grass stained with slick scarlet. Corpses of nymph recruits surrounded him, the *planets and stars loomed in the night sky* scent of gore and death assaulting his nostrils. Arrows whistled past his head, inches from *he had to run for his life* piercing him. He dodged the assaults or *Anteros was chasing him again, and if the god caught him this time, he was done for* sent them bouncing off the shell of the Helm and the shaft of the Trident.

Two Huntresses approached him from *his muscles screamed at the effort of maintaining speed* his either side. One had a long brown braid flying out *he didn't know long he'd been running, but it felt like forever* behind her, the other with choppy blonde hair flittering wildly around *"Stop!" Anteros boomed from behind him* her face in the wind.

Against his will, Andy donned the Helm, and

"We must finish the convergence!" Anteros yelled chills charged through him as he turned invisible. Anteros forced him to *up ahead, the voices of Mom and Dad and Mel-Mel and Mark and Spencer echoed through the air* skewer the Huntresses with the Trident, then *"Jump off the edge, Andy!" Spencer cried. "Before it's too late!"* shove them off the prongs so he could *he reached a clearing, the edge of the garden* keep using the weapon.

Darko, Kali, and Prometheus *he sped up, sprinting toward his lost loved ones* arrived at Andy's side. Six more Huntresses noticed their arrival, and the young women *he stopped dead* pulled back from their fight with the recruits, hurdling over the piles of corpses toward *he now stood at the edge of a jagged cliff overlooking space* Andy's companions.

As the six Huntresses neared, Prometheus, Darko, and Kali lunged *he glanced between the trees behind him* toward them. The Titan god slung his chains around two of their necks *and the galaxy before him* and pulled the links tight, strangling them, while Darko launched multiple arrows *his heart pounding* at two others, piercing them through their chests, and Kali stabbed *his hands growing slick with sweat* her spear through the last ones' guts.

"There are twenty Huntresses," Anteros shouted through Andy. "We must temporarily kill them and get their bodies into one concentrated area. Once they are all together, I will perform the Descent!"

Andy's companions offered him nods, then started after *"Do not jump!" Anteros shrieked* the rest of Artemis's cronies. Anteros forced Andy to stay close *"If you sever our connection now, we won't be able to defeat the Huntresses!"* to the bodies they'd already gathered, presumably to ensure they remained "dead."

Within seconds, seven other Huntresses *the trees behind Andy rustled* swarmed Darko, Kali, and Prometheus up ahead, daggers in hand. Kali tore her spear through two, and *he chanced a glance over his shoulder* Darko pierced his arrows *to make sure it wasn't Anteros* through three. Prometheus got ahold of the last ones with *thankfully, the god hadn't reached him yet* his chains and choked them until they went limp.

In his peripheral, Andy spotted a shimmering silver object soaring *"Is Anteros telling the truth?" Andy asked his loved ones down below* straight for Darko. It must be one of *"Or is he lying so he can gain control of my body for good?"* the Huntresses' arrows! Twitching, Andy tried to open his mouth *"You're not ready, kiddo," his dad said* to cry out, to warn the satyr. But Anteros *"You need more time to understand it all, sweetie," his mom added* kept Andy quiet and *"Just jump!"* rooted in place.

In the end, Darko never *he didn't hesitate to listen to his mother* got pierced by the shimmering silver arrow. Kali yelped out the satyr's name, shoving *he jumped off the edge of the cliff* him out of the way. He toppled *Andy fell into space, soon tumbling into the ghostly arms of his loved ones, and they hugged him tight* to the side, and the projectile impaled Kali *and soothing warmth spread through his chest, and then they released him from their embrace* through the stomach.

The sight of Kali being shot must have helped Andy snap himself out of Anteros's control, because his jarring transitions between what was happening outside of him and what was happening in his head came to a screeching halt. His grip on the Trident tightened—this time of his own accord. "Kali!" he screamed, panic coursing through his veins. He bolted forward.

The final five of the twenty Huntresses slipped out from behind the trees and piles of corpses. They surrounded Darko, Kali, and Prometheus, malevolent grins on their lips as they nocked their arrows and took aim.

"What have you done?" Anteros howled in Andy's head. *"I told you not to jump off that cliff. I told you we needed to finish the convergence. You imbecile! You've severed the connection!"*

But Andy wasn't listening to Anteros. The only thing he could focus on was his companions. With no thought other than *I have to save my friends*, he furiously flapped his wings and soared toward them.

CHAPTER THIRTEEN
EVERYONE

Karter's muscles ached, his skin and robes and hair soaked with sweat after a second day of training for Diana's execution with Zeus, Heracles, and Dionysus. He shuffled down the hall toward his bedchamber, every muscle in his body burning. He intended to draw a bath and soak away the day's aches and pains.

When he finally reached his chambers, he did just that. He undressed, filled his tub, and slipped into the water. He dipped his head down, down, down until he was submerged in the hot liquid, the back of his head touching the bottom of the tub. He stayed there until he had to come up for air, allowing himself but a few moments of complete silence, of peace. It was the only place he didn't have to think of lightning and gods and war and immortality.

After allowing himself some quiet, he scrubbed his hair and skin with shampoos and soaps, and once the bathwater grew cold, he decided it was time to go to bed. Tomorrow night he would execute Diana. Not only that, but the day would be filled with more training. He needed to rest so he could—

He paused as he exited his bath chamber, catching sight of someone sitting on his bed. A black shadow behind the canopy. He figured it could only be one person, but it was best to check. "Hello?" he called. "Violet, is that you?"

"Of course," Violet said. She slinked out from behind the canopy, wearing a silk dress the colors of a Narcissus flower. In one hand, she held a plate of meats and bread; in the other, she had a chalice full of what Karter assumed was some sort of drink. "You must be utterly exhausted from the day you've had," she continued. "Heracles told Iro all about it. She suggested I bring you something for dinner, as you didn't get a proper meal today?"

"I didn't, no." He caught sight of Violet's

opalescent eyes flashing in the darkness. It looked as if she might be smiling, but the expression brought him no warmth. "Thank you," he forced out. She nodded, strolling toward him, and handed him the cup and plate.

Even in the semi-dark, Karter could see that the cup was filled with what must be some of Dionysus's wine. *She didn't pick an aphrodisiac, did she?* he wondered. *Then again, even if she did, that might not be such a bad thing.* Shoving aside his thoughts, focusing only on how hungry and thirsty he was, he inhaled the food and drink.

"Why don't we go to the garden tonight?" Violet asked as Karter chugged down the last of the wine. It was red and sweet, tasting of crushed berries on his tongue. As the liquid hit his stomach, it filled him with pleasant warmth, his head growing light. "Like old times," she added.

A part of Karter wanted the day to be over. A part of him was so exhausted that he wanted to crawl into bed, nestle himself within the sheets, and sleep forever. However, another part of him felt suddenly vibrant—giddy, almost. And "old times" with Violet did sound nice.

A memory crossed his mind, the memory of the last time he'd gone into the garden for a rendezvous with the Daughter of Aphrodite. The night Spencer and Syrena had attempted to escape

Olympus so they could visit their fathers, the night Karter had taken on the punishment meant for them.

"Maybe the garden isn't such a good idea," Karter said. "Could we stay in?"

She smiled coyly. "Oh, no. Don't tell me such a powerful Son of Zeus fears the dark? Wouldn't you like to play outside with me, Karter?"

Her jest was enough to put Karter at ease. Or, at least, to temporarily distract him from painful memories. A familiar, lustful sensation tugged in his stomach. He laughed, set aside the plate and chalice, and took Violet's hands in his. "Of course."

She giggled, and so did he. Together, they scampered out of the bedchamber, into the halls of Zeus's palace, toward the Garden of Olympus.

They crept down the hallways lined with statues of gods and doors leading into other demigods' bedchambers, no more than tiptoeing so they didn't wake a soul. "Shhhh," Violet whispered when Karter failed to suppress a chuckle. He pressed his free hand over his mouth, stifling himself as best he could.

It wasn't long before they reached the garden, and Violet dragged him past cypress trees standing a hundred feet tall, past bushes of potent-smelling flowers, past fountains whose water splashed into ponds swimming with exotic fish, until finally they reached a marble gazebo concealed by greenery on all sides.

Once they stepped beneath the gazebo's curved ceiling, Violet threw herself at Karter. She pressed her lips against his mouth, buried her fingers in his hair. Allowing his hands to fall to her waist, he kissed her back.

Karter wasn't sure how long they kept on like that. All he knew was that after an extended amount of time, Violet began tugging at his robes and whispering in his ear. At first, he couldn't quite make out what she was saying. As he listened more closely, he started to decipher her words.

"We will be together for all eternity, don't you think?" she murmured. "In love until the very end of time. A god and goddess second only to Zeus and Hera."

Karter paused to look at her. Had he heard that right? "A god and goddess?" he asked. "What are you talking about?"

She gazed at him longingly, her opalescent irises flashing again. For some reason, the sight made all the heat in Karter's body drain away. "Why yes, of course," she said. "Once you are made a god and the Chosen Two are destroyed, we'll marry. And then, like Dionysus did for Ariadne, you'll make me a goddess so we can be together for all time."

He pulled out of her embrace, his head spinning. This was how she talked to people who were under her love spell. In fact, it almost sounded as if she was giving him an order.

"You . . . you lied to me," he said, backing away from her. "You said you weren't trying to force me to fall in love with you, but you are, aren't you? I told you before, I'm not under your spell. I don't know how, but . . . maybe it's because you broke my heart before?"

The pining expression on her face morphed into one of frustration. "That's not how it works, you idiot." She bared her teeth and turned away to pace and yank at her hair. "Who do you have feelings for? Is it Iro? Layla? Some other demigod?"

He scrunched up his nose in disgust. Not that anyone she'd mentioned was disgusting, but the thought of being with them in *that* way was. "No, no! None of them."

"Then who is it? Where did you meet her?"

"I haven't met anyone." And he hadn't. Right?

Violet snarled. "When I find out who she is, I'll kill her for stealing this opportunity from me. I really thought she was harmless, that if I gave you a bit of time to work out your feelings, continued pursuing you, offered you a drink to fuel your lust . . . Ugh, I was *sure* you'd fall for me again!"

Head spinning, Karter leapt into the air and flew back toward the palace. Violet called after him, begging him to let her explain, but he didn't give her so much as a backward glance. *I can't deny it any longer*, he thought. *I knew it all along, but I didn't want to face it. She never cared for me. Not when we were younger, and especially not now.*

The whole time, she intended to use me for her own gain.

The events of the past two days played out in his head, over and over and over. The gods' uncharacteristic kindness toward him, their patience even as he failed to do as they asked, their speeches at the party last night . . .

Everyone did.

Old memories he shared with Spencer and Syrena and his mother tumbled through his mind. For some reason, even the memory of Zoey risking her life to save him—of the time they shared in the Hephaestus City jail cell—played out in his head.

Well, maybe not everyone.

When he made it back to his room, he shut and locked the door. He collapsed on his bed and put his face in his hands. *I've made a terrible mistake*, he thought. *A terrible, terrible mistake. I should have never listened to Violet and Layla and Xander. I should have never helped them bring Diana to Olympus. I should have never betrayed Zoey!*

His chest grew tight. Hot tears welled in his eyes

and slipped down his cheeks. *No, no, stop. I can't think this way.* And he couldn't. Although he knew he'd never forget Spencer and Syrena and Mother, and what he'd done to Zoey and Diana, Zeus and Heracles and everyone else had already asserted that this was his fate. That he was destined to execute Diana, destined to become an immortal god among the rest.

But wait . . .

Hadn't Heracles said something else about fate, too?

That it was a choice?

How it was a result of a series of decisions people make throughout their lives, along the journey from when their threads of fate are first spun, all the way to when the threads are finally cut?

"In a way, you determine what happens next," Heracles had told him. *"You decide whether this war on the gods ends or continues."*

What was it Zoey had told him when he'd betrayed her? *"Everyone has a choice. No one can make you do anything you don't want to do."*

The question was, what *did* he want to do? Did he want to end the war on the gods? Or did he want to prolong it? Because the choices he'd make within the next day would help determine the outcome of it.

For what felt like an eternity, Karter agonized over questions such as this, but he found that uncovering the answers was not so simple. In the end, he knew his true desires could never be fulfilled. Because what he wanted most in this world was to have Spencer and Syrena back. To have his mother back.

But why? Even in life, they couldn't give him what the gods could. They couldn't erect a city full of worshippers for him. They couldn't offer him a throne on Olympus. They couldn't award him with immortality for his great deeds.

No, he realized, *they couldn't give me any of those things.*

They gave me something better.

With that thought, Karter shot up in bed.

For the first time in a long while, he knew what he had to do.

What he *wanted* to do.

Thank God for the Helm of Darkness and Poseidon's Trident, and thank God for Andy's wings, because if it weren't for those things, Andy was sure Darko and Kali would have been screwed.

Because the Helm cloaked him with invisibility, and because the last five of Artemis's Huntresses couldn't track him by his footprints, it was pretty easy to fly over to them and skewer them with the Trident. They did manage to shoot some of their arrows at Darko, Kali, and Prometheus before Andy got there, but Prometheus used himself as a shield for the other two, and they ended up being okay.

Well, other than the arrow in Kali's gut.

Andy held his breath as he landed next to Kali and threw the Helm of Darkness and Poseidon's Trident aside. Prometheus tore the arrows from his arms and legs while Darko rested Kali against a grassy mound. She clutched her injury, and blood trickled out from it, coating her fingers.

Tears already burning his eyes, Andy dropped to his knees beside Kali. "Aww, don't cry," she said with a weak smile. "I'll be fine." Darko put his face in his hands and burst into a fit of sobs.

For some reason, Darko's reaction only seemed to strengthen Andy. Rather than crying himself, he forced down the tears threatening to escape his eyes and began ripping strips of cloth from his outfit. He still wore the one he'd stolen from the outskirts of Aphrodite City for a disguise, and for the first time he wondered whether whomever he'd stolen it from was missing it.

Once he was satisfied with the amount of cloth he'd gathered, he applied pressure to Kali's wound. "We just—we have to stop the bleeding first. And then, um, we need something to keep it from—from getting infected."

"As much as I hate to say it, I'm not sure we have time for that," Prometheus said. Though his words were cold, his tone was gentle. "Tomorrow night, the Son of Zeus executes Diana. We have to reach Olympus and free her. Otherwise, we'll lose this war."

Darko shot Prometheus a glare, his face already red and puffy, snot dripping from his nose. "We patch up Kali, and then we go."

"No," Kali croaked, shaking her head. "Prometheus is right. Diana needs you. Please, go and save her."

A lump formed in Andy's throat. "What about you?"

"Don't worry about me," she replied. "All I want is for Diana to be okay. If to save her you have to leave me behind, then . . ." She trailed off.

Despite how well Andy had held himself together up until this point, tears started to slip down his cheeks. After everything he'd been through, after all the people he'd lost—he wasn't sure how much more he could take.

With one hand, he kept the pressure on Kali's

wound. "If we go without you, you have to promise us you'll still be here when we get back." Kali rolled her eyes, but Andy could see how watery they'd become.

Darko sniffled, placing one of his hands over one of Kali's. "Why?" he asked her, his voice cracking. "Why would you do that? Why would you save me?"

"Because I care about you, you dolt," Kali said, and started coughing. Blood escaped her lips, sprinkling her chest. "Don't feel too special, though. I would have done it for anyone in our little crew." She gestured at Prometheus. "Except for you. I like you, but you can take care of yourself."

"One of us has to stay with you," Andy said. "We can't leave you alone with the nymphs. Not that I don't think they can take care of you, but . . ." He wasn't sure where he was going with that, so he just shut up. In truth, he only wanted Kali to be with someone she knew. Someone who knew her, too.

"I'll do it," Darko said. "I'm not important. All I seem to do is mess things up. I lost Medusa's head, I fell in love with that Daughter of Aphrodite and got us captured, and now Kali is injured because of me . . ." He paused, smiling sadly. "I couldn't even avenge my own brother's death."

"Wow, I have so much confidence that you can keep me alive," Kali remarked.

Darko shook his head. "I didn't mean it like that. I meant—I meant that I can't seem to get anything right, so let me get *this* right. Let me be the one to keep you safe. I promise, I won't fail you."

"I don't think you should stay with her," Prometheus said, and hurt flashed in Darko's eyes. "And that's not because I don't think you can do it," the Titan added quickly. "The thing is, you're a satyr, and you were training to become an *astynomia* in Hermes City. You have insider knowledge about the cities. If it weren't for your quick thinking in stealing that thread and using it to track where we'd been in the Labyrinth, it would have taken me years to find my way outta there. You're not as big of a screwup as you seem to think you are, kiddo."

Andy put his free hand on Darko's shoulder. "Everyone makes mistakes." As he said it, he thought of how much he'd hurt Zoey before. "You're more important to all of us than you know."

"Don't worry, Darko," Harmony's familiar voice said from behind them. "Narcissa and I will care for Kali while all of you go to Olympus."

Andy turned to see Harmony, Narcissa, and Chloe. They stood alongside two of the other nymphs who'd come with the group to Artemis City that were still alive. Harmony and Narcissa carried Zoey, who was still unconscious, with their vegetation, while the others hauled a still-lifeless Asteria and the group's supplies with their own vines and water.

"We'll do everything we can to ensure she stays alive until the Daughter of Apollo can heal her," Chloe added. "Just as we'll do for our recruits who were injured in the conflict."

Andy gazed out at the battlefield—he'd been so distraught about Kali that he'd almost forgotten there were others who were hurt—and sure enough, he spotted hundreds of nymphs around him as they cried and clutched their wounds. Some of them hobbled toward one another and hugged for a long while, but many more would never do so again, because they had perished.

Andy couldn't count the dead from here. There were simply too many. As their companions recovered their bodies, anguished sobs pierced the air.

Strangely enough, however, the nymphs' corpses didn't stick around for long. Within moments their blood evaporated. Their bodies trembled, then shrank, and then it looked as though they were joining the nature around them, their skin and hair and even their clothes morphing into or melding with vegetation. Some deceased Dryads twisted and lengthened at odd angles until they'd transformed into vines, bushes, or little trees, while others dissolved into the grass closest to their bodies and began sprouting wildflowers. At the same time, the lost Naiads metamorphized before Andy's eyes, their remains liquefying into clear freshwater to nourish the greenery beneath them.

"Wait a second," Andy started, turning to Darko. "Isn't that what happened to the satyr and centaur *astynomia* in Aphrodite City? The ones we had to fight and kill? Didn't they return to nature after death, too?"

"Yeah," Darko replied, wiping some tears from his face. "Like I told you then, satyrs and centaurs and nymphs are all a lot alike. We're nature spirits, but in physical form. So after death, our souls return to it."

"That's right," Harmony added with a small smile. "When we pass, we're not really gone. We just . . . become something else." Her voice cracked as she finished her sentence. She put her face in her hands and wept, and Chloe embraced her.

Narcissa cleared her throat, and as she spoke, sadness laced her tone. "Yes, well. We will care for the wounded and mourn the dead, obviously, but we must stay the course. Their sacrifices will not be in vain. That said, it appears we'll need to take Artemis's Huntresses as our prisoners and ensure they cannot regenerate for the time being." She looked to Andy. "Unless you still planned on sending them to the Underworld?"

"Right," Andy said. He grabbed the Helm and Trident and closed his eyes. *Okay, Anteros,* he thought. *You can take over my body again. You know, to perform the Descent Spell.*

As the seconds ticked by and Andy heard nothing from Anteros, his stomach twisted and turned with anxiety. What was it the god had said to him just a short while ago? *"I told you not to jump off that cliff. I told you we needed to finish the convergence. You imbecile! You've severed the connection!"*

C'mon, Anteros. I know you didn't mean that. Listen, I could really use your help here.

Crickets.

Andy opened his eyes and faced Narcissa. "I'm sorry. I don't think I can do the Descent without Anteros. For one, I don't know the words." He turned to Prometheus. "Do you know them? You said something about how Asteria was talking to you about this convergence stuff. Did she say anything about how to cast the Descent Spell?"

Prometheus shook his head. "She only talked to me about your and Zoey's convergences with

Anteros and Calliope—which we're going to need to discuss while she's still out, by the way. At any rate, I had no idea a spell that could open a portal to the Underworld even existed."

"Well, were you paying attention to the words Calliope said through Zoey when they cast the Descent earlier?" Andy asked.

The Titan god scowled. "I didn't exactly have the *time* to do that, Bird-Boy. I was busy fighting one of the most powerful goddesses to ever exist."

"We will simply take the Huntresses as our prisoners, then," Narcissa said. She turned to the nymphs around her. "We must gather the others and round up the Huntresses' bodies. We'll have to work in shifts to ensure they cannot regenerate."

"We also need to take a head count to find out how many recruits were killed," Harmony added. "Then gather the wounded and start for New Mount Olympus."

Andy, Prometheus, and Darko stood. "That sounds like a lot," Andy started. "So we'd better get going."

Zoey rushed through the garden, her lungs aching, her heart hammering in her chest. She had to get away, had to run for her life. She didn't know who or what was chasing her, but she knew if she was caught, she would lose herself forever.

She also knew she'd never been in this place before, but for some reason, it was oddly familiar, with its cypress trees, marble fountains, golden paths, and bushes of flowers. Above her, there was a fantastical view of space, its stars and planets levitating so closely it was as if she could reach up and snatch them from the dark atmosphere.

"Zoey," the painfully familiar voice of a young man called to her again, from somewhere up ahead. His words were muffled slightly by the trees, but there was no mistaking who it was. "You need to hurry. Come to us."

"Spencer!" she cried out. "Spencer!"

Behind her, a woman—no, it had to be Calliope— shouted, "Stop! Do not go to that dreaded Son of Hades. He will only hinder us. Come back here. Come back to me!"

Although she knew Calliope couldn't see her, Zoey shook her head. Calliope had to be the thing she was running from, which meant the goddess must be dangerous to some extent. Besides, Zoey didn't care if Calliope was a part of her or if she was a reincarnation of Calliope or whatever it was that was going on. Spencer was calling for her, and she would find him no matter what.

It wasn't long until Zoey reached a clearing. She sprinted just a short distance more before she reached the edge of a jagged cliff. However, rather than overlooking land, it appeared to be hovering over space itself. Vibrant planets orbited the burning sun, stars of the galaxy sparkling. The edge of the garden, *she thought, though she wasn't sure* how she knew that's what it was.

"*Do not jump off the edge!*" Calliope screamed from far behind her. "*We must complete the convergence if we are to defeat Zeus! We must become one!*"

"*Don't listen to her,*" Spencer said. *His voice sounded* as if he was somewhere far beyond the cliff, out in space. "*Jump before it's too late. We'll catch you.*" We? Zoey wondered. Who else is with him?

But there was no time to ask. Instinctively, Zoey glanced over her shoulder. Calliope burst from the trees, arms outstretched toward Zoey.

That was enough for her.

She leapt off the edge of the cliff and fell into the galaxy.

Up above, Calliope bellowed in rage, but Zoey didn't care. Why would she? The farther she plummeted, the more she could begin to see them.

There were three of them. The first one she recognized was Spencer, and a beautiful young woman stood beside him. Syrena. Yes, Zoey recognized the Daughter of Poseidon from the visions Spencer had given her and Andy. And then there was an older man, an older man she hadn't seen in years, other than in the vision Spencer showed her of his death . . .

Her eyes filled with tears. "Dad!"

Yes, their forms were unmistakable, although they were

all blue and misty, shimmering and phantom-like. They're ghosts, *she realized. They stretched their arms out, reaching up toward Zoey to catch her, and she readied herself to embrace them all. She missed her father and Spencer dearly, and although she'd never met Syrena, the Daughter of Poseidon was the reason she was alive—a hug seemed justified when she thought about it like that.*

When she tumbled into the spirits' arms, they hugged her tight, and soothing warmth spread through her chest. More than that, though, memories flashed before her eyes.

First, her mother and father when they told her they were getting a divorce.

Then her mother beating her on the night she thought of a way to pay their apartment rent. "Why don't you just let me live with Dad?" "Your father doesn't want you."

Her old boyfriend, Jet Weaver. Him and her cuddled in his bed at his parents' house. This was the day she shared her darkest secret with him.

The kids at school taunting her relentlessly after Jet told them what she'd admitted to.

Andy getting bullied by Jet on the day of the Storm. Zoey stepping forward and stopping Jet from assaulting the boy.

Her grabbing Andy by the hand and driving him out to his car in the junior parking lot. "You're really cool, and I hope we can be friends." "I'd like that, Andy. See you around?"

Spencer's voice sounded as the next few hours of that day

played through her head like a movie on fast-forward. "This is who you were before you were part of the Prophecy."

"You had a hard life," her father added. "I wish I could have made it easier for you. Even so, you were going places. You were special, hon. Real special."

"What does this have to do with anything?" she asked, able to see nothing but these memories as they continued unfolding in her mind.

Syrena was next to speak, her voice as pretty as her face. "It's important that you remember who you are before you decide whether you want to go through with the convergence."

There was that word again. "I'm so confused. What do you guys know about the convergence?"

Suddenly, the memories faded away and Zoey was sitting on a bench in a garden between two cabins—this was the place where Spencer had taken her back when they'd been in Kali's village. Spencer sat on her right, her father on her left, and Syrena stood before the three of them. Blue mist curled and twisted off their ghostly forms, their hazy skin and clothes shimmering beneath the lights strung up above.

"Despite what Calliope and Anteros say," Syrena began, clasping her hands together, "you and Andy are not one with them."

"They'd like you to believe you're one and the same," her father said. "But it's just not true. They seem to want to kick you out of your own bodies, or at least take them over."

"What they don't know is that if you and Andy go through with the convergence, they'll be lost, too," Spencer

explained.

Zoey looked over at Spencer. Even as an apparition, he was painfully handsome. "What do you mean 'they'll be lost, too'?"

"He means that once the convergence is complete, Calliope will no longer be Calliope, and you will no longer be you," Syrena said. "Not only that, but Anteros will no longer be Anteros, and Andy will no longer be Andy. The four of you—well, you'll have joined with Calliope, and Andy will have joined with Anteros, but you both will have also become something else. Something new."

"Something new," Zoey repeated. "I see."

Syrena nodded. "Yes. Not gods, but not humans, either. Divine but not immortal. Just . . . new."

"What if I don't want to become something 'new'?"

Dad, Spencer, and Syrena shared grave looks. After a long stretch of silence, Syrena opened her mouth to reply. However, before she could say anything, she dissolved into tendrils of blue smoke.

Zoey gasped, turning to Spencer, then Dad, only to find them disappearing as well. She grabbed for her father, but her hand went straight through him. "Wait!" she yelped. "Please, don't go! Don't leave me!"

"They have already accomplished what they came for," *Calliope said, her voice sounding only in Zoey's head now.* "They have no reason to speak with you any longer."

"What do you mean?"

"Figure it out on your own, since you have decided you do not need me." *Calliope's voice grew fainter with each passing moment.* "Farewell for now, little girl, and prepare yourself for what is to come. I can no longer protect you." *By the time Calliope finished her sentence, her voice had petered out. Her last words echoed in Zoey's head in the form of a hushed whisper, and then she said no more.*

Heart pounding, Zoey forced her eyes open. The sound of chains clanking and footsteps crunching against grass filled her ears, the spicy smell of pine permeating her nostrils. The sun hovered high in the sky, but she remained cast in shadow, and soon she realized why: Prometheus held her in his arms. The Titan god's massive form blocked any rays of light from reaching her. *Thank goodness*, she thought, exhaling in relief. *I was only dreaming.*

"Good afternoon," Prometheus said. He grinned down at her, and she realized he was walking, carrying her along with him. "How was your nap? Are you feeling well enough to make this hike on your own?"

"Hike?" Her throat was dry, her voice hoarse. "Where are we going? What happened?" Memories of Artemis discovering them as they flew back to camp from Artemis City, of Calliope convincing Zoey to let her take over so they could save the nymphs from the Moon Goddess and her Huntresses, of Calliope forcing her to kiss Andy again and sending Artemis to the Underworld, tumbled through her mind. "Did we—did we win? I know we got rid of Artemis for a bit, but what about the Huntresses? Are the nymphs okay?"

"Some of them," Prometheus replied. "Why don't you see for yourself?"

She looked around and spotted hundreds of Dryad and Naiad recruits as they walked around her and Prometheus through the trees. Hundreds more were carried by vegetation directed by dozens of the Dryads, and what Zoey assumed to be their injuries were covered with wrappings.

Zoey sighed in relief, but then she remembered Prometheus saying only some of the nymphs were okay. A pit of dread formed in her stomach. "How many lives were lost? Are Andy and Darko and Kali all right?"

"Those three are fine. Kali is wounded—"

"*Wounded?*" Zoey shot up in the Titan's arms. "Wounded is *not* fine."

"I promise you, she'll be okay," Prometheus said, but Zoey raised a skeptical brow at him. "We've already determined that the arrow didn't hit any vital organs. It's a miracle, but it's essentially a deep flesh wound. The biggest things we have to watch for with her are blood loss and infection.

Harmony and Narcissa are doing all they can to keep her and everyone else with injuries well and comfortable until Diana can heal them up." He let out a long breath. "As for casualties, nine hundred and forty-eight nymphs are dead, and it only took twenty of Artemis's Huntresses to kill that many."

Zoey's breath caught in her throat. "How? There were over three thousand recruits. How did only twenty Huntresses—"

"The Huntresses are enchanted by Artemis," Prometheus said. "They're not immortal by themselves, but as long as they fight alongside Artemis and follow her rules, they regenerate after death like the gods, and they don't grow old. Every time the nymphs managed to kill one of them— which is a difficult feat, I'll admit—they'd just regenerate. Andy ended up not being able to send them to the Underworld, like you did to Artemis, so we took the Huntresses as prisoners, and as they come back to life, the nymphs on duty kill them again."

"Zoey!" she heard Darko call. "You're awake!" He clopped toward them through the horde of nymphs, Andy close behind, and Prometheus set her down. At first she felt a little wobbly, but after a moment she stood by herself.

Darko threw his arms around her neck, hugging her, and she embraced him back. Andy stepped up next to them. "What all do you remember?" he asked.

"Not a whole lot," she lied, her cheeks growing hot. She didn't want to talk about their second kiss, not even a little bit.

Andy turned bright red. He started nibbling on his thumbnail. "Just so you know, Anteros possessed my body at pretty much the same time Calliope did yours. I'm super sorry about what happened."

Darko pulled away from Zoey, and she fidgeted with a curl that framed her face. "It's fine, Andy. Seriously. I'm sorry too." Eager to change the subject, she continued, "Anyway, I remember letting Calliope take over, and then her having me send Artemis to the Underworld. After that, I felt awful. Everything went black, and then I had a really, really weird dream." She shivered.

"Wait, weird dream?" Andy said. "Was it the one where you're running through a garden away from Anteros? Er, I guess in your case, it would be Calliope? And your dead loved ones are calling out for you, asking you to jump off a cliff that leads into space?"

"That's the one," she replied.

Prometheus crossed his arms, raising a brow at them. "That is *oddly* specific."

"That's because it's the same dream I had,"

Andy explained. "After I sent Circe to the Underworld. Anteros told me it was real, but honestly, I still don't know for sure if it was. I had it again while he made me fight the Huntresses. I guess in that case it would be considered more of a vision . . . Anyway, when I first had the dream, I jumped off the cliff, but a bunch of stars caught me and then I woke up. But when I had it the second time, when it was more of a vision, I jumped off the cliff and reunited with everyone down below. My mom and dad, my little sister and best friend, Spencer—"

"Hey, Spencer was in mine too," Zoey interrupted. She paused, contemplating what them having the same dream could mean. "Wait a second. After you reunited with your dead loved ones, did they say anything to you? Anything, uh, concerning?"

"No. I didn't get the chance to speak with them, although the first time I had the dream, they said they needed to discuss something with me. The second time, the vision just . . . ended. I'm guessing because I was in the middle of a fight when it happened?"

That sounded right to Zoey. "Yeah, I'm sure that's it," she said.

"Why?" he asked. "Did they say anything concerning to you?"

She swallowed hard, trying to recall the details. "Yeah, actually. They said we're not really Calliope and Anteros—which I kind of already figured out. Also, they said Calliope and Anteros want to take over our bodies? That that's what this whole convergence thing is all about? Us joining with the gods inside of us?" Prometheus's expression darkened, and Zoey continued, "They also said that if we go through with the convergence, we'll no longer be ourselves. I won't be Zoey, but Calliope won't be Calliope, either. You won't be Andy, and Anteros won't be Anteros. We'll be something else. Not gods but not humans. Divine but not immortal. We'll just be . . . new."

"Asteria talked to me about your convergence situations," Prometheus said. "She's still regenerating after using so much power and burning herself up, by the way. It should take a while, considering how badly she overtaxed herself."

"Do you think this situation is what she was referring to when she said that visions of the future showed her she'd be arriving late to the execution?" Zoey asked. "Do you think it'll take her until we're already on Olympus to wake up?"

"Probably," Prometheus replied with a shrug. "Anyway, I'm glad she's out. I can say what I really think about this convergence nonsense without her trying to stop me." He walked forward, gesturing for them to follow. The nymphs still hiked all around them. "C'mon, let's walk and talk. We've gotta wash up, dress up, and infiltrate New Mount Olympus by the end of the day, so we don't have time to stand around."

CHAPTER FOURTEEN
BETRAYAL

Andy hadn't heard from Anteros since last night during their fight with the Huntresses, and honestly, after everything Prometheus had said about the convergence stuff, he was glad for it.

Apparently, Asteria had told Prometheus something similar to what Zoey had been told in her own weird garden dream, but with a few differing details. She said that Anteros and Calliope were definitely trying to take over Andy and Zoey, but that that was "beneficial," and that it needed to happen "for the greater good." According to the

Titan goddess, this whole god-possessing-a-human thing had happened before, and it was pivotal for Anteros and Calliope to become their "most powerful selves" again so that the gods could be defeated.

Yeah, Andy was never trusting Asteria again.

Not. Ever.

"Who does she think she is?" Andy cried as they continued trekking through the forest toward New Mount Olympus. "Seriously, is it not enough that we died and got brought back to life five hundred years later in this whacked-out postapocalyptic hellscape? Is it not enough that we're pushing ourselves so friggin' hard all day, every day, to steal the gods' magical toys so we can defeat them? Is it not enough that we try to save everyone we can, while putting our own lives at risk? And now she wants us to give up our bodies and 'converge' with these assholes who can't even respect our personal boundaries? Ugh!" He kicked a pile of pebbles as they passed it, sending them flying.

Zoey bit her lip as she walked beside him. "Yeah, I don't know. How did Calliope and Anteros even get inside us? I think I had some brief flashes of Calliope's memories from when it might have happened, but I don't really understand them. I'd need to ask Calliope about them, but I haven't heard from her since I woke up."

"You don't understand them because they're unreal," Prometheus replied. "I've never heard of a situation so ludicrous, yet at the same time, I know it must at least be partially true, because ever since your powers started developing, I've seen divine essences growing within you." He paused for a moment and tilted his head at them. "Yeah, I see them now. They look like they've shrunk a bit, but they're there."

Darko shrugged. "On the bright side, you haven't heard from Anteros and Calliope, right? Maybe they realized how awful it was to expect you guys to just give yourselves over to them. I mean, it's not your fault they somehow got trapped in mortal bodies, and I think you can still defeat the gods without their help."

"Oh, most definitely," Prometheus said. "I'm not sure how the two of you are going to do it yet, but you know what? Ever since I met you, you've surprised me time and time again. I'm sure you'll surprise me when you figure out a way to win this thing, too."

A while longer passed before they were close enough to Olympus that they needed to bathe, get into their disguises, and travel the rest of the way on their own as "aristocrats." Narcissa and Harmony had already appointed twelve new nymphs that would be going with them, since

Eugenia and several others had been killed, and since Harmony and Narcissa were going to stay behind to tend to the wounded.

One by one a trio of Naiads took Andy, Zoey, Darko, Prometheus, and the twelve new nymphs away from everyone else. The Naiads had them strip naked, and then they were hosed down with cold, clean freshwater until they were squeaky clean.

After the Naiads finished directing all the water off each of them and they were completely dry, they put on the nice clothes they'd bought in Artemis City. The nymphs braided one another's hair, and one of them even styled Zoey's. When Andy saw her all dolled up and in her blue gown, he had to focus on keeping his jaw from dropping.

When it was finally time to go out on their own, Andy, Zoey, Darko, and Prometheus made sure to hug Kali and the pegasi (who had flown away during the fight with Artemis's Huntresses and had come back a while after it ended). Thankfully, Kali seemed to be doing kind of okay, but her brown skin had turned ashen, and she was way less snarky than usual. The sooner they rescued Diana and got her to heal up Kali, the better.

"Good luck, Darko," Harmony said, embracing the satyr. She pecked him on the cheek. He brushed his fingers where her lips had touched his skin, his cheeks going from deeply tanned to scarlet. Andy gave him a high five as they marched off into the trees.

Pretty soon, they started catching sight of other people—really, super nicely dressed people in horse-drawn chariots who had their noses stuck in the air and acted self-important even as they rode by. *The actual aristocrats*, Andy thought, and Prometheus must have been thinking the same thing, because he concealed Andy's wings and Darko's horns and furry goat legs, and he made the nymphs look like regular young women. He also shrank himself down and transformed his chains into jewelry and Poseidon's Trident into a cane. Andy assumed he probably even concealed Andy's and Zoey's divine essences, too.

About a half hour after Prometheus concealed everyone's magical nature, the trees began to grow sparse, and a pearlescent columned palace that stood high atop a giant mass of floating rock came into view in the distance. Storm clouds hovered around the palace. It glistened under rain and lightning.

Beneath the huge floating boulder was a long line of aristocrats, and Andy and the others scurried over to the end of the line to wait their turn to be transported to their seats by Heracles, the Gatekeeper of Olympus. As the others in front of them eyed what looked like invitations, which were handwritten upon rolled-up pieces of papyrus, Prometheus studied the papers carefully. When the group neared the front of the line, he took the liberty of snapping his fingers. Light sparked in their hands, and then they all had their own invites.

Finally, it was their turn, and Andy couldn't help but get nervous when he laid eyes on Heracles. The hulking dark-haired god was bigger and more muscular than even Prometheus, and that was saying something.

"Invitations, please," Heracles said to all of them since they were clearly together. He held out his hands. They relinquished the doctored papyri, and Andy held his breath as Heracles examined each one.

Finally, Heracles said, "Great. Next." Andy released the breath he'd been holding, his lungs aching, and the massive god snapped his fingers. In the blink of an eye, Andy and his companions were sitting in one of the coolest pieces of architecture Andy had ever seen.

It had to be half the size of one of the gods' cities, with a temple on the far end of it that looked as if it led into the palace, and a sprawling dirt floor surrounded by hundreds of rows of seats made of sloping gray stone that was curved into a sort of crescent shape. The seats were already filling up with who Andy assumed were gods, demigods, nymphs, and aristocrats. There had to be thousands of them; in fact, it was kind of baffling.

Andy leaned over to Zoey beside him. "Don't all these guys have better things to do?" he whispered.

"No," she whispered back. "Probably not, if they're as petty as the gods."

Darko shushed them, and no one said anything else as they waited for the execution to begin.

Karter spent the day of Diana's execution training relentlessly alongside Zeus, Heracles, and Dionysus, and the night came quickly.

As he waited to be summoned for the event, he sat alone in his bedchamber, thinking of his plans for tonight.

There was a knock at his door, and he answered it. Violet, Layla, and Xander stood in the doorway.

Karter made it a point to barely look at Violet. He hadn't spoken to her since last night, and if he had things his way, he never would again. "The king sent us for you," Xander said. "It's time for the Daughter of Apollo to die. Are you ready?" He and Violet snickered. Perhaps they suspected Karter would fumble his task again.

Not this time, he thought, and stepped out of his chambers. He pushed past the other demigods. "I am."

As they walked, Karter noticed that the halls of Olympus looked so much longer and darker than they ever had before, but he didn't mind. For the first time in his life, he knew he was exactly where he was supposed to be, doing exactly what he was supposed to do.

Soon they reached the long, twisting stone staircases leading into the jail located deep within the belly of Olympus. Flaming sconces that hung from the walls lit their path. Karter and Layla started down the stairs, Violet and Xander close behind them. "I request a word with the Daughter of Apollo," Karter said to Layla, his tone ice cold. "Before the execution."

Layla stared straight forward, a blank expression on her face. "The king insisted we were not to be late to the execution. Are you sure?"

"Layla, are you some kind of half-wit?" Violet hissed from behind them. "Why would you allow him to speak with her at all? He's meant to kill her, not make friends with her."

Karter shot Violet a quick glare over his

shoulder. He halted, straightened his posture, and turned around to face her. "You would do well to remember your place, Daughter of Aphrodite." He gestured at Layla and Xander. "In fact, all of you would do well to remember your places. Tonight, I will be made an immortal god, and you'll be below me. I thought it was polite to ask first, but now I'm not asking anymore. Daughter of Ares, hand over the key to the cells. *Now.*"

Layla didn't hesitate. She handed him a ring, a single bronze key hanging from it. Violet and Xander scowled at him.

Go ahead, he thought. *Suspect me of every crime under the sun, and especially of betraying the gods. At least this time you'd be right to suspect. But try anything, and I'll kill you.*

He gripped the ring tightly. "Thank you. Now, when I go in, be sure to stand guard outside the door in case the Daughter of Apollo manages to attack me."

"Surely you don't need anyone to protect you," Xander mocked. "Why would such a powerful Son of Zeus need worthless, lesser demigods to defend him?"

Karter wiggled the fingers of his free hand. Pulsing, hot power burst in his chest. It snaked down his arm, and then sparks of green electricity danced in his hand, crackling between his fingers.

Xander's eyes went wide. He took a step back, almost stumbling over the stair behind him as his calves ran into it. "I don't need any of you to protect me," Karter said. "But if for some reason I have to execute the Daughter of Apollo in her cell, I want witnesses of my kill." They all remained frozen in place.

Karter didn't say another word. He simply nodded at them, then continued down the steps.

Once they reached the jail—a cavernous chamber constructed of stone—Layla directed Karter to Diana's cell. From out here, he couldn't see her, as the cell doors were fashioned with slabs of solid rock.

Karter stuck the bronze key into the keyhole and unlocked the cell door, then conjured his child-of-Zeus strength to shove it open.

Sucking in a deep breath, he stepped inside.

He shut the door behind himself and conjured a red lightning bolt to illuminate the jail cell before him. He spotted Diana among the mottled, uneven stones making up the room right away.

The last time he'd seen her, he'd thought that was the smallest and weakest she'd ever look. However, he was almost certain he'd been wrong. The smallest and weakest she'd ever look had to be right now in this cell.

It seemed the gods had only permitted her to

have the least amount of food and water possible to keep her alive until her execution. She'd definitely lost a few pounds, her skin dull with dehydration. Shackles were secured around her wrists and ankles, the chains attached to the floor. A chalice full of water and a plate filled with bread and fruit sat on a nearby table, but there was no way Diana could have reached the refreshments; the chains weren't long enough. Someone must have purposely left those there, weakening her further before the execution.

Diana looked up from the floor and glowered at Karter. "Come to gloat?"

He shook his head, hurrying over to the food and drink. He grabbed the cup with his free hand, hastened to her side, and held it to her lips. She quickly gulped down the liquid. "No," he whispered. "Listen, I know that—that I've had trouble picking a side in the past. But over the course of the last few days, I . . . well, I've come to realize a few things. Some of those things are about fate and destiny, but most of them are about— about myself."

"What are you talking about?" Diana whispered back, her gaze softening ever so slightly, though she still looked suspicious.

"Let me explain." As he continued, he hardly believed what he was saying. It wasn't until this moment that he'd been able to verbalize how he felt. "Listen. I, um—I thought I didn't have a choice in all this. Whether I execute you, I mean. And I thought I was fine with the gods telling me what to do, so long as it meant becoming one of them. So long as it meant forgetting about the hardships I've experienced. But . . . as it turns out, I *do* have a choice in what happens next. What's more, pain is not so—so easily buried." He thought of how he'd wanted to let go of and forget about Spencer and Syrena and his mother. How even the gods could not completely shut out the memories of the people they'd loved and lost. "Pain is something you just have to learn to live with."

He paused to clear his throat. "I guess my point is, I know I've hurt the people I love most. I've harmed them beyond measure, and now that they're gone, I can never make up for it. Even still, I won't be able to live with myself if I kill you tonight, or even if I let you die at all. So my plan is to get you and the grandchildren-of-Hephaestus out of here. Alive."

Diana's green eyes brightened with hope, and Karter went on. "I'm going to undo your chains, Diana. Take a few minutes to eat and gather your strength. You're going to need it if we're to save Troy and Marina and escape Olympus." He freed her of her shackles, and within less than a minute she inhaled all the bread and fruit on the plate.

A knock sounded at the door. "I hate to disturb you," Xander started on the other side, sarcasm lacing his tone. "But Zeus is waiting on us, and if I know him at all, he isn't doing so very patiently. Let's get going."

Karter and Diana shared a frantic look. "Are you ready?" he whispered.

"I don't think I have a choice," she replied.

"Besides, *love*, we shouldn't be keeping the people waiting for their show all night," Violet said mockingly.

Layla added something else, then Xander, and then it seemed all three of the demigods outside the cell were talking at once, because Karter couldn't understand a thing they were saying. He allowed his red bolt to disintegrate, then conjured two green ones, one in each hand. He turned to face Diana. She was already in a fighting stance, balls of golden sunlight glowing in her palms.

Neither of them had to say anything. Although they hadn't been part of the same demigod warrior team, they'd still fought together before, and they'd fought one another, too.

"Layla!" Karter yelled, and everyone outside the cell went quiet. "Open the door. I'm ready to take the prisoner to the amphitheater for her execution.”

When Layla started opening the cell, Karter jumped into the air, focused on his strength, and kicked the hunk of rock open all the way. The force sent the Daughter of Ares flying backward. Violet and Xander cried out in surprise.

Karter soared above them, brandishing the green lightning bolts. “Quiet, all of you! Keep your mouths shut, or I’ll be forced to kill you!”

That was enough to silence them, but Violet and Xander glared at Karter with their fists balled at their sides. Layla stared up at him in shock.

Diana slipped out into the open. Boldly, fearlessly, she stepped up below Karter, readying her spheres of light.

“Karter?” Layla asked in a low voice. “What—what’s gotten into you? I don’t—I don’t understand. You’re to be made a god. Why would you do something like this?”

“I’ll tell you why,” Xander snapped, not bothering to keep his volume down. “It’s because of his precious Spencer and Syrena. He’s always allowed his weakness for them to cloud his judgment, and now he’s—”

Before Xander could finish his sentence, Karter swooped down and brought a green lightning bolt so close to his face it almost touched his nose. Xander yelped, stumbling back.

"You're right," Karter said through clenched teeth. "I *am* doing this for Spencer and Syrena. They loved me despite my shortcomings. They stood beside me even when I was considered a disgrace. While everyone else pretended to care, and only when it was convenient for them, no less. And I . . ." He swallowed back tears. "I fell for it. I fell for the lie, because I wanted to believe that one day, I could forget all the hurt and have the life every demigod dreams of. But I can't. So instead, I'll have to learn to live with myself for what I've done. I'll have to—to make up for it as best as I can. I'll have to try to be the man I should have been for Syrena on the night of her execution, and for Spencer long before his stepmother betrayed him."

"I can't believe I wanted to make you fall in love with me a second time," Violet said off to the left. "Not only did that repulsive scar ruin your looks, but you've become pathetically emotional over the years." Karter turned to see Violet as she raised a few of the darts she kept hidden in her dress.

A ball of golden sunlight rammed into Violet's stomach, sending her spiraling to the floor. Her head ricocheted off the stone. With a soft sigh, she fell unconscious.

Xander grabbed a dagger from his belt. Layla put her hands up. "No," she said. "If we fight

Karter, we die. Let them go."

"I'd rather die than let traitors roam free," Xander replied. Before he could rush toward Karter or Diana, Layla leapt up behind him and rammed a fist into the side of his skull, knocking him out. She used the trick often in battle; it involved channeling her super-strength, which she'd inherited from her father. She grabbed Xander by the arms, shoved him into Diana's cell, and slammed the door shut.

"Go," she said to Karter and Diana. "Get out of here."

Diana took a tentative step toward the Daughter of Ares. "Layla? Why would you—"

"I said *go!*" Layla shouted in desperation.

Karter shook his head. "Not before we have the grandchildren-of-Hephaestus, too. Where are they being held?"

Layla quickly led them to a cell located within an adjacent jail-chamber, and Karter didn't waste any time. He unlocked the door, opened it, and, using his free hand, illuminated the cell with red lightning. Sure enough, Troy and Marina were in here. They lay on the ground only a few feet from one another, their wrists chained to the floor. A table with empty plates and cups stood between them, and Karter breathed out a sigh of relief. *At least they're not starving like Diana.*

Marina groaned, lifting her head. When she saw Karter, she glowered at him, crackling orange flames forming in her palms. Troy was next to spot him. The Grandson of Hephaestus's jaw clenched.

Karter raised his hands as if in surrender, jangling the key. "I'm here to save you."

"Yeah, right," Troy said.

"He's telling the truth." Diana entered the cell. Graceful as ever, she jumped up to snatch the key from Karter, then jogged over to Troy and Marina and unlocked their chains. "All right, get up," she said, offering them each a hand. "We have to hurry and escape."

Marina laughed coldly, and Karter's stomach bubbled with nausea as he recalled what Zeus had done to the grandchildren-of-Hephaestus. *If my punishment went as planned,"* Zeus had said, *"and my punishments generally do, Troy and Marina will be paralyzed from the waist down for the remainder of their miserable lives."*

This is all my fault, Karter thought. *They're paralyzed because of me.*

"What's wrong?" Diana asked, still holding out her hands for them. "Come on, we have to go."

"You weren't awake for it, were you?" Troy asked.

"Awake for what?"

Marina glowered at Karter, then looked up at

Diana. "Zeus struck our backs with lightning. He made it so we can't—can't move our legs. We can't walk."

"Maybe I can heal you," Diana started, her tone frantic. "Maybe I can—"

"No," Troy said, his lip quivering. "I don't think this is something that can be reversed. I'm afraid we'll only burden you."

"Let me try." She knelt and placed one hand on each of them. Her body blazed with golden light, and the glow spread into the twins.

Almost a full minute passed before she pulled away from them, all their illumination fading away. "Well?" she said between gasps of breath.

They knit their brows and grunted in effort, but nothing happened.

"I'm so sorry," Marina said. "I think it's better if you leave us here. We wanted to do more for you, but—"

"No," Karter interjected. "I refuse to leave you to die." He stepped toward them. "Let me carry you out of here. After we escape, we'll do something for your paralysis. Diana's in a weakened state. Surely, once she's had time to rest and she's back to full strength, she can do something about it."

"And if she can't?" Troy asked.

Karter averted his gaze from theirs. He ran a

shaking hand through his hair, pressing his lips into a thin line. Finally, he looked at them once more. "The fact that you're here . . . it's my fault. It's a result of my decisions." He thought of Zoey. Of how she'd asked him to join her group, and of how he'd chosen to bring Diana to Olympus instead. "If it weren't for me, neither of you would be here now, and I'm going to have to find a way to make it up to you. If Diana can't help you, *I will*."

"How can we trust anything you say?" Marina replied. "Zoey and Diana tried to save you, and you repaid their kindness with betrayal."

The words spilled from Karter's mouth before he could think about how he sounded. "I understand why you can't be certain whether to trust me. However, none of that matters right now, because you can be certain of one thing: if you don't let me help you, you'll die."

Troy and Marina shared a somber look, then nodded at Karter. Tapping into his strength, he bent down, picked them up, and hoisted them over his shoulders. "Are you ready to go, Diana?" he asked.

"More than you know."

Together, they exited the cell. Layla waited for them outside.

Diana grabbed the Daughter of Ares's hand. "Layla, come with us."

Layla glanced down at her hand in Diana's, then at Diana's face, with wide eyes. Her skin turned the same burgundy shade as her coil-y hair, as it usually did when she grew upset, but strangely enough, she didn't seem mad. "I—I can't," she stammered. "You know . . . you know what he'll do to me if he discovers I even thought about helping you. Don't you remember what happened when I tried convincing him to just *consider* resurrecting Pearl?" Karter raised a brow. He'd never heard anything like this from Layla before. As far as he'd known, she'd never argued with the gods about the decision to leave Pearl dead.

"He taught me to—to honor the gods no matter what," Layla continued. "That my duty must always be to them. That my destiny has always been to serve them. If he finds out about this, he'll see it as the ultimate betrayal, and he'll pun—"

"Ares can't hurt you anymore if he's defeated along with the rest of the gods," Diana interjected, seizing Layla's other hand.

I see, Karter thought as Diana paused for a few seconds. *I'm not the only one with a cruel father. Why am I not surprised?*

Diana continued, "I don't understand why even now, you still feel like you have to stay here and be loyal to the gods." She jerked her head toward the chamber where Violet and Xander lay unconscious. "Besides, won't Xander remember you were the one who attacked him from behind? You can't stay here. It's too dangerous."

Layla shrank in on herself, though she held tight to Diana's hands. "I have to. Besides, I can just tell the gods the truth: Xander would have died by Karter's hand if I hadn't knocked him out. It's better to regroup and fight smart later rather than get yourself killed in the heat of the moment, right?"

"Please, come with me," Diana said, her voice pleading. "Let's do this together, Layla. Like we should have all along. I know you loved Pearl as much as Syrena and I did. She was your best friend, and . . . and so was I."

At this, the color drained from Layla's face. Karter thought he saw tears forming in her eyes.

The Daughter of Ares pulled away from Diana. She hung her head. "I . . . I can't. I'm sorry. Please go. Get to safety, before someone comes down here and sees what's happened."

Diana's bottom lip trembled. She turned away from Layla, clenching her fists at her sides, before finally running toward the jail exit. Karter followed close behind.

As they started up the winding staircase, Troy asked, "How exactly do you plan on getting all of us off this cursed hunk of rock, Son of Zeus?" He patted Karter's shoulder blade. "I know you can fly, but it doesn't seem like you've got room for more than two."

"Not an issue," Karter said. "We just have to sneak through the palace to my bedchamber. I stole a pegasus that Diana can ride down. It's stationed outside my window."

"You stole a pegasus?" Diana wiped a few tears from her cheeks. "You planned this out ahead of time, didn't you?"

"I did."

They reached the top, and a quick scan of the halls confirmed they were alone. Karter bolted in the direction of his bedchamber, while Diana raced toward the amphitheater.

Karter halted, almost tripping over his feet. "What are you doing? My room is *this* way."

"Yeah, but Andy and Zoey aren't," Diana replied with a shrug.

"What in all the gods' names are you talking about?" Karter cried. "There's no way those two are here. They might have escaped Poseidon's palace and stolen the Trident, but—"

"You clearly don't know them very well," Diana remarked. "Thanks, by the way. For confirming they got Poseidon's Trident. If anything, that only makes me surer about them being here. If I know them, they're waiting for you and me to enter the amphitheater so they can save me."

"So what do you propose we do? Go out and face my father? He'll kill us!"

Diana smiled mischievously, her eyes brightening ever so slightly. "Not if you 'kill' him first. Didn't you learn how to make green lightning?"

Karter's jaw dropped. "You can't be serious. Zoey and Andy—they—"

"They're here," Diana finished for him. "Not just to save me, but to steal your father's Master Lightning Bolt too. And they're going to need our help."

"What about Troy and Marina? They can't fight right now."

"Leave us," Marina said. "Here, in the hall. We might not be able to use our legs, but I can still conjure flames. If someone sees us, I'll use my fire-powers to protect us."

Troy nodded. "And once you meet up with the Chosen Two, you can come back for us. We'll all escape together."

Karter couldn't believe what he was hearing. What they were suggesting. Even still, he set Troy and Marina behind a pillar, trying to hide them as best he could. Then he sprinted after Diana as she rushed for the amphitheater, his pulse pounding in his ears.

Zoey grew more and more restless, practically bouncing in her seat with anxiety. The crowd in the amphitheater whispered among themselves; Zeus had announced that the execution would start whole minutes ago, yet there was still no sign of Diana.

Andy leaned over to Prometheus. "Should we start without them?" he whispered. "Maybe storm the palace? Find everyone and break them out?"

Prometheus sighed. "I'm not sure that's the best idea."

"But what if it's our only choice?" Darko asked.

"If it comes down to that, then—" Prometheus never finished his sentence. He didn't have to. A woman in the front row screamed. Then someone else did, and someone else, and someone else, until it sounded as though everyone in the audience were yelling.

Zoey looked out at the amphitheater and couldn't believe what she saw. Karter was flying above the audience, two peridot-green bolts crackling in his hands. What was strange, however, was that he was supposed to be using them on

Diana, and she was nowhere to be seen.

Multiple people in the audience shrieked, "What is the Son of Zeus *doing*?" and Zoey found herself wondering the same thing.

"Now?" Andy asked.

Prometheus kept Andy from getting up. "Hold your pegasi. We haven't located our girl yet."

"Where is the prisoner, son?" Zeus boomed from the center of the dirt floor. He sounded aggravated, as if he'd written a script for tonight's show and Karter had decided on improv instead.

The King of the Gods jumped into the air, his robes billowing around him as he soared to Karter's level. Thunder roared in the distance, green lightning crackling in the sky. "Look at all the lovely citizens who came to watch the execution." Zeus gestured at the crowd. "It's not necessary to drag this out any longer. Why don't you go get the Daughter of Apollo now, my boy?"

It was then that Karter did something that shocked Zoey to the core. He narrowed his eyes at his father and yelled over the thunder, "Today, Diana lives!" As the words left his mouth, he chucked his green lightning at Zeus.

In an instant, the bolts hit Zeus—one in the chest, the other an arm. He screamed and convulsed, smoke rippling off his skin, and plummeted to the floor of the amphitheater. He landed hard on his back, his mouth lolling open, his unblinking eyes staring up at the roaring black sky.

As the audience screeched in terror, Zoey finally spotted Diana. The Daughter of Apollo ran into the amphitheater and looked out at the crowd as if desperately searching for someone or something. Karter swooped down to her side, and what appeared to be the other gods of Olympus piled out from the front rows of the audience. The gods advanced on Diana and Karter. Diana began chucking golden spheres of sunlight at them, while Karter conjured green lightning and shot at them with it.

"Zoey, now," Prometheus said. "Subdue them, before they trample any of us."

Zoey focused on her voice-powers, on what she could say to calm these panicked people. However, the familiar tingling sensation in her throat never came. Not only that, but her body didn't feel as though it was thrumming with power, as it usually did when she tapped into the abilities.

"It's all right," she yelled, hoping that if she went ahead and spoke anyway, her powers would show up. "This must be part of the event. Zeus wouldn't have allowed for it otherwise, don't you think? There's no need to panic."

Even the citizens closest to her didn't stop

shrieking, nor did they calm down, as she'd hoped they would. Soon everyone had begun to stampede out of their seats.

Zoey swallowed hard. "Sorry, you guys. I guess Calliope's still recovering from our encounter with Artemis. It doesn't seem like she's going to lend me any power tonight." Prometheus nodded, and with a snap of his fingers, he allowed all their disguises to melt away, then whipped his chains in warning at the scattering citizens if they even threatened to get too close.

In seconds Andy returned to himself, feathered butterfly wings and all, as did Darko, Prometheus, and the nymphs. "Andy, fly with Zoey over to Zeus," Prometheus barked. "If he's really dead for now, steal that Master Lightning Bolt from his robes. Dryads—get me and Darko and the Naiads down there, too. This is about to be the fight of our lives."

Zoey retrieved the Helm of Darkness from their pack and put it on. Prometheus handed the Trident to Andy, and Zoey threw her arms around Andy's neck. As she touched him, he disappeared with her. Tightening one arm around her waist, Trident in his free hand, Andy flew them toward Zeus's body. To Zoey's surprise, he seemed a lot more wobbly than usual, as if he was having trouble keeping his balance in the air. Thankfully, though, they didn't crash to their deaths.

Behind them, the Dryads made a bridge of vines above the audience that led down to the dirt floor of the amphitheater. Darko, Prometheus, and all twelve nymphs scrambled up onto it and started sprinting across.

Even when Andy landed, Zoey didn't let go of him. She slid her fingers down his arm and grabbed his free hand. "We stay invisible for as long as possible," she said.

"Agreed."

Together, they raced toward Zeus.

CHAPTER FIFTEEN

COLUMN

Karter wasn't sure whether he could fight the gods. He'd already shot down Zeus with a green bolt, temporarily killing him, but Hera and Heracles had him cornered. His only chance of escape was to fly into the sky or back to the palace—except he had no intention of abandoning Diana.

Hestia, Dionysus, and Aphrodite surrounded Diana. "If one of us kills the Daughter of Apollo instead of Karter, the war on the gods will still end, right?" Dionysus said, glowering at her. He raised his hands, his vines slithering all around him.

Heracles pointed a finger at Dionysus. "Don't you dare. We can't do anything that might compromise the future. In Father's visions, Karter was the one to kill her, and the war ended quickly thereafter. If anyone else does so, the outcome is unclear."

Hera summoned her battle scepter with a clap of her hands and stalked closer to Karter. Although she stood a few feet taller than him, he didn't back down from her glare. He stared up at her in defiance. "The future is already unclear," she said. "This was not supposed to happen. However, we'll still wait. The king should regenerate shortly, and when he does, I have no doubt he'll order Karter's and Diana's deaths immediately." She bent down to meet Karter's gaze. "You will no longer get away with defying the gods, you filthy ingrate. We offered you immortality, power beyond your imagination. For gods' sakes, I was going to accept you as my *son*. Even before that, we gave you all you could have wanted. And this is how you repay us?"

Fury unlike anything Karter had ever felt brewed and boiled in his gut. His heartbeat quickened, a hot, tingling sensation rising from his toes to his face. "Gave me all I wanted? You must be joking, Hera. Since I was a child, the gods have made it a point to destroy everything I care about. But you know that better than anyone, don't you? Because you're the one who murdered my mother." He scoffed and, without thinking, spit in her face.

The other gods around him gasped. Hera took a step back, her expression an impassive mask. She wiped the saliva from her skin with the back of her hand, then narrowed her eyes into slits. "I suppose you're right about a few things, bastard child." She raised her scepter. "But whether you like it or not, the whore deserved to die. As do you." Hera brought down her weapon. Karter darted to the right, barely dodging her attack.

Just then, the ground began to quake. The Queen of the Gods stumbled to the side, and so did everyone else.

Regaining his balance, Karter conjured his power of flight and soared over to Diana. He pulled her into his arms and flew high above the immortals.

All the way up here, he could see what had caused the shaking, though he could hardly believe his eyes. "Andy!" Diana cried with pure joy. Sure enough, it *was* Andy. The boy stood guard before Zeus's body, and he had Poseidon's Trident in hand. He slammed the prongs against the floor of the amphitheater, over and over, causing the earth to shudder. He also looked different from how Karter remembered. He wore the white robes and golden sandals of an aristocrat, and a pair of feathered butterfly wings had sprouted from his back.

Where's Zoey? Karter wondered, and that was when he saw her—well, he didn't really *see* her. Rather, he saw where she must be. One moment, Zeus's body was visible. The next, it disappeared. *She's wearing the Helm of Darkness, and she plans to steal the Master Lightning Bolt.*

Just like Diana said.

"It's them!" Heracles bellowed. He seized one of the columns holding up the amphitheater temple and tore it from its place. He brandished it like a weapon, bounding toward Andy. "The Chosen Two of the Dreaded Prophecy!"

The rest of the gods howled in rage, following Heracles's lead. They charged for Andy. Heart in his throat, Karter flew toward the mortal boy.

Dionysus was first to reach Andy. The god used his vines to propel himself forward, and soon greenery slithered around Andy's ankles and wrists. Andy jolted his limbs, trying to free himself of the vegetation's grip. It held fast. *Almost there, almost there*, Karter thought.

Andy cried out as Dionysus made a vine curl around his neck. He jutted the Trident's prongs in Dionysus's direction, but the god stayed just out of reach. "I've got the boy," Dionysus shouted over his shoulder. Another vine wrapped around the handle of the Trident. "And the Trident, too."

Karter swooped down toward them. But before he could attack the god himself, Diana leapt from his arms, spheres of sunlight blazing in her hands. Her foot collided with Dionysus's temple. He toppled sideways.

Like the nimblest of dancers, Diana flipped in the air and landed on the ground. She spun around and pitched her balls of light at the other gods charging for them. At the same time, the vines Dionysus wrapped around Andy came undone. They wriggled back to his side as he let out a pained groan, trying to get up from the dirt.

Karter landed beside Andy. The boy raised Poseidon's Trident, rushed toward Dionysus, and plunged the prongs through the god's chest. Dionysus went limp. Golden ichor leaked from his wounds.

Andy tore the Trident from Dionysus's body and turned to Karter. "So, did you *actually* decide to join our side this time? Or do I have to use this Trident on you?"

"I'm here to help you," Karter said. "I swear."

Andy didn't look convinced, and Karter couldn't blame him, but there wasn't time to explain. Heracles grew closer and closer to them, the rest of the immortals in tow. It appeared Diana hadn't hit any of them with her missiles, or if she had, the attacks hadn't deterred the deities.

Karter readied two green lightning bolts. Diana created more fiery spheres. Andy brandished the Trident.

Heracles approached, still clutching the broken-off pillar. Karter chucked his lightning at the god, while Diana hurled her glowing spheres at him. Heracles ducked beneath the attacks. The gods behind him didn't see them coming in time. Diana's light rammed into Hestia's stomach, sending her barreling backward. Karter's bolts struck Aphrodite, the peridot electricity whizzing across her skin. She toppled to the ground, dead for the moment.

Karter darted forward to meet Heracles head-on before the god could attack Diana and Andy. Heracles swung the column at Karter like a massive club. Channeling his strength, Karter caught the column.

Heracles released a battle cry and shoved the column against Karter. The veins in his arms bulging, Karter stood his ground to the best of his ability, holding tight to the pillar. The heels of his sandals dug into the dirt beneath him.

On Karter's right, Diana launched two fiery spheres at Heracles. They struck him in the ribs. He stumbled to the side, losing grip of the column. Karter yanked it out of the god's reach and tossed it aside.

Hera appeared thirty feet in front of Karter, lifting her scepter. Hestia seemed to have recovered; she followed Hera closely, brandishing a pair of twin daggers.

Karter conjured two green bolts. He hurled one at Hera, the other at Hestia. They dodged the projectiles with ease and continued to advance.

I got lucky with Zeus and Aphrodite because they weren't expecting my attacks, Karter thought, gritting his teeth as he conjured more peridot lightning. His chest had begun to burn at the exertion. *So how am I supposed to fight the others? How are any of us supposed to fight them? We're just mortal. It's only a matter of time before—*

An arrow *whoosh*ed past them. It pierced Hera through the shoulder, and she screeched in pain. Another arrow went flying, this one into Hestia's stomach. She yelped, keeling over.

The sounds of chains clanking penetrated the screams of the dispersing crowd, and Karter looked over his shoulder. To his surprise, the Titan

Prometheus—still in shackles—and Zoey and Andy's satyr companion—a bow in hand and a quiver of arrows slung over his back—careered toward them. Behind the Titan and satyr, a dozen nymphs used shields of plants and water to block the other gods and demigods from coming closer.

Hestia snarled at Prometheus and the satyr, then launched a dagger at Diana. The Daughter of Apollo tried to get away, but she wasn't quick enough. The weapon pierced her thigh. She cried out, falling to the ground.

Andy glanced between Diana and Hestia. He scowled at the goddess, leapt into the air, and flew toward her and Hera in a slightly unsteady manner, clutching Poseidon's Trident.

"Diana!" the familiar voice of a young woman exclaimed, and Karter's stomach did a flip. *Zoey.* Had she revealed herself? Despite the circumstances, he swung around.

Zoey had in fact revealed herself. Like Andy, she was dressed as an aristocrat, her floor-length dress the same bright-blue color as her irises. She had the Helm of Darkness tucked under her handless arm. With the hand she had left, she held a humongous drawstring sack. Golden electricity arced around the brown fabric, and Karter recognized the bag as the one Zeus kept the Master

Lightning Bolt stored within, under his robes. *She got it.*

Not only that, but behind her, Zeus still lay "dead," ichor spilling from fresh wounds in his throat, chest, and sides. She must have wanted to keep him incapacitated for as long as possible.

Zoey rushed to Diana, and Karter realized the sight of her was making his chest hurt. The last time he'd seen her had been when he betrayed her. If they managed to get out of this alive, would he ever be able to make it up to her?

As Zoey helped Diana rip the blade from her thigh and Diana healed the injury, Prometheus wrestled with Heracles. The satyr hurried over to Andy, presumably to aid the boy in fighting Hera and Hestia.

"Retrieve the objects of power," Hera ordered, her words carrying over the chaos. "And do not allow any of these traitors to escape, unless you care to be punished with the utmost severity."

Another voice that Karter knew all too well, a voice he had not expected to hear again—the voice of a Titan goddess—echoed from above. "You never were a merciful queen, were you, Hera?"

Asteria!

Thousands of miniature stars floated down from the sky and into battle. They twirled around Hera's and Hestia's faces, twinkling brightly in their eyes as if to distract them from Andy and the satyr. If that was Asteria's intent, it worked, because the duo took advantage of the immortals' disorientation. Andy stabbed Hera in the chest with the Trident, and Darko shot Hestia through the throat with an arrow.

"Hey, Son of Zeus!" Prometheus called from off to the side. Karter looked over to see he was still wrestling Heracles, and he seemed to be losing. "Since you decided you're a good guy now, you mind givin' me a little help?" Karter sprinted toward them.

Heracles and Prometheus suddenly stopped wrestling. They stared at something behind Karter. Heracles's expression was awed, while Prometheus's was panicked. Had the other gods and demigods fought their way past the nymphs?

Karter looked back to find something much worse.

Zeus climbed to his feet, his body fully regenerated, his flesh free of lightning burns and blade wounds. He conjured peridot lightning as he glared at Karter.

The King of the Gods heaved a green bolt for Karter. Karter lurched to the left. The lightning blasted the dirt next to him.

Karter glanced at Zoey and Diana—were they okay?—but it seemed they'd already disappeared, taking the Helm of Darkness and the Master Lightning Bolt with them.

As Zeus reared back to shoot Karter with his other bolt, thousands of glittering stars sped in front of Karter. Asteria materialized before him, shielding him from Zeus. Prometheus managed to squirm out of a stunned Heracles's grip and bounded up to Asteria's side, his chains at the ready.

"Go, Karter," Asteria said. "Follow the Chosen Two. Help them retrieve the grandchildren-of-Hephaestus, escape Olympus, and finish their war on the gods. Your destined greatness awaits."

Behind Zeus, the fortification of plants and water the dozen nymphs had created came undone, the minor gods and demigods erupting through. They made a break toward Zeus, while the nymphs scattered, trying to dart out of harm's way. Some of them didn't make it, though. In seconds, one Dryad and two Naiads were shot down.

Zeus began to laugh. It was a horrible, maniacal sound. The sky darkened, thunder rumbling in sync with his cackling. He heaved his peridot lightning in Prometheus's direction.

Karter never found out whether the bolt hit the Titan god. He jumped into the air, intending to fly back to the temple, then into the palace. That was the only direction Zoey and Diana could have gone. Hopefully, Andy and the satyr were already with them.

Karter spun around and was met with the broken column barreling toward him. Narrowly dodging the assault, he soared around Heracles toward the temple.

When Karter reached the temple, the first thing he saw was Zoey, Diana, Andy, and the satyr as they dashed toward the palace. Karter flew to the group's side, then dropped to the marble floor to run with them. "What took you so long?" Diana asked as they sped into the palace halls and headed in Troy and Marina's direction. "Why didn't you fly away right when you saw Zeus?"

"I did," Karter replied. "Sort of."

Zoey rolled her eyes at him. She no longer clutched the sack holding the Master Lightning Bolt; it seemed she'd handed it off to Andy. The boy had it slung over his shoulder, the Trident still in his hands. However, Zoey did hold another pack, which, judging by the shape and size of it, contained the Helm of Darkness. "What are you even doing here?" she asked.

He tried not to let his heart sink at the sharp tone in her voice. "Helping all of you."

"You realize if you'd done that back in Hephaestus City, we wouldn't be in this mess, right?" she barked. "Diana already told us about Troy and Marina. If it weren't for you, they wouldn't be paralyzed, Diana wouldn't be half starved to death, and Kali wouldn't be wounded and stuck back in the forest. Not to mention the fact that hundreds of nymphs were killed on this mission." Karter didn't reply. He couldn't. Zoey was right. If he'd only known then what he knew now, it would have changed the trajectory of all their paths.

"Uh, guys?" Andy piped up. "The big dude with the column isn't far behind us. I don't think this is a good time to argue."

"That's Heracles," Karter said. "My immortal half-brother. We need to pick up the pace. You can fly now, even if you're still learning, right?" He leapt into the air, snatched up Zoey and Diana, and hoisted them over his shoulders.

"Hey, what do you think you're *doing*?" Zoey screeched, flailing in his grasp.

"Keeping Heracles from pulverizing you," Karter said flatly. "Also, don't let the Helm touch me, even while it's in that bag. Unless you want it to suck away my life force, in which case I wouldn't be able to get you away from Heracles."

"Don't tempt me," she snapped in reply.

Karter did his best to ignore her, looking down at Andy. "Get the satyr and let's go. We have to hurry!" Andy nodded and handed the satyr the Trident, then grabbed him under the armpits and jumped into the air alongside Karter.

As Karter watched Andy fly, he became sure that the boy was still honing his flight skills. Andy had some trouble staying high up, and he grunted and groaned and knit his brow in exertion as he did so. Even still, this was faster than running. *It's the only way we'll escape Heracles*, Karter thought. *He might be a Son of Zeus, just like me, but he didn't inherit the gift of flight.*

"You can call me Darko, by the way," the satyr said after they'd already soared through a couple of hallways toward the grandchildren-of-Hephaestus. "Also, what's the plan? How are we going to get ourselves plus Troy and Marina off Olympus?"

"I stole a pegasus and stationed it outside my bedchamber window," Karter explained. "If I fly the twins down, two people can ride the pegasus, and Andy can carry whoever's left."

"Oh, that sounds a lot better than our first plan," Darko remarked.

"What was your first plan?" Diana asked.

"The nymphs who came with us were supposed to make a bridge back down if Asteria couldn't fly us," Andy answered. "But they, um . . . there's no telling whether any of them are gonna make it outta here now."

Karter couldn't hear anyone behind them. He tried looking over his shoulder, but Zoey's and Diana's backsides blocked his view. "Did we escape Heracles?" he asked them.

"I haven't seen him since three hallways ago," Diana said.

"Good." Karter rounded a corner, then stopped dead when a flash of white light blinded him. *Oh, no. It's a god.*

When the light faded, Heracles stood in the center of the hallway, the massive broken pillar in his burly hands. *I'm such an idiot*, Karter thought. *He must have guessed where we were going and intercepted us!*

The trick now was escaping Olympus and going somewhere Heracles wouldn't suspect. The god couldn't reach them when they were this high up, but he could certainly club them down or squish them against a wall with the column if they weren't quick enough.

Heracles stared up at Karter. "Why?" he asked. "Why do this, little brother?"

"Let us through without any trouble," Andy shouted, flapping in place. "We have all three objects of power. You don't stand a chance."

Heracles sneered at Andy and Darko. "Is that so?" He swung the column at them. Andy swerved to avoid it, but the movement was clumsy. He and Darko crashed sideways into a wall and tumbled to the floor. "If you're so unstoppable, then why are you running away? Why not use the objects of power to their full potential and destroy the gods?" The immortal raised the column once more.

"Leave them alone!" Karter yelled. He swooped down in front of them. Zoey and Diana scrambled off his shoulders and hastened toward Andy and Darko. Karter held out his arms, trying to shield them all from Heracles.

Heracles brought the pillar to his side. "I can do as you ask, I suppose."

Karter furrowed his brow. "What? Really?"

"Of course." He gestured at Diana. "So long as you admit your folly and kill the Daughter of Apollo."

Karter set his jaw. "Never."

The god clucked and shook his head. "I don't understand why you're doing this. You could live forever, an immortal among the rest. You could fulfill your *destiny*."

"You said it yourself," Karter replied. "I have a choice."

"What a pity it is, then," Heracles hissed, "that you chose wrong."

He raised the pillar, prepared to bring it down. Karter braced himself to catch it.

The column slammed against Karter's hands. The impact sent shock waves of pain through his body, and he slid backward toward the others. Tapping into his strength, he replanted his feet and, using all his might, shoved the pillar against Heracles.

The god fell to the side, losing grip of the column. It careened toward him, then rammed into the floor beside him. Chunks of marble and precious metal spiraled through the air at the collision.

Burning, blazing pain seared through Karter's chest. But that didn't stop him from conjuring a green lightning bolt in his trembling hands. He couldn't give up now. He had to stop Heracles, had to get the others out of here.

His godly half-brother still lay on the floor. This could be his only chance.

He pitched the peridot bolt at Heracles.

Heracles ducked. The lightning blasted into the wall behind him. He rolled over and jumped to his feet. He seized the column. Stomped toward Karter.

Gasping for air, Karter collapsed to his hands and knees. *I have to get up. I have to . . .*

An arrow shot toward Heracles. The god dodged it. Two spheres of golden sunlight soared toward him next. He easily swerved out of their paths.

Heracles grunted in pain, halting in his tracks. Ichor began dribbling from the side of his broad neck. There was a wet tearing sound, and the flesh of his throat opened to reveal the muscles and tendons and ligaments beneath. *It must be Zoey!* Karter thought. *She snuck up on him using the Helm of Darkness!*

Whatever relief Karter felt from this realization didn't last long. Heracles jerked out an elbow. Zoey cried out. A few seconds later, she reappeared on the floor ten feet from Heracles, the Helm of Darkness rolling away from her. Although her dagger remained lodged in Heracles's throat, the god regained his balance and raised his column above Karter.

As Karter prepared to roll out of the way, he saw someone dashing forward in the corner of his vision. He looked over. It was Andy.

The mortal boy struck Poseidon's Trident against the floor. Shudders rocked the hallway. Stumbling to the side, Heracles brought down the column.

With a rush of panic, Karter realized the blow meant for him was about to flatten Andy instead.

With no thought other than *I must save Andy*, Karter leapt to his feet and vaulted toward the boy.

In the end, he wasn't quick enough.

But someone else was.

Darko shoved Andy out of the column's path, and rather than crushing the boy, the marble crushed the satyr instead.

CHAPTER SIXTEEN
FLOWER

Andy dropped the Trident and reached for Darko, watching in dumb shock as Heracles's broken column came down upon his friend.

It happened so quickly.

There was nothing he could do.

One moment, Darko was alive and well.

The next, mangled beyond repair.

Gobs of warm red splattered Andy's face, Darko's horns and skull and the rest of his bones crunching under the force of the marble.

Time seemed to slow, and Andy fell to his

knees. He thought he heard someone else screaming Darko's name, but when he tasted blood coming up from his throat, he realized he was the one howling for his friend.

There was shouting all around him. A pair of legs running past him. Then someone—Karter, maybe—lifted the pillar off Darko.

Andy couldn't bear to gaze at what remained of him. *No, you have to*, he thought. *You have to make sure.*

When Andy looked, he wished he hadn't. Darko was no longer there, a mound of bloody skin and fur riddled with crushed organs and shattered bone left in his wake. If Diana couldn't heal Pearl after her decapitation, or give Zoey back her hand after Persephone chopped it off, there was no way the Daughter of Apollo could fix this mess.

A pair of arms flew around Andy's neck, and a face pressed into his chest—Zoey, they belonged to Zoey, it was Zoey. Her body was racked with something that sounded like sobs. Or, at least, Andy thought that's what they sounded like. He couldn't hear much over his own wailing.

Andy wasn't sure how long they stayed like that. All he knew was that suddenly someone else grabbed him by the arm and tried to drag him away. And although he knew they had to get out of the palace, although he knew they had to escape

Olympus, something told him he couldn't leave Darko.

He yanked himself from their grasp and wrapped his arms around Zoey, tighter than ever. He rested his head on hers, and they cried together. Someone came up behind him, rested a hand on his shoulder, and squeezed, as if trying to be comforting.

That was when Darko's blood evaporated into the air. His body—what remained of it—trembled, shrinking into the size and shape of a small pot. Then its texture and color shifted into that of rich brown soil, and it began sprouting healthy green grass.

Finally, a stem with a little bulb emerged from the vegetation. As quickly as the stem had risen, the bulb burst open, revealing the scarlet petals of a flower.

Andy relinquished some of his hold on Zoey to gently brush the flower's petals—velvety soft beneath his fingers. He gulped down a cry, his vocal cords ripped raw from all the screaming. He wasn't sure whether he'd be able to talk for a while, but at the same time, he didn't care whether he could.

"It's a poppy," Diana whispered from behind Andy, her voice cracking with anguish. She must have been the one holding his shoulder. "Darko—

he turned into a poppy flower."

Zoey lifted her head from Andy's chest and pulled away from him. Her eyes were already puffy, her cheeks soaked with tears. Tentatively, she picked up Darko's red poppy by the soil housing it. She sniffled and said, "We can't leave him here."

"I'll carry him down," Andy croaked, staring hard at the flower. "When all of this is over, I'll plant him somewhere amazing."

And just like that, Darko was in Andy's arms, smaller and more breakable than ever.

Before Andy knew it, all of them were running down the halls of Zeus's palace again—Karter in front, Diana in back. They left Heracles behind; the god lay "dead" on the floor, stab wounds and lightning scorch marks riddling his body.

Someone had also put the bag holding the Master Lightning Bolt on Andy's back, though he didn't know who had done it or when they had done it. Beside him, Zoey ran with the sack holding the Helm of Darkness on her own back, the Trident in her hand.

Soon they reached Troy and Marina, who were hiding behind a pillar. Karter threw the twins over his shoulders, and then they fled to the Son of Zeus's room.

Once they made it to Karter's room, the demigod punched the glass out of the window.

Outside, a gray pegasus whinnied at him. After everyone climbed outside, Diana and Zoey mounted the creature, while Karter continued carrying Troy and Marina. Andy simply held tight to the flower.

On the other side of the palace, the screams of battle roared on, but Andy hardly processed the sounds. Instead, as he and the others flew off Olympus and soared toward solid land, he could think of nothing but the people he'd loved and lost.

First Dad.

Then Mark, Mom, and Mel-Mel.

After that, Spencer.

Now Darko.

He wasn't sure whether he'd been crying minutes ago, but he was now. Tears slipped down his cheeks as he held Darko's poppy flower close to his chest, protecting it from the biting wind.

The clouds around him suddenly cleared, and he caught sight of Zoey as she rode the gray pegasus with Diana. Her long curls flew around her in the most beautiful way he'd seen yet. The sight only made him cry harder, and he stumbled in the air. *Never*, he thought, catching himself, regaining his balance. *I'll never lose her. I won't let it happen.*

Clinging to that comforting thought, Andy sobered up. He held his head a bit higher, managed to quell his tears.

Soon they reached the trees below. What they would do next, he had no idea. But he did know one thing: They now had all three objects they'd set out to steal. The Helm of Darkness, Poseidon's Trident, and the Master Lightning Bolt.

It was time to put those objects to good use.

It was time to end this war on the gods.

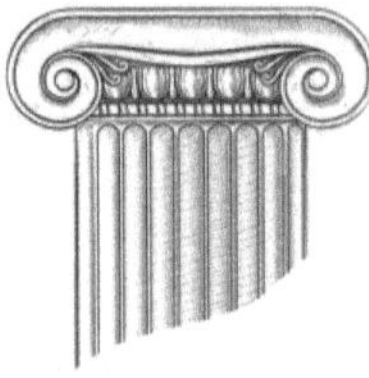

Persephone's eyes snapped open as she gasped for breath. She cried out in terror, though she had no idea why.

The familiar scents of mold and mildew and death and decay assaulted her nostrils, and although her head spun, rendering her surroundings a blur of red and black, she immediately knew where she was. *Hades's castle in the Underworld.*

"Shhh, sweet daughter, shhh," the familiar voice of her mother whispered to her. A hand stroked her cheeks, her hair. "It is all right. Catch your breath, and understand that you will never burn in Tartarus again. I will make sure of it." *Tartarus?* Persephone thought, a vague image of its massive pit and the cerulean fire within flashing across her mind. *Who said anything about—*

It was then that the memories came surging back.

First Spencer summoning her to ask her for help. She lied to him, of course, agreeing to aid him on his quest to help the Chosen Two of the Prophecy steal the Helm of Darkness from her husband. She'd been plotting for years to kill her wretch of a stepson without facing punishment by Hades, and this situation presented her with a more-than-perfect opportunity to do so.

Next Hades as she stabbed him in the back and sliced his head from his neck. Spencer as she heaved her sword through his innards. She slipped the Helm of Darkness over her head and started toward Tartarus with her husband's head, intending to hurl it into the pit, where it could never reunite with the rest of the body and regenerate.

Last, the Chosen Two and Karter, Son of Zeus as they battled her at the edge of the pit of Tartarus. *"You're fighting for the wrong side,"* she told them. *"Join me, all of you, and I can assure you you'll live to see another day. We'll steal Poseidon's Trident. We'll steal the Lightning Bolt. Together, we'll take down the Olympians, and I'll rule as your queen. Queen of the world."*

The impertinent mortals refused her offer. They cast her into the scorching blue flames.

Then she was falling, falling, falling. After what felt like forever, she crashed into a cluster of sharp rocks. There was burning, blinding pain, and she saw her blood—yes, *red blood*, not the golden ichor that usually flowed through a god's veins—and entrails splattering all about. And after that, nothing.

Until now.

Persephone blinked hard, trying to fix her vision, and soon she could see she lay in a cave-like chamber, the high ceilings and wide windowless walls lodged with skulls and precious gems. The throne room. *I must have died in Tartarus*, she thought, *then regenerated when Mother retrieved me and brought me here. But how . . . how did she manage it? How did she free me from Tartarus? It's practically impossible, even for gods.*

Demeter's face came into view, hovering over Persephone's. The goddess's lustrous, spiraled brown hair was tied back in a severe bun, but even so, several curls had escaped the ties and clips. The loose strands stuck out every which way, as if the goddess had been standing out in violent winds for hours. Not only that, but thermal burns peppered her forehead and cheeks. Persephone assumed her mother obtained those injuries during her time in

Tartarus.

What struck Persephone the most, however, was the crazed look in her mother's hazel eyes. She had not seen Demeter so frantic in millennia, not since the goddess had first retrieved Persephone from the Underworld after Hades kidnapped her and forced her to marry him.

Another familiar deity appeared in Persephone's line of sight, one that made her stomach sick. As usual, his dark hair was greasy, his cheeks as sunken and pale as a corpse's. *Hades.*

Although Hades seemed concerned for Persephone as he gazed down at her, she knew better than to fall for his manipulations. Whenever she had resisted him in the past, he had beaten her down with unending cruelty. It was only after she had resigned herself to being his obedient wife—his dutiful Persephone, Queen of the Underworld—that he had shown her any love or tenderness.

She was sure he didn't know of her betrayal and murder of his bastard son. Otherwise, he would have already re-banished her to Tartarus in a fit of rage without consulting the other gods first. Even still, she didn't plan on hiding her treachery from him. *I will never serve him again. Not after everything he put me through.*

However, one question burned through

Persephone's mind. Why had her mother saved Hades from Tartarus, too? Demeter loathed Hades—at least, she acted like it and said as much. What in all the gods' names was going on?

Persephone shot to her feet, shoving Demeter and Hades away even though they towered over her. "Mother, why?" she cried in indignation. "Why did you save him? *How* could you? You know of the horrors that revolting demon has committed against me." Her eyes filled with hot tears, electrifying magic coursing through her veins as she prepared to battle them both. She knew she was no match for them, but that didn't mean she would go down without a fight. Blackened vines and grass crunched as they twisted and curled out of her palms. "I finally rid myself of this sham of a union, and you decide to ally yourself with the god who forced it upon me?"

"Calm yourself, Persephone," Hades said with a condescending smirk. "You are hysterical. Your mother has always wanted to keep you to herself. Do you really believe she'd forfeit the opportunity to do just that? Or did you consider the possibility that she had orders to save me, as well?"

Persephone bared her teeth. "My mother always advocated for my freedom, not to 'keep me to herself.' Don't you recall, or is your memory truly so feeble? She did all she could to protect me from *you.*" She launched her plants toward her husband's neck and limbs. He didn't flinch, didn't even blink.

Before the vegetation could reach Hades, the blade of a sword sliced through all of it. Persephone's pulse quickened as she stumbled backward. Who else was here?

She looked over to see who the sword belonged to: Ares, God of War. Ares was unmistakable even beneath all the armor, his scarlet flesh and hair peeking out from under the coverings. Behind him stood more gods she knew: blue-skinned Poseidon, cunning-eyed Hermes, silver-haired Athena, and deformity-ridden Hephaestus. They all wore armor like the God of War's. Persephone glanced back at her mother to find that Demeter had donned similar metal attire, though the Goddess of Harvest had her helmet tucked under one arm.

Athena strolled ahead of the other gods toward Persephone, shoulders back, head held high. "Persephone, Zeus sent the six of us on a mission to Tartarus not only to banish Apollo, but also to save you and Hades." Persephone's heart fell to her feet. Apollo had been banished to Tartarus? Despite the history they shared, and despite the fact that he was an Olympian, she'd never wished for him to suffer such a fate . . .

What all had transpired in her absence?

"Our king knows about the little stunt you pulled recently, too," Ares said, brandishing his sword. "How you conspired against the gods with Spencer, Son of Hades, to steal the Helm of Darkness. How you murdered the boy and took the Helm for yourself. How you tossed your husband's head into the pit of Tartarus so he could never again regenerate."

At these words, Hades's expression lit with fury. A low growl escaped his throat. "How dare you." He stalked toward her. "How dare you disobey me."

She raised her arms, readying herself to fight, but there was a blur of movement—Hermes using his super-speed. He stopped in front of Hades, blocking the god from coming any closer. Demeter did the same.

"Now, now, brother," Poseidon began, sauntering forward, "you mustn't act rashly. We're going to need dear Persephone for the upcoming battle, you see."

Hades glared at Poseidon. "Battle? What battle?"

"The Daughter of Apollo and the late Daughter of Poseidon somehow resurrected the Chosen Two of the Dreaded Prophecy," Hephaestus explained in his grumbling way. "The Chosen Two then stole your Helm of Darkness. They also managed to take Poseidon's Trident."

The King of the Underworld balled his fists at his sides. "*What?*"

"Don't forget the Master Lightning Bolt," Hermes added. "Just a short while ago, I made a call to Zeus to let him know our mission was successful and that you both would regenerate shortly. He told us the Chosen Two stole the Lightning Bolt earlier this evening, during what was supposed to be Diana, Daughter of Apollo's execution. Apparently, my demigod half-brother had a change of heart. Rather than executing Diana and becoming an immortal god, as he was supposed to, Karter saved her and helped the Chosen Two instead. Together, they all escaped Olympus."

"You *imbeciles!*" Hades bellowed, the walls and ceiling trembling at his screams. "How could you have let this happen?"

"We might ask the same of you, Uncle," Athena snapped. "This debacle began in your domain, after all. You could have nipped it in the bud right here in this castle, but you didn't."

Hades yelled something at Athena, but Persephone couldn't register what was said. She shrank back, swallowing hard, the hairs on the back of her neck standing straight. *The Chosen Two have all three of the pantheon's most powerful objects. What does this mean for the gods? For Mother and me?*

Footfalls echoed from somewhere behind Poseidon, Athena, Ares, and Hephaestus. Everyone looked that way, and Persephone sucked in a sharp breath at who she saw enter the chamber.

"I see the mission to banish my twin to Tartarus and rescue Hades and Persephone was successful," Artemis said bitterly as she approached them. She wore no armor, no coverings. Just her regular old tattered dress, her bow and quiver of arrows slung over her back.

Athena's jaw dropped. "Sister, what are you doing here? You're supposed to be hunting the Chosen Two."

Artemis halted at Athena's side. "I was, and I found them. But before I could capture them, the girl used the Helm and Trident to perform a variation of the Descent Spell and sent me to one of the farthest reaches of the Underworld. I traveled here, hoping to find the lot of you before you transported home."

For a long while, the gods seemed to be holding their breaths, not saying a word.

Finally, Hades spoke. "How did they discover the Descent Spell's existence in the first place? How did they uncover the secrets of our magical objects? Harness the divine power to use them?"

"The girl claimed she was Calliope incarnate," Artemis replied. "She also said the boy was Anteros. I sensed their divine essences, but it cannot be true. They are only mortal humans. Besides, Calliope and Anteros faded away centuries ago."

Athena snapped her fingers and turned to Poseidon. "Wait a moment. Uncle, didn't you and Triton and Amphitrite say something like that? Didn't you tell Zeus about the Chosen Two resembling Anteros and Calliope, and that you thought they might have come back from the dead?"

Poseidon stroked his beard as if considering the question. "I did, but he dismissed my claims. He says it's impossible. That we must have been mistaken."

"And what if you were not mistaken?" Demeter asked. "What if Calliope and Anteros are alive and well, hell-bent on destroying the pantheon for some godsforsaken reason? Don't you think it would prove that we never truly die, even if we fade away from lack of worship?"

"It would prove nothing," Poseidon retorted. "If those mortal nuisances *are* Calliope and Anteros, that means they never really faded away in the first place. No, if they are Calliope and Anteros, then something greater is at work here."

Ares pointed his sword at Poseidon. Persephone could see his skin growing an even more vibrant shade of scarlet in the places it was visible. That happened whenever he worked himself up, which was often. "Who they are is irrelevant," Ares spat. "The fact remains: they are waging war on us. They have stolen our greatest weapons, and they have discovered our secrets."

Athena rested a hand on Ares's shoulder as if to calm him. "Fear not, brother. The Chosen Two cannot defeat us even with such advantages. Just as Zeus says, it is only through fantastical strokes of luck that they've come this far." She glanced at all the gods in the room, her gaze falling on Persephone last. A shiver snaked down Persephone's spine as Athena went on. "So long as we work together, we will destroy them once and for all."

To be continued

in the fourth installment of

the War on the Gods series . . .

THE THREADS
OF FATE

A. P. Mobley is a YA fantasy author with an undying love for Greek mythology and epic, magical tales. She grew up in Wyoming and currently lives in South Dakota. She considers herself a huge nerd, loves coffee a little too much, and can be found snuggling with one of her pets into late hours of the night.

Thank you for reading *The Master Lightning Bolt*! If you enjoyed this book, please consider leaving it a review on Amazon, Goodreads, Bookbub, or wherever it is you like to get your books from.

I say this because reviews are the best way to thank authors for writing the books you love. The more positive reviews a book has, the more new readers websites show it to. I do not have a big publisher paying to promote my books, so reviews are the most important component in spreading the word about my stories.

A review doesn't have to be lengthy; just a few words or a sentence or two is amazing.

Thank you again for reading *The Master Lightning Bolt*. It is an absolute dream come true to be able to publish my stories for you to read.

Follow A. P. on Instagram, Twitter,
and TikTok:
@author_apmobley

Like her Facebook page:
facebook.com/authorapmobley/

Sign up for her newsletter, get free short
stories, and MORE:

ACKNOWLEDGMENTS

There are several people who helped bring this book to fruition, people I truly can't thank enough.

Tory, my husband, thank you so much for reading the earliest, messiest drafts of this story. This was difficult to get down from beginning to end, and without you, it would have taken me much longer to get right. I love you so much, and I truly appreciate how dedicated you are to helping me make my books the best they can be, even though you aren't the biggest fan of reading.

Dillan, my writing buddy and author (as well as real-life) friend, thank you for listening to my struggles as I wrote and published this book. It's so wonderful to have you around, not only because you're awesome, but also because you understand how difficult and isolating this author life can be. Every writer needs a fellow writer friend to help pull them through the hard times, and for me, that friend is you!

Nikki Mentges, my editor—as always, I couldn't publish anything without you. Your thorough feedback and assistance really helped me bring this manuscript to the next level, not to mention gave me the confidence that I'm setting things up correctly for the finale. I'm so grateful to have you by my side on this author journey of mine.

Gabrielle Ragusi, my cover illustrator—wow, it's really been you and me since the beginning of this series, hasn't it? Even before I'd finished writing the first book, you were working on art for it, inspiring me to make my words worthy of your paintings. I'm beyond grateful for everything you've done for these books, for all the support you've given them both publicly and behind the scenes. Just one more book to go, at least in this series.

Matt, my baby sibling, thank you so much for doing the watercolor painting of the series map. I'm so proud of the strong, amazing person you've grown up to be, and I can't wait to see all that you accomplish. I know you're going to change the world with your brilliant mind and extraordinary talent.

Finally, Giggles and Kelsey, two of my best friends, and my Stylish B******—thank you a million times over for your advice on the interior design and character art I did for these books. I must have sent you both hundreds of photos asking for your feedback on those things, and you always helped me figure out what wasn't quite right so I could move forward to make them better.

www.ingramcontent.com/pod-product-compliance
Lightning Source LLC
Chambersburg PA
CBHW051312190726
48290CB00001B/124